THE PARDONER'S CRIME

1322. Sir Richard Lee, Sergeant-at-Law, is sent by King Edward II to Sandal Castle to preside over the court of the Manor of Wakefield. Sir Richard and his assistant Hubert of Loxley are forced to investigate a vicious rape and a cold-blooded murder. As the township prepares for the Wakefield mystery plays, the strangest case is brought before him. The Pardoner, Albin of Rouncivale, confesses to a crime, believed to have been committed by the outlaw Robin Hood. Sir Richard must quickly discover the truth — the stability of the realm and the crown itself may depend upon it.

KEITH SOUTER

THE PARDONER'S CRIME

Complete and Unabridged

ULVERSCROFT
Leicester

First published in Great Britain in 2008 by
Robert Hale Limited
London

First Large Print Edition
published 2009
by arrangement with
Robert Hale Limited
London

British Library CIP Data

Souter, Keith M.
  The pardoner's crime
  1. Murder- -Investigation- -England- -Wakefield- -Fiction.
  2. Great Britain- -History- -Edward II, *1307 –1327-* -
  Fiction. 3. Detective and mystery stories.
  4. Large type books.
  I. Title
  823.9′2–dc22

  ISBN 978–1–84782–672–5

Published by
F. A. Thorpe (Publishing)
Anstey, Leicestershire

Set by Words & Graphics Ltd.
Anstey, Leicestershire
Printed and bound in Great Britain by
T. J. International Ltd., Padstow, Cornwall

This book is printed on acid-free paper

To Andrew who shares my enthusiasm for medieval England. With happy memories of our walks and talks around ancient battlefields.

Contents

With him there rode a gentle Pardoner
Of Rouncivale, his friend and companion,
That straight was come from the court of Rome.
Full loud he sang 'Come hither, love, to me!'
This Summoner bore to him a stiff burden . . .

A voice he had as small as hath a goat.
No beard had he, nor never should have;
As smooth as it was as it were late shave.
I trowe he were a gelding or a mare.
But to his craft, from Berwick into Ware
Never was there such another Pardoner.

The Pardoner's Portrait
The Canterbury Tales
Geoffrey Chaucer (1343–1400)

Prologue

Albin of Rouncivale, he who proclaimed himself a Pardoner, a granter of indulgences from His Grace the Bishop of Rochester himself, pulled his damp cloak about him and tossed his hood back to shake his lank yellow hair free. He was uncomfortable. His buttocks ached from his long ride to Pontefract; he was wet from a fresh drizzle that had only just abated, and his stomach had been urging him to stop to break his fast for at least an hour. He halted his donkey for a moment to straighten his cap, on the front of which he had sewn a vernycle, a copy of the handkerchief with which St Veronica had reputedly wiped Christ's face on the way to his crucifixion. Then he again shouldered his staff, a stick of beech capped by a cross of base metal studded with glass beads, which was his badge of office, or, as he liked to think of it, his crowd-drawer. Finally, he hawked and spat to clear his lungs.

'There is money to be made this day,' he said to the back of the donkey's head. 'I can

1

feel it in my bones.' And so saying, he wheezed as he rattled the sack which contained his jar of small pig bones that did him such good service in his daily trade. 'By the bones of St Peter, let us see what stirs in Pontefract today. And from the sound of it we have hit the town upon a special feasting day.'

Cresting the rise, the great limestone castle of Pontefract with its corbelled turrets came into view. The land dropped from where he was to rise again to the great mound on which the castle stood. And at its base arose a clamour that was greater than the Pardoner would have expected even upon a market-day in the height of summer, let alone on a crisp morning in March.

As he began the descent into the town he smiled with smug satisfaction as he began to gather the inevitable following of urchins and loafers. He knew that they were attracted by his ornate staff, and his sack of relics, indulgences and pardons.

An unholy crowd of sinners, he thought to himself, as if mentally assessing their potential for trade. He nodded at some of the dirty faces looking up at him with expressions of awe and curiosity.

'Beati paupers spiritu!' he piped up in his thin reedy voice. Then, sure in the knowledge that none of his followers would have any

2

knowledge of Latin, he added for their benefit: 'Blessed are the poor in spirit.'

This occasioned laughter, though he doubted if many of these simple folk considered themselves to be blessed.

'Have you come far, Master Pardoner?' cried one.

'Aye, from Ware, on my way to Berwick.'

'Come for the execution, have you?'

Albin of Rouncivale was as used to seeing hangings as any traveller. He shrugged non-commitally. He would probably wait to see what poor soul or souls were going to have their life choked out of them, or if they were lucky, their necks snapped by relatives or by ruffians paid to jump on them as they dangled. On balance executions were usually good for business. Lots of guilt, lots of sins to be pardoned *in absentia*. And fear of a similar fate at the end of the day made many a neighbour pay for a precautionary pardon.

The road began to climb towards the castle mound and the Pardoner was grateful of his stout little beast.

'There hasn't been anything like this as long as I have lived here,' said one oldster, who looked, the Pardoner thought, as if he had spent his years working in the liquorice fields that surrounded the area. 'The king himself is here.'

And at the name of the sovereign there came mutterings of disgust and what sounded like curses of blasphemy. The Pardoner turned his head as if scandalized.

'King Edward? Here?' he asked, with a frown. 'But Pontefract Castle belongs to Thomas, Earl of Lancaster!'

There was general laughter. Then: 'Where have you been, Master Pardoner? The King's army under Sir Andrew Harclay, the Warden of Carlisle cut off the earl's army at Boroughbridge. They say old Thomas had been trying to get help from the Scots.'

'But instead he was captured and brought here in chains, to his own castle. Two days ago six rebel barons were hanged, drawn and quartered before this castle. They made Lancaster watch, then the King and that dog John de Warenne, the Earl of Surrey, the Dispenser Lords and Edmund FitzAlan the Earl of Arundel tried him in his own hall yesterday. And just as Lancaster had denied Piers Gaveston, the King's former favourite any defence, they didn't allow him to speak for himself.'

'He's to die for treason!' cried a youngster of about eight. 'God save the King.'

The Pardoner's eyes widened. 'Treason? That means he will be hanged, drawn and quartered?'

'No!' exclaimed a whitebeard, who had been limping alongside the donkey. 'The earl is cousin to the King. Royal blood. It is the axe for him.'

The tumult had been getting louder as they approached the crowd that milled about the walls of the castle. Then the noise of the rabble was drowned out by the sound of numerous trumpets and the beat of side-drums. The crowd murmured and gradually fell silent as a procession emerged from the gatehouse. Men at arms formed a column around a group of drummers, followed by a mail-clad messenger bearing the royal flag. Behind him a youth led an ass upon which sat Thomas, Earl of Lancaster, with his hands lashed behind him and a friar's hat upon his head.

Albin of Rouncivale joined the throng, urging his donkey on with a few jabs with his heels. The earl was paraded through the streets of the town, his head hung on his chest as his former vassals jeered, gesticulated and threw dirt and refuse at him. Then once again the parade started to climb a gentle rise.

'It is the Monk's Hill,' an urchin informed the Pardoner. 'They always hack their heads off there.'

And indeed, waiting there, his face concealed behind a black mask, his thick torso covered in a leather apron stood the executioner. His arms were bare to the shoulders, the biceps rippling.

The earl was hauled from the ass and prodded towards the block of wood.

He looked up at the castle — his castle — and saw several richly dressed figures looking down from one of the turrets of the keep. Even from that distance there was no mistaking the crown that the middle figure was wearing. King Edward II, of Caernarvon, Lancaster's cousin surrounded by his new-found lackeys. They were drinking wine and seemed to be enjoying this ignominious end to the man who felt that he should have been King of England.

'As the Lord is my witness — ' the Earl of Lancaster began.

But, at a signal from the King's mail-clad messenger, he was immediately silenced by a gag that was thrust into his mouth.

Gasps and protests rang out from a few members of the crowd, but they were soon silenced by a show of steel from the men at arms, and gradually a dominant jeering noise rang out as the mob began to bray for blood. The drummers continued a slow, sonorous beat of their drums. Then, as the messenger produced a proclamation, the drumming abruptly stopped.

'By order of His Majesty, King Edward Plantagenet the Second of Caernarvon, on this day, the 22 March 1322, Thomas of Lancaster, cousin to our sovereign, has been tried by his King and his noble peers, the Earls of Surrey and Arundel, and their lords, the Dispensers, and found guilty of high treason against the person of his sovereign. He is duly stripped of his titles, and his lands, possessions and honours are forfeit to the crown — as his life is committed to the Lord.'

A nod from the messenger and Lancaster was thrust down over the block.

'Wait!' cried the messenger. 'It is the King's order that he must face north, to Scotland, where he had tried to seek help from the murderous Bruce!'

No longer defiant, his body shivering from either cold or fear, he had to wait until a priest appeared and mumbled over him in Latin.

Then the headsman's axe rose, fell and severed the earl's head from his body in one horrifically bloody moment.

The headsman bent and lifted the head by its hair and held it aloft, the eyes still eerily twitching as blood gushed from the severed vessels upon the ground and the mouth hung open, while below it the decapitated body still sprawled over the block convulsed for a further moment then lay still.

Slowly the crowd began to recover itself; gasping, cursing, and laughing.

Then the messenger went on with his proclamation, announcing that all members of Lancaster the traitor's army who had not surrendered would be outlaws and would suffer the pain of immediate execution. No concession would be given to rank or title.

But few people were listening intently. They were either ogling the gruesome scene on the execution ground or trying to imagine what was going through the King's mind at that moment, for the party in the turret seemed to be making merry.

Albin of Rouncivale was no longer listening either. Although he had been shocked by what he had seen, that shock did not last long. He made a silent sign of the cross as he watched the Earl of Lancaster's head dangle from the hand of the executioner.

His mind saw profit ahead.

1

The Outwood

It was a hot morning in June and travelling through the Outwood, the great forest of oak, holly, beech and hazel to the north of the township of Wakefield, was a welcome retreat from the sun for the two riders. They had been making their way slowly from town to town and from village to village in order to familiarize themselves with this part of their liege lord, King Edward II's northern holdings. The ride from Sherburn-in-Elmet to Methley had left them hot and uncomfortable and they were all too aware of the weight of their chain-mail hauberks that they wore under their surcoats.

Sir Richard Lee, Sergeant-at-Law and newly appointed Circuit Judge of the King's Northern Realm wiped the patina of perspiration that had formed on his brow and leaned down to rub his left calf muscle.

'Does the wound still pain you, my lord?' Hubert of Loxley, the tall broad-shouldered, clean-shaven man riding at his side, asked concernedly.

'I fear it festers, for it throbs so,' returned Sir Richard. He too was tall, although more willowy in physique than Hubert, his friend and assistant. He had a short well-groomed beard, as befitted one of his class and position, and would have been considered handsome by most women, his eyes blue and piercing, his nose slightly bent, having been broken in a joust some years previously.

'Those accursed bowmen!' said Hubert. 'I suspect that they dip their arrows in poison and have them cursed by witches before they go to war.' He turned his head and spat, then immediately made the sign of the cross over his heart.

They were of about the same age. Richard knew that he was precisely thirty-one years old at his last birthday, while Hubert had an idea that he was within a year or two of that. Hubert had, like his father before him, been groomed in all manner of fighting as one of Sir Jasper of Loxley's personal men at arms. As such he had followed his master whenever he had been called to take up arms and had seen action against the Scots at Stirling when he was a youngster of thirteen, and actually saw the rebel William Wallace taken in chains south to his grisly fate. When Sir Jasper's daughter, Lady Eleanor was given in marriage to Sir Richard Lee he was assigned to escort her and stay as her personal bodyguard. Strong, well built and skilled in hunting and fighting he had readily formed a bond with his mistress's new husband. Hubert had been able to teach Richard much about hunting and weaponry, while Richard, a scholar and Sergeant-at-Law had taught Hubert the rudiments of reading and writing. Unfortunately, when tragedy struck Sir Richard's house and Lady Eleanor died in childbirth, and their baby son died a few days later, the bond between them was strengthened far beyond that of master and servant. Within weeks Sir Richard answered his sovereign's call and fought against the Marcher Lords at Hereford, Pembroke and Shrewsbury. Later, they had been involved in the rout of the Earl of Lancaster's army at Boroughbridge, as they tried to cross the River Ure.

Richard had been assigned a troop of his own and, seemingly without fear, had led from the front. Unfortunately, an arrow had caught him in the left calf, penetrating his leg greave and the muscle itself to embed itself in his horse's belly, so it fell, literally pinning him under it. Then at the mercy of Lancaster's infantry with their bollock daggers, which were used to such effect to slit the throats or slip inside the helmet eye slits of unhorsed knights, he was saved by Hubert's timely intervention as he dispatched two men with two swipes of his great sword.

After the battle Richard was taken to the Abbey of St Mary in York where he lay raving in the hospital with pain and fever for two weeks. And when he recovered, there was Hubert watching over him, ever suspicious of the potions with which the Benedictine monks were wont to ply him. When he was sufficiently recovered, Hubert gave him the sealed orders from the King himself, craving his presence at York Castle. It was then, in a private audience with King Edward that he was given his special commission as Circuit Judge of the King's Northern Realm. It was the sovereign's wish to introduce just law to his realm, and Richard, as an already honoured Sergeant-at-Law, had been an obvious choice. That had been the start of their laborious and lengthy round of all the towns and villages in the area of the Manor of Wakefield and the Honour of Pontefract.

Richard tossed back his head with his mane of coal-black hair and laughed. 'Hubert, how many times must I tell you not to be so fearful of witches, sorcerers and the like. It is all nonsense. All superstition.'

Hubert was not so easily convinced. 'Aye, well, you may say so, Sir Richard. I have not so much learning as you, but I have seen things with these eyes of mine, and I don't intend taking any chances.' He patted his chest. 'I wear an arrowhead around my neck that was pulled from the back of a Crusader at the Siege of Antioch.'

'Antioch, eh?' Richard repeated, with a good-humoured twinkle in his eye. 'That means it must be well over two hundred years old.'

'Aye, old and valuable it is, my lord,' returned Hubert. 'And priceless it is at deflecting arrows. Mayhap you should have worn one at that skirmish at Boroughbridge then you wouldn't have taken that arrow wound.'

Richard ignored his man's seeming logic. 'By valuable I take it that you bought it with good money?'

'It cost me several . . . groats,' Hubert replied evasively.

'And it deflects arrows? How then was it taken from the back of a crusader?'

'Why I suppose — '

There was the sudden whoosh of a missile travelling at great speed then a whumping noise a few feet ahead of them as an arrow embedded itself in an oak tree at the height of their heads.

'Outlaws, Hubert! To arms!'

Both instantly reached for and drew swords as they wheeled round on their horses, in readiness for an attack.

'Hold!' came a voice from nearby. 'There are ten bows aimed at you at this moment. Attempt to escape and your horses will be brought down first.'

'Show yourself, wolfshead!' cried Hubert. 'Know you that we are fighting men and that this is — '

Richard had silenced him with raised hand. 'What do you want, master bowman?' he cried. 'And by what authority do you hold up honest and harmless travellers?'

There was a high-pitched whistle, which was followed moments later by another arrow striking the same tree, but from a different direction. This was immediately followed by another whistle and yet another arrow from another direction.

'By the authority of the power of might,' came the mocking reply. 'Now you can see that there are several of us. Throw down your weapons or fall with them.'

Hubert cursed, but Richard smiled. 'Do as he says, Hubert.' And by example he cast his sword down.

'But Sir Richard?'

'There is a brain behind these men,' Richard explained softly. 'Had they merely wished to kill us they could do so easily.'

With a surly oath Hubert acquiesced.

'Now dismount and walk away from the swords,' came the commanding voice.

When they had done so there was a rustling of leaves and a hooded bowman stepped out from the dense undergrowth. He was of about the same age as Sir Richard, with several days' growth of beard on his tanned and grimy face. He was dressed in a short hooded cloak with a leather doublet underneath, with arms bared from the elbow. His forearms were muscular above leather wrist strappings. From a low slung belt hung a heavy sword and dagger, and upon his back he had a full quiver of arrows.

'Why have you assaulted us like this, fellow?' Richard demanded. 'And why have your comrades not revealed themselves?'

'I ask the questions,' returned the other. 'There is no need for my men to show their faces. And in case you had not noticed,' he said with an amused smile, 'I am the one with a bow and an arrow trained at your chest. So my first question to you is a simple request for your names. My second is to know your purpose for travelling through our woods.'

'I am Sir Richard Lee, Sergeant-at-Law and Circuit Judge of the King's Northern Realm. This is my man, Hubert of Loxley.'

He raised a quizzical eyebrow. 'And what mean you by saying this is your wood? All woods in England belong to the King.'

'He may think they belong to him, but we say they do no longer. Any man passing through here must pay a toll. This wood now belongs to the brothers of the Greenwood.'

'A fine name for thieves and robbers!' growled Hubert.

The bow was instantly turned on Hubert, the stance and steadiness of the holder leaving them in no doubt but that if he wished, the bowman could dispatch instant death.

'I am a patient man,' said the archer calmly, 'but that much cannot be said for my comrades. Do not risk your life more than you are already doing.'

'You are not a King's man, I take it?' Richard asked.

The other sneered. 'King's man, earl's man, what do these matters mean to slaves, serfs, villains and even freemen like myself? Ordinary people are told to follow armies, they cannot choose.'

'You are outside the law, then? I take it you fought at Boroughbridge. On the side of the Earl of Lancaster? Which mayhap makes you a contrariant?'

Again the bowman laughed. 'Aye. Being on

the losing side puts one outside the law. And contrariant makes you both outlaw and traitor!' Very deliberately he turned his head sideways and spat. 'Whatever property or things that one might call one's own are confiscated and you are declared outlaw, common wolfshead that may be killed by any that choose to do so. Just another piece of sport for the rich and powerful.'

He flicked his wrists, pointing the arrow to the nearby shrubbery where the carcass of a doe deer lay with a grey-goose feathered arrow still protruding from its heart. 'Just like that.'

Richard's eyes narrowed slightly. 'That is a hanging offence, to kill the King's deer.'

The archer shrugged. 'We are outside the King's law, but we must still eat. The deer belong to the wood and we claim the woods, so it is ours, not the King's.' His mouth curled into a smile. 'Although if he should care to pardon us we would let him sup with us and feast on our good fresh venison.'

Richard was perspiring still and his calf throbbed. He ran a hand across his brow, striving to seem as casual as he could lest the outlaw perceived him to be afraid rather than in pain. In truth, he had little fear of death, or even very much of a taste for life since his Eleanor had died in childbirth. When his son died a day later he had for a time even hoped for death. That was why he had been perhaps less careful than he needed be at the battle of Boroughbridge.

'You have a wound, Sir Richard,' the archer said. 'I can tell the signs. It may be festering. You may sit down on that tree bough.'

Richard did as he was bidden. 'I thank you — whatever your name is.'

'My comrades call me Hood. I am Robert Hood of Wakefield.' Once again he gave a wan laugh. 'Or rather I was of Wakefield.'

Richard nodded comprehendingly. 'And I imagine you have guessed that we were also at Boroughbridge, but with the King's forces under Sir Andrew Harclay.'

The Hood nodded without betraying any emotion. 'Mayhap you had more choice than we did.'

Richard put a hand on Hubert's wrist as he sensed an outburst from his man. 'And what would you have of us, Robert Hood?'

'A toll for using the Outwood. A mark for each man and his horse. And you will also tell us where you are going.'

Richard opened the pouch that hung from his belt and drew out money, which he lay on the bough beside him. 'There is your toll, Master Hood. As for where we go, know you that we are on the King's business and are going first to Wakefield then to Sandal Castle. It is my mission from the King to sit at the Manor Court and administer the law.'

The Hood tossed his head back and laughed disparagingly. 'Why, there is no law in Wakefield — and then again, too much! Yet it amounts to the same thing. There is no justice and little humanity.' His eyes suddenly became serious. 'Yet I and my men may soon see that it is otherwise.'

'It is not for those outside the law to take the law into their own hands,' returned Richard. 'What riles you that you rant so?'

'Apart from the merry state that you find us in,' said the Hood, relaxing the tension on his bowstring and bringing it down so that it pointed harmlessly at the ground. 'Since Earl Thomas of Lancaster was murdered, Wakefield has fallen into greedy hands. The bailiff is a lackey, the constables are a bunch of dullards and drunks and the new steward is a buffoon. There have been two hangings, a spate of floggings and too many people put in the public stocks for the merest of trifles. My woman's kinswoman was raped and they have charged no one with the crime.'

Richard nodded his head in concern. 'At difficult times order is often lost. Brutality and ignorance often make easy bedfellows. I will change this.'

'I hope so, Sir Richard,' replied the bowman. 'Or I and my men will wreak a savage revenge if the man who took away Lillian's maidenhood is found and goes unpunished.'

'I am a Sergeant-at-Law, Master Hood, but you should understand that I will dispense the law, with no help from anyone outside it.' He rubbed his calf. 'May we go now?'

The Hood stared suspiciously at him for a moment. 'Do not think that you can send anyone after us. We come and go in the woodland and forest as we please. Barnsdale Forest stretches all the way to Sherwood and an army could get lost in there. Yet I shall be keeping watch on what happens in Wakefield. And there had better be justice for my Matilda's Lillian. As for you, Sir Richard, I advise you to seek out Wilfred Oldthorpe the apothecary. He has a shop on the Westgate. He has snakestones and the like and is skilled in treating wounds that fester.'

The knight inclined his head in thanks. 'And so tell me where I can question this kinswoman of your lady. I am mindful of showing even those outside the law that the law of the land works. I will do what I can.'

'Ask at the Bucket Inn near Jacob's Well. The mistress there will tell you all.' And stepping backwards he disappeared into the greenery.

Five minutes later, as Richard and Hubert made their way onwards, Richard was puzzled to see Hubert grinning to himself. 'I did not think that you were amused by our little adventure, Hubert.'

'Oh that! Pah, we could have dealt with the fellow and his rabble if needs be, yet I could see that you planned to talk to the fellow and that you had the matter well in hand without me, my lord. No, I was just pleased to have given you proof.'

'Proof of what?'

'Why, of the power of my talisman! It deflected all three of those arrows they fired at us.'

★ ★ ★

The road from the Outwood that led towards Wakefield was gated but unmanned. It led first across heathland with the Pinder-fields to the left, the undulating pastures where the township kept their cattle. Beyond that it broadened out into the wild heathery land of the Old Park which contained the East Moor, the Park Hills and the Wind Hill, upon which could be seen one of the several windmills that served the locality. To their right they passed cultivated lands, divided up into ridges and furrows, upon which several handfuls of smock-clad peasants could be seen working. And beyond that could be seen the half-wooded Great Park which was famously well stocked with deer, partridges and boar.

Hubert had been ruminating in silence until they were well clear of the wood and the habitations of Wakefield came into view. 'So tell me, my lord, what do we know of this town of Wakefield?'

Sir Richard wiped his brow again. 'I was well briefed before we began our journey and read up about it last night. It is an ancient town that the Saxons built on an eminence that slopes down to the River Calder, although they say that some of the townships around it were actually Viking settlements.' He pointed along the length of the rough track they were making their way down. 'There are four main roads, each with a toll-gate which closes at the eight bell curfew. This is the Northgate, the others being Kirkgate, Westgate and Warrengate. The main three roads meet at the market-place, which is called Birch Hill. It is said to be of a goodly size, with a pond, a market cross and a great circular area that they call the Bull Ring, for obvious reasons. The prison is also there, as is a church and the Moot Hall, where I shall preside over the Manor Court.'

Some distance further they passed a wayside chantry chapel, bearing the markings of St John the Baptist. Its door was closed, but beside it was a carved trough full of water, presumably blessed, and an offertory box in which some wag had left the body of a drowned rat.

Hubert snorted. 'It looks as if there are some irreverent dogs around this town, my lord.' He made the sign of the cross as they passed. 'And what of Sandal Castle? Will the new steward accommodate us?' Hubert asked.

'He has been ordered by the King's messenger to receive us. Sir Thomas Deyville is thought to be an able enough fellow, but he has no knowledge of law and there is concern that he may have been over-zealous in settling in. His majesty wanted a firm hand, yet he knows that he must not make enemies of his own people. That is why I have been given this roving commission, to introduce fair law into the Manor of Wakefield.'

'And this Sandal is it far from Wakefield?'

'A couple of miles on the other side of the river.'

They had reached the gate of the Northgate road, on either side of which were a couple of humble dwellings. The gate itself was a stout timber on great hinges that barred their way. A middle-aged woman with a closed eye appeared from one of the hovels, wiping her hands on a dirty apron.

'Good day, masters. I am Alice-at-the-Bar and I and my son are charged with letting in those as wants to come and keeping those in that mustn't stray.' She immediately burst into a cackle that sent a shiver through Sir Richard's spine. 'It is a toll to enter, unless you tickle my fancy.'

Sir Richard eyed Alice-at-the-Bar dispassionately. 'Know you that I am Sir Richard Lee, the Circuit Judge of the King's Northern Realm and by his warrant I and my man must enter Wakefield immediately. I shall be presiding over the court,' he said meaningfully. 'I would treat any news that the town gatekeepers were taking bribes, or worse, with appropriate severity!'

Alice-at-the-Bar's one good eye shot open wide in fear. 'I meant nothing, sir. I jest a lot, but I mean nothing.' And with a manly whistle she called her son, a spindly youth, and together they raised the bar and let the two riders through.

'Where can I find first the Bucket Inn near the Jacob's Well and then Wilfred Oldthorpe the apothecary?' Richard asked, tossing a farthing, which was caught nimbly and thankfully by Alice-at-the-Bar, despite her one eye.

'That would be easy, sir. Like as not at this time of the day Master Wilfred Oldthorpe will be drinking ale at the inn. You won't get a finer brew in the whole of Yorkshire than at Mistress Quigley's Bucket Inn.'

And after she had given Sir Richard directions she winked at Hubert, who winced and unconsciously touched the arrow-head beneath his surcoat.

★ ★ ★

Wakefield was a straggling town of gabled wooden houses, most of which had under-crofts on the ground floor for keeping animals or storing supplies, and which were roofed with either thatch or reeds. The main streets were wide and well rutted by ox-carts and pack-horses, with side streets and narrow alleys leading off them. Dung heaps, puddles and refuse of various sorts made walking in a straight line difficult, the result being that the streets were full of animals and folk going about their business in an erratic, almost zig-zag manner. As Sir Richard and Hubert rode down the Northgate they passed open doors from whence emanated the odours of wood smoke, baking bread and cooking. All this mingled with the smell from a nearby tannery and of ground corn from the two water-mills and a great windmill visible on the Westgate.

They found their way to the lane on which the Jacob's Well was sited. This provided fresh water to the east end of the town and, as it happened, to the brew-house of the Bucket Inn. The inn itself was the most conspicuous and impressive building on the lane. It was a two storeyed affair, with a thatched roof, two outhouses and a large brew-house. On either side of the door were two half-barrels containing mulberry bushes, while from a joist above the low doorway hung a bucket from which trailing roses seemed to cascade out.

The smell of beer, cooking meat and onions made Hubert's stomach gurgle. 'A comely place, this Bucket Inn looks,' he said to Sir Richard. And then hopefully, 'would we have time for a mug of ale and a bite, my lord? It would mayhap help to wash away the taste of that rogue who robbed us in the Outwood.'

Richard smiled as he dismounted and handed the reins of his mount to an ostler who suddenly appeared from behind the brew-house. 'We were not robbed, Hubert. We merely chose to pay his toll.'

Hubert frowned. 'But it was illegal, my lord. Surely you — '

But Richard had stopped listening. He pushed open the door of the inn, bent his head under the lintel and entered the smoky interior.

It was a large noisy room, one end of which was taken up with barrels from which a couple of maids were pouring mugs of ale, while two more girls and a surly looking potman were dispensing them and platters of steaming food among the various heavy wooden trestle tables. A roaring fire, despite the heat of the day, kept a large iron pot above the flames steaming away, filling the inn with a pleasing aroma. This was enhanced by the smell of beef and roast chicken coming out of the open door of a kitchen.

'A popular place, right enough,' Sir Richard said over his shoulder to Hubert, as the latter closed the door behind them. 'I think refreshment would be a good idea before we begin work.'

The potman passed them and grunted at an empty table by the fire. They sat and removed their gauntlets. Richard was looking round the inn at the assorted clientele when a pleasant female voice demanded his attention.

'Good day, gentlemen, welcome to my inn. And what can I get you today?'

Richard had barely looked at a woman

since his Eleanor had died, but this woman immediately struck his attention. She was a large-breasted woman of about twenty-five with a narrow waist, hazel-eyed with wisps of brunette hair escaping from her simple cap. Her skin was too tanned for a lady, yet it suited her pretty and healthy looking face. Her smile revealed strong white teeth with a slight gap between her two front ones.

He noted that although she talked directly to him, yet her glance had by-passed him and fallen upon Hubert, whom she graced with a smile that lit up her face. Richard smiled inwardly, for he had long been aware of Hubert's attraction to women.

'You are I take it Mistress Quigley, the owner of this inn?'

'That is me, Beatrice Quigley. You have heard of my inn, sir?'

'The old woman, Alice-at-the-Bar told us when we came through the Northgate. She said that you would be able to point out a local apothecary by the name of Oldthorpe.'

Beatrice smiled and pointed to a far corner where a portly, middle-aged man wearing a battered liripipe hat was staring into a large pot of beer. Before him were the remains of a meal. 'Master Wilfred enjoys a hearty lunch,' she replied. 'But if you need his medical skills I would suggest waiting a couple of hours, until he gets over his — refreshments!'

Both Hubert and Richard smiled. 'I may do that,' said Richard. 'But I would also like you to tell me where I might talk with a girl called Lillian.'

'Who told you that I would know that, my lord?'

'I heard of it from a man who called himself the Hood.'

He watched and saw the slight widening of her eyes, as if in alarm. Then her face registered suspicion. 'And why should you want to talk to this girl Lillian, my lord?'

'I am Sir Richard Lee and I — '

A scream suddenly rang out from somewhere upstairs and a moment later a handsome, bare-headed blonde woman appeared at the top of a flight of stairs. She looked shocked, her head turning right and left as if searching for someone. Then they fell upon the mistress of the inn. 'Beatrice!' she cried. 'Come up. You are needed.' She held up her hands which were covered with blood. 'And bring that apothecary!'

The inn customers mostly fell silent at this entry, but no-one seemed particularly interested. Or rather, no one seemed eager to get involved when blood was apparent.

Richard and Hubert watched Beatrice hitch up her dress and rush through the crowded inn to grab the sleeve of Wilfred Oldthorpe the apothecary and half drag him towards the stairs.

'Come, Hubert!' Richard said, as they disappeared upstairs. 'I am always nervous when I meet someone for the first time with blood on their hands.'

Hubert followed his master with alacrity. He was not so much aware of the blood, as the fact that the women of Wakefield seemed uncommonly attractive.

2

Trouble at the Bucket Inn

Albin of Rouncivale was feeling pleased with himself. Things had been going well for him ever since his venture in Pontefract, following the execution of the Earl of Lancaster. He had spent a highly profitable week in the town and only left when the local priest had actually offered him physical violence for poaching on his territory. The fat, useless fool! He had no idea of how to feed off the wages of sin, unlike himself. He guessed that he had seen and counselled more of the Pontefract folk than ever ventured into his church in a month of Sundays. And at that he had laughed, for he called every day a *sinday*, and Sunday just an extra big day to harvest the crop of sinners, perverts and those who were contemplating sinning.

From there he had meandered around the hamlets and villages of the Honour of Pontefract, setting up a temporary pulpit in each and then retiring to the local inn or hostelry where he was usually able to obtain a back room or an outhouse to receive the sinful. And he grinned at just how many of them there were. Enough to make him a rich man some day, he hoped.

Eventually, he had come to Wakefield, which seemed to be a veritable den of iniquity, incest and just plain ordinary dishonesty. In fact, a place no different from anywhere else in King Edward's realm. Except that it boasted a market, a regular fair and the prospect of a great deal of trade as the feast of Corpus Christi approached, when the town guilds would be putting on the Mystery Plays that the town prided itself upon. Yes, he reflected, there was much to look forward to.

'Good day, Master Pardoner,' cried one of a group of five maids who were busily treading laundry in a trough at the back of one of the great timber-framed houses behind the parish church of All Saints. 'Are you preaching or pardoning this day?'

'A little of both,' he said with a smile, turning in his saddle and waving the cross that he had balanced against his shoulder, like a pikestaff. 'But you already bought a pardon from me yesterday, didn't you?'

'I did. But I think I might need another after what me and my man got up to last night.'

She was a comely, buxom girl, as indeed

were the others. They worked away, showing off their legs and arms as they trod the linen of the great house in the trough of urine and lavender, giggling merrily among themselves.

'Perhaps I shall be seeing you later then,' he said over his shoulder. 'I shall be preaching near the Bull Ring this afternoon.'

'We might all be there, Pardoner,' cried the forthright one again, and they all trilled with suggestive ribald laughter.

Albin of Rouncivale grinned and stroked his smooth beardless chin. Yes, the wenches of Wakefield seemed to be a healthy bunch with good appetites in matters pleasurable.

He coaxed his donkey towards the Bull Ring, where the bull-baiting was held every fair's day, but which now was packed with temporary market-stalls. He threaded his way through the throng then passed the all but deserted square by the Tolbooth, which served as the town gaol, and the nearby Moot Hall. The town stocks and pillory were in the middle of the square. A miserable, unkempt-looking fellow plastered with rotten vegetables and dung was sitting there, with his feet ensnared by the great hinged boards. Beside him was a flask of water and a crust of bread. He looked up beseechingly at the sound of the donkey's feet.

'Bless me, Father?' he asked.

Albin of Rouncivale stared at him then slowly shook his head. A cruel smile passed over his thin lips. The fool had committed a crime and he was being punished. That was only right. After all, if he was stupid enough to get caught, that was his problem. The Pardoner made a point of never being seen doing wrong. He had no intention of ever getting caught and suffering the humiliation of the stocks or the pillory — or worse.

★ ★ ★

For all of Wilfred the apothecary's portly, middle-aged build, and the fact that he had been dragged up the stairs by Beatrice when he was actually faced with a situation requiring his skills in medicine, he responded with admirable swiftness. Although Richard and Hubert were only mere moments behind them, yet already the apothecary had assessed the situation and pitched in.

It was a spectacle that Hubert of Loxley had not been prepared for. Despite all of his battle experience, when he had seen men's bodies hacked, maimed and dismembered, the sight of a young girl bleeding profusely on a pallet bed from knife cuts to her own wrists made him feel weak at the knees. Richard noticed and steadied him until he regained his strength and straightened himself with a combined look of gratitude and embarrassment.

'What has happened here?' Richard asked. 'Why has this girl taken a knife to herself?'

Beatrice had been standing with her arm about the shoulders of the woman who had called her upstairs, while the apothecary was applying tourniquets that he had taken out of the shoulder bag that he had discarded on the floor. At the sound of Richard's voice she turned, her face grim and challenging.

'And exactly what business is it of yours?' Beatrice demanded. She had disengaged her arm from the other's shoulder and now stood with her hands on her hips, effectively barring the entrance to the room. 'Who might you be anyway?'

'I am Sir Richard Lee, the Circuit Judge of the King's Northern Realm and this is my assistant Hubert of Loxley. And since taking one's own life is a crime against the King's Law and against the Church, it is very much my business.'

The girl was about seventeen years old and a blonde beauty by anyone's standards. She was unconscious, her face almost alabaster pale, and her breathing fast becoming laboured. A glance at her and the woman with corn-blonde hair who stood wringing her bloodstained hands told Richard that they were not distantly related.

'The girl is not yet dead, my lord,' said Wilfred the apothecary. 'And she will not die this time, if I have anything to do about it.'

'Well said, Master Apothecary,' returned Richard. 'How can we aid you?'

'By helping me get her to my premises on Westgate. I have need of my wife, who will help me cauterize these wounds. Then I will prepare a restorative.'

'Has . . . has she lost much blood?' Beatrice asked, anxiously.

Wilfred pointed to the blood-soaked blankets on the pallet bed. 'A few minutes longer and she might have lost a mortal amount.' He clicked his tongue. 'But I think that she will recover well. By bleeding herself she has probably removed much of the black melancholic humour that had made her feel so wretched.'

Beatrice shook her head. 'It is not a disease humour that made her do this, Master Apothecary. It was the crime committed on her person, as we all know.' Then before he could reply she turned to the other woman. 'There, Matilda, you can rest easy again. She will live and grow old.'

The woman called Matilda heaved a sigh of relief and bent to stroke the younger woman's brow. 'May the Lord be praised,' she said. 'I will not let you out of my sight after this.'

The apothecary heaved himself to his feet and looked at Richard and Hubert. 'Then if one of you gentlemen would carry her I will lead the way.'

Richard was about to move forward, but Hubert stayed him with a hand on his arm. 'I will take her, my lord.' And, bending, he gently scooped her up as if she weighed nothing at all, then he followed the apothecary down the stairs.

'This girl is called Lillian, is she not?' Richard asked of the two women.

They both exchanged looks of amazement.

'How . . . how do you know this, my lord?' Matilda asked.

'I talked with a man in the Outwood. He is your man, I believe.'

Matilda gasped and covered her face with her hands. 'My Robin? You . . . you saw my Robin?'

Beatrice quickly interjected. 'Robert Hood is a good man. You have not harmed him, have you, sir?'

Richard shook his head. 'He was well and was looking at me from the other side of a longbow when we talked. He told me that your kinswoman had been raped, and I said that I, as the Circuit Judge of the King's

Northern Realm would investigate. I am a man of my word.' He turned to the stairs. 'My man and I shall take Lillian to the apothecary's and I will call back later. There are certain things that I must know about here.'

★ ★ ★

They rode up to the Birch Hill, passed the busy market with its many stalls and booths of timber and plaster, the superior ones having dwelling quarters above them. As they made their way through the noisy throng of people, pigs and sheep, they caught the characteristic smell of blood and offal from the shambles, where the butchers plied their trade and the odour of fish and the noise of poultry as they neared the market cross. Finally escaping the crowd they arrived some moments later at Wilfred Oldthorpe's establishment on the Westgate. All the while Hubert had ridden with Lillian in his arms. He kept looking at her concernedly, as if worried that the journey could cause fresh haemorrhaging.

There were trays of fruit and vegetables and bundles of herbs on a wooden table outside the premises, and above the open door there was a signboard with a painting of a flask of wine beside a pestle and mortar. Through the large open-shuttered window a young woman could be seen measuring a quantity of some sort of powder and pouring it into a jug which was being stirred by a man in his mid-twenties who was bent almost double and who had the hump of a hunch-back over his right shoulder. His open mouth dribbled saliva and he seemed to move slowly as if his wits were impaired.

'Emma!' the apothecary called through the window. 'I have a patient. Get the cautery irons.'

Richard stood aside to let the apothecary inside, and then Hubert followed carrying the girl in his arms.

'Is your daughter used to treating wounds, Master Apothecary?' Richard asked, as the woman responded immediately and moved quickly through into a back room.

'Emma is my wife,' the apothecary replied drily. 'And yes, she assists me in many things. She is also skilled in midwifery, the preparation of herbs and the spicing of wines.' He spread a hand out to indicate the shelves that reached to the ceiling of the room. They were laden with labelled jars of herbs and spices, bundles of liquorice roots and sticks of rhubarb. Against the counter were open sacks of various grains and cereals and against another wall were hogsheads of wine and shelves full of a variety of flasks. The floor was covered with reeds, lavender and fleabane stalks.

'And this is our grocery business,' he went on, with a note of pride in his voice. 'Bring the lady through here if you would, sirs.' Then, to the simple-looking servant, 'Look after any customers, Gilbert.' But seeing the flustered look on the man's face, he snorted, then said, 'Just call out if anyone comes in.'

They went along a narrow corridor and entered a room with a desk, shelves with more bottles and flasks of medicines and heaps of scrolls. A small fire was burning and Emma, the apothecary's wife was bending in front of it, prodding some instruments with a gloved hand. Wilfred Oldthorpe pointed to a couch beside a shuttered window. 'Lay her down gently, sir.'

Hubert laid her down and stroked a wisp of corn-coloured hair from in front of her eyes. 'I would feel better if the girl would wake up,' he said, anxiety written across his face.

'She will wake as soon as I cauterize her wounds,' said the apothecary. 'You see if she doesn't.'

'Good, for I mean to talk to her,' said Richard.

Emma turned from the fire to face them. 'I

have the instruments all ready, Husband. They just need a moment longer.'

Richard found himself studying her, for she was a singularly attractive woman of about twenty-eight. Perhaps half the apothecary's age, he guessed. She was dressed in a green gown with an apron covered in flour and some sort of paste. Her long raven hair was braided and looped twice about her brow. Her skin was pleasingly pale with just a hint of colour in her cheeks. Her features were fine and her lips were full. Her eyes settled upon him and she smiled.

The apothecary immediately set to work and unbandaged Lillian's wrists. As soon as he released the tourniquets blood started flowing again. 'Hmm, I had hoped that I would have got away without doing this, but the blood will not stop unless I seal the wounds with heat.' He redid the tourniquets and then took the glove that his wife proffered him. 'Hold her, Emma,' he instructed.

Emma did as she had been bidden without question. Clearly, she knew what was needed and he had little doubt that she realized that Lillian had just a short time before attempted to take her own life.

Wilfred Oldthorpe took one of the cautery irons from the fire in his gloved hand, then

41

removed the temporary dressing and moved closer with the red hot metal. 'Hold her hand will you, sir,' he asked Hubert, who winced, but immediately grasped Lillian's hand.

As soon as the cautery iron touched and seared her flesh, Lillian's eyelids flickered. And as the apothecary worked the instrument to seal the wound the air was filled with the stench of burning flesh. Then Lillian's eyes opened wide with a start, her mouth gaped and she screamed. It was but a short scream, for her body bucked most violently, only to be restrained by the surprisingly strong hands of Emma Oldthorpe and Hubert. Then she swooned and lapsed into unconsciousness again.

The apothecary had kept working through all this. 'Now take her other hand and I will seal the other wound.' His eyes rose to meet those of the horrified Hubert. 'I told you she would wake,' he said, with a smug professional grin.

Richard had been watching Lillian closely. Now he was all too aware that his leg was beginning to pain him quite badly again, and he could feel perspiration dripping down his face. He looked up to see Emma Oldthorpe appraising him with interest. Immediately she tapped the apothecary on the shoulder.

'Husband, I think that once we have

finished with this patient, you had better see to this gentleman, too. He looks as if he may have a fever!'

* * *

Half an hour later, while Emma and Hubert sat with Lillian, Richard let the apothecary examine his leg wound.

'It is festering, but the fester has not reached the bone,' Wilfred Oldthorpe informed Richard. 'I have just the right treatment for this.' And after he had cleaned the wound to remove the film of pus that had collected, he pulled a pot off a shelf and from it drew out a foul-smelling piece of rotting cowhide, which was covered in a green mould. He smoothed it over the calf wound then bound it with a bandage. 'This mould will cleanse the pus and inflammation away. I have seen it work on many a festering wound or sore. This was an arrow wound, I take it.'

'Aye, it happened at Boroughbridge. It has been fine and was healing well until a couple of days ago.'

'It is damp that does it,' Wilfred said, standing and wiping his hands on his sides. 'It acts upon the fire element and makes a steamy humour which makes the flesh fester.'

Sir Richard nodded. As an educated man

he was aware of the Doctrine of Humours, the principle upon which medical men worked out what sort of ailment someone had. 'Bleeding you a little might also help,' he suggested, somewhat doubtfully.

Richard produced some coins and left them on the desk. 'I think not, Master Oldthorpe. I lost enough blood at the hands of the monks at the Abbey of St Mary in York. It feels more comfortable already. Now, when can I talk to the girl?'

'You may talk to her now,' came Emma Oldthorpe's voice from the door. 'She is awake and a trifle groggy. I have given her some of your best nostrum for her pain, Husband.'

Hubert was still sitting beside Lillian's couch. She was leaning against a bank of cushions that Emma had provided, her wrists neatly bound, an empty goblet on a small table by her side.

Richard introduced himself and sat down in the chair that Hubert vacated for him.

Lillian immediately covered her face with her hands and began to sob. 'I am such a fool,' she whispered. 'I . . . I . . . am so sorry. I just feel so . . . so unclean. I am so guilty.'

'Lillian, I make no judgement about you trying to take your own life, although I am sure that you understand that the Church considers it a sin. I believe it is a matter for your own conscience,' Richard said gently. 'I will say that there is no reason for you to feel guilty if you have been raped. That is someone else's crime, and if we find out who did it, I shall see that they are punished as the law decrees.'

'But I am tainted! I will never be able to wed.'

Richard put a hand on her shoulder. 'You are not tainted. You have been wronged. Now tell me, what did you see of your assailant?'

'N . . . nothing, my lord. It was dark and I was caught from behind. He threatened me and . . . and . . . he — '

'Go on,' Richard coaxed.

'He used me from behind! Like a dog! Then he told me to be still and not look after him. I was too afraid to move a muscle until I thought he had gone.'

'The villain!' said Hubert between grated teeth. 'I would like to meet him — face to face.'

'Did you get any sense of him?' Richard persisted. 'Was he big or small? Old or young? Did he smell of anything?'

'I sensed nothing about him at all, my lord.'

Richard pursed his lips. 'And where did this take place?'

'In the parish cemetery, my lord, three days ago.'

'And it was dark. So it was after the eight bells curfew,' Richard reasoned. 'Why were you abroad then? You know that is against the law?'

Lillian bit her lip. 'I was there on my cousin's business, my lord. She was unwell with a flux and was vomiting her insides out. I was there to meet her betrothed.'

'You mean the outlaw, Robert Hood?'

Lillian looked uncertainly from Sir Richard to Hubert. Then her lower lip began to tremble and she once more burst into tears. At the sound of her misery Emma Oldthorpe the apothecary's wife came into the room and threw a comforting arm about Lillian's shoulders. Lillian's sobbing gradually settled down and she sniffed and finally calmed.

'Yes. Robin Hood. We call him Robin,' she explained. 'And that is why I feel so dirty. So guilty. I — I fear that it might have been my cousin's betrothed who ravished me.'

★　★　★

A miller's cart was parked outside the Bucket Inn when Richard and Hubert returned. The miller himself, a work-hardened fellow of some sixty summers, bow-legged, pug-faced

46

and ruddy of complexion was struggling through the inn door with a sack of flour. Hubert had dismounted and was a step behind him when he stumbled and went headlong, the sack slumping beside him.

'Let me help you, father,' said Hubert, helping the miller to his feet and then lofting the sack effortlessly upon his shoulder. 'Where would this need to be taken?'

But the miller dusted his knees and shook his head. 'I thank you, sir, but I am no father to thee and I shall do my own work.' And saying, he took the flour sack from him and made his way through the busy inn towards the kitchen door.

'A sour fellow,' Hubert whispered to Sir Richard.

'He is not sour by nature,' said Beatrice, the landlady, appearing from behind the door. 'That is Midge the Miller, who runs the mill beside the bridge over the Calder. He is surly because his son followed Thomas of Lancaster and was deemed a contrariant and outlaw — like so many good men — by the King.'

Richard put a hand on Hubert's elbow to silence any remonstration. His assistant had a strong sense of loyalty and was apt to react swiftly. Too swiftly at times, Richard felt. Then turning to Beatrice, he said, 'Lillian is

47

well and sleeps at the apothecary's house, cared for by his wife.'

'Ah, the lovely Emma,' Beatrice replied cryptically. 'Matilda will be well pleased. Can she go to see her?'

'Soon,' returned Sir Richard. 'After we have a talk.'

Beatrice nodded as if expecting his words. She led them up the stairs to the room where Lillian had been lying. The linen had been changed and fresh lavender strewn about the floor. Matilda was standing by the shuttered window, a willowy woman in a mustard yellow gown, now with a plain white wimple covering her head and throat. At their entry she whirled round, concern on her face.

Richard told her of her cousin's treatment. 'Master Oldthorpe is a skilled apothecary,' he added, admiringly.

'I thank you for your intervention, my lord. Lillian has been through the torments of hell!'

'But now I think it is time that you told me more of these torments,' said Richard, gesturing for them all to sit. 'First, I understand that you are close to the outlaw Robert Hood?'

Matilda's chin came up and she met Sir Richard's regard. 'We are betrothed, my lord. We would have been wed this summer, but for the wars of the mighty. It was only through following his feudal lord, Thomas of Lancaster, that he was outlawed.'

'As was Much, the Miller's son. You met his father Midge as you came in,' Beatrice explained. 'He, too, was pressed into serving the earl and was outlawed after the battle of Boroughbridge.'

'That explains his annoyance when I called him father,' Hubert commented.

'My Robin had built a house on Birch Hill, a five-roomed dwelling that was to be our home for life. It had cost him a fine of twenty pence in the Manor Court in 1316, because he had refused to join the old Earl de Warenne's army when he went north against the Scots. This time he did not dare refuse when the Earl of Lancaster demanded an extra seven hundred bowmen from the Manor of Wakefield when he was moving north to avoid the King's army.'

Richard nodded his head understandingly. 'And his house has been repossessed. This would have been by William de la Beche, who was temporary custodian of Sandal Castle, before it was handed over to Sir Thomas Deyville, the Deputy Steward.'

'No, it was the new one, Sir Thomas Deyville,' said Beatrice. 'He is a man with a heart of stone.'

Matilda put a hand on Beatrice's arm. 'If it had not been for my friend Beatrice here, I would be destitute.' She hung her head. 'And my Lillian with me.' She sighed, then raised her head proudly again. 'She is my cousin, but I have been more sister to her. I have to look after her.'

Beatrice interrupted. 'You may not have had time enough to see for yourself yet, my lord, but Wakefield is under law such as we have never had before. There have been hangings and floggings. The Deputy Steward has a heavy hand when it comes to meting out punishment. William Scathelocke, one of the town pinders has been in the stocks for two days for not clearing cattle out of the corn fields. Every few hours he is plastered with cow dung. He is a mischievous rogue, I have to admit, but he doesn't deserve that.'

Richard scowled. 'I will be having words with the Deputy Steward of the Manor soon enough and I shall be taking court matters in hand. I take it that this crime of rape has been reported?'

Matilda nodded. 'We reported it to the Westgate constable and to the Deputy Steward's clerk. There was a pitiful hue and cry, but what else could we do? We are but women. And nothing has happened yet.'

Richard and Hubert looked at one another, both equally unimpressed at this information about the sort of protection offered to women, or the manner in which such cases were handled throughout most of England.

'Lillian told me that this crime took place after curfew in the parish cemetery. Why was she there?'

Matilda shook her head guiltily. 'She was going on my behalf, to meet Robin. I was too ill with a flux of the bowels to go. But, as it happened, he could not make it in time. And when he could get there he was unable to get past the constables into the town. The hue and cry was that effective, at least.'

'And some evil villain ravished her!' said Beatrice angrily. 'There are many undesirable types lurking about in the darkness and the constables and their men cannot cover all of the town wards.' She looked at her friend and pursed her lips. 'We realize it was madness to let a young girl like Lillian go.'

'You are sure that Robert Hood could not get into the town? You have seen him since?'

Matilda nodded as she wrung her hands. 'He . . . he is my betrothed, my lord. He is an honourable man and . . . and I do not think that he should have been outlawed.'

But Richard was thinking of what Lillian had told him. What she believed to have happened. He would investigate the case and reserve his opinion about Robert Hood, the contrariant and outlaw.

3

Sandal Castle

A goodly crowd had formed at the edge of the Bull Ring where Albin of Rouncivale had set up his temporary pulpit. He had stuck his staff with the brass cross into the ground and tethered his donkey to it. As usual he had babbled a few choice Latin sayings at them, sung a hymn and then harangued them with the parable of the sheep and the goats.

'Yes, hearken, my brethren,' he cried out. 'There are few among us who are without sin. Sin has been inherited from your fathers, from your mothers and it grows within each and every one of you like a canker.' He watched the faces of his audience and suppressed a smile as he saw folk wince and shuffle uneasily. He prided himself on being able to spot guilty looks and the credulity of the God-fearing. He had a trick of opening his eyes wide to glare and glower at individuals, as much as if to tell them that he could see the sins within them. He knew that if he let that glance linger momentarily upon a suitable listener then he would be assured of a customer.

He turned and pulled his saddle-bag from his donkey. 'I am Albin of Rouncivale and I bring pardons to those in need.' He delved inside his bag and pulled out a small piece of parchment with an ornate Latin inscription upon it. 'This can bring absolution from the Bishop of Rochester, himself. Why risk being without one? An accident on the way home, a sudden illness visited upon your house and you could rue the fact that you go to Judgement without a pardon.' His hand delved inside the bag again and came out with a small casket. 'And for those who have sinned badly I bring things blessed by having been touched by the sainted. In this box I have a piece of the sail of the boat that St Peter himself fished from. And more, I have relics of saints that by their touch may heal the sick, cast out demons or save the darkest of souls. I have bones of St Thomas himself. And I have other gifts from the saintly.'

Richard and Hubert had stopped to listen to what was going on as they made their way back from another visit to the apothecary's before leaving to complete their journey to Sandal Castle. Richard watched in amusement as members of the crowd hailed and closed in on the Pardoner, their hands going to pouches and purses.

'I fancy that a pardon might be a good investment, my lord,' said Hubert.

To his surprise, Richard put a hand firmly on his own as he reached for the purse that hung from his belt.

'No, Hubert. You have your arrow-head. Let that be enough,' he whispered. 'Anyway, what need have you of pig bones or horses' teeth.'

'Pig bones, my lord?' Hubert's eyes suddenly grew in size and a growl threatened to escape from his lips. But this also was stopped when Richard put his forefinger to his lips.

'Of course. A lot of these Pardoners are charlatans. They play on people's fears, on their guilty little secrets. No, put away your money, good Hubert, and let us away to Sandal.'

Hubert gave the Pardoner a rueful glare and then turned his horse to follow his master.

The afternoon sun was starting to go down by the time they rode down the Kirkgate, passed the King's Mill, one of the soke-mills within the town of Wakefield, and crossed the great timber-buttressed bridge over the Calder. On the south side of the river, the stench of a tallow works, so important to the manufacture of precious candles, was so bad that they had to cover their noses and mouths with their neckclothes and urge their mounts to speed up the gently rising, meandering road towards the village of Sandal Magna. On their way they passed groups of merchants, itinerants and shepherds herding their flocks to the wool market on Birch Hill.

The terrain was gently undulating, intermittently wooded or cultivated in the characteristic strip farming of the area. Each field was divided into strips or selions, measuring about thirty feet in breadth by a furlong in length. Each of these were divided up by green unploughed balks for the serfs to walk upon and lead their oxen, as indeed several were doing as they passed. The land looked lush, with the usual rotation of crops that was practised throughout the land. Yet in addition to the cereal and root crops, Richard noticed that there were also fields of rhubarb and liquorice, both specialties for which the manor was famous. To the east was a great expanse of heathland.

'My lord, before we arrive at Sandal Castle, lest I show my ignorance to the Deputy Steward, could you explain again about why we have been sent to this centre of rebelliousness?'

Richard grinned. 'Hubert, I believe that you pretend to be more ignorant of politics than you really are!' Then seeing his assistant's face drop into an expression of wounded chagrin he shook his head good-humouredly and continued.

'You must first understand that the Manor of Wakefield, and the Honour of Pontefract are two great estates that were deliberately woven together when they were granted to their respective lords by King William the First, he that they called the Conqueror. The Manor of Wakefield was given to the de Warenne family and the Honour of Ponte-fract to the de Lacy family. Each of these holdings is huge and roughly of the same area. The Manor of Wakefield extends from Normanton in the east to distant Halifax in the west, some thirty miles of land that takes in about one hundred and twenty towns, villages and hamlets, with Wakefield as its centre and Sandal Castle as the lord's stronghold. For the most part the two houses have lived in harmony since then, until the last incumbents took over each manor.'

'That would be the eighth Earl Warenne, the Earl of Surrey who held the Manor of Wakefield.'

'That is correct, Hubert. And the Honour of Pontefract passed from the de Lacy family to Thomas Plantagenet, the Earl of Lancaster through his marriage to Alice de Lacy. Earl

Thomas was cousin to King Edward himself.'

'Aye, and we fought against the Earl of Lancaster's army at Boroughbridge.'

'True again, but we need to go back a few years to understand all that has happened. Earl Warenne was a man whose temperament was ruled by Mercury, tempered by Venus. At the age of nineteen he was wed to Joan of Bar, old King Edward Longshanks's ten-year-old granddaughter, but the marriage was doomed to fail and was never consummated. Before long he was living in sin with one Maude de Nerford.'

Hubert laughed. 'So, he needed a woman not a girl. There is too much marrying early among nobles in my opinion.'

'That is as maybe. Yet there is more to hear. Neither Earl Warenne nor his neighbour Earl Lancaster approved of the new King Edward the Second's favourite, Piers Gaveston.'

'He who became the Earl of Cornwall? Why was that, my lord?'

'For the reason that the king doted on him and favoured him above all the rest of the nobility. Gaveston was the son of a Gascon knight in service to the old king, and, as a youth, he and the present king, when he was still the crown prince, declared themselves brothers-in-arms. Old Longshanks was furious about this and had him banished. Yet the

58

banishment lasted only until the king died and King Edward of Carnarvon, our present king, brought him back, conferred on him the title of Earl of Cornwall and married him off to Margaret de Clare. But it was not a match made in heaven.

'And then the king left to marry Isabella of France. When he did so he made Gaveston Regent of England and gave him a seal of absence, so that he was effectively king in Edward's absence. Because of that twenty of the great barons, the Lord Ordainers, rose up and forced the king to banish him again, this time to Ireland as Lord Lieutenant. He was not there long, however. Edward brought him back and the two picked up on their relationship.'

'As brothers-in-arms. What of that, my lord?'

'Do not be naïve, Hubert. It is said that they knew each other, as a man may know a woman.'

Hubert's eyes widened for a moment, as if he was surprised to hear this news. But then he shrugged. 'It is natural to many I suppose, but for me, I would prefer the firm body of a wench.' His face fell into a grin and he chortled. 'Especially if I was a king and could have whatever woman I chose.'

Richard shook his head at Hubert's sense

of humour, then he went on, 'After a failed military campaign against the Scots he was banished again, after pressure from the nobles, including Earl Warenne and Earl Lancaster. And once again he returned swiftly, although it seems it was to see his newborn daughter.'

'A goodly and true thing for any father,' commented Hubert.

'But dangerous for him and the king. The country was on the verge of civil war, so Edward and Gaveston left London for the north, taking with them the royal wardrobe. They travelled to York and then on to Newcastle, but the nobles had divided and pursued them. Earl Lancaster came over the Pennines and almost caught them. He did take the Queen and it is said that he found and kept the royal treasure that they had been forced to leave. Edward and Gaveston fled down the river to Tynemouth and then took a boat to Scarborough. There King Edward left Gaveston at Scarborough Castle while he hurried to York to try to raise an army.'

The road levelled out and they came to a great fishpond which abutted another field system where serfs were still at work. Richard dismounted and led his horse to the water and let it lap some up. Hubert followed suit, patting his mount affectionately. As they stood there they heard the cadence of a galloping horse upon the road. Moments later a rider in the livery of the Manor of Wakefield passed them, his sweating horse's hoofs kicking up a trail of dust as he went. Their own horses were unsettled for a few moments and they calmed them as the rider disappeared up the road towards Sandal.

Hubert sucked his lower lip pensively. 'I like this tale of Gaveston less the more I hear of it.'

'Still listen, Hubert, for it explains much of the two lords' enmity to each other. Earl Lancaster's army blocked the King's path, which allowed a group of the other barons to lay siege to Scarborough Castle. Among those barons were Pembroke, Henry Percy and Earl Warenne of Surrey. After a fortnight, Gaveston surrendered on the terms that he would be delivered unharmed to York Minster for the judgement of Parliament.' Sir Richard's face clouded. 'And that is where it turned really nasty.'

'How so, my lord?'

'Treachery! Nothing but treachery. Pembroke, Henry Percy and Warenne had intended to keep their promise and moved Gaveston to the Earl of Pemboke's castle at Wallingford in Oxford. There they thought they had him held in safe custody, but when

61

the Earl of Pembroke left him one night to visit his local rector in Deddington, Lancaster, Warwick and Hereford pounced and stole off with him to Warwick.'

'Infamy!' gasped Hubert.

'There is worse. After a few days Warwick turned a blind eye and let Earl Lancaster arrange for him to be taken to Blacklow Hill where two Welsh assassins despatched him. One ran him through with his own sword and then, as he lay dying, the other hacked off his head.'

Hubert gulped. 'Methinks that this Earl of Lancaster deserved his fate at Pontefract.'

Sir Richard shrugged non-commitally. 'King Edward was, of course, furious. And many of the barons, including Earls Warenne and Pembroke sided with the king. Lancaster and Warwick had no option but to make a public apology in return for their amnesty. But as regards Warenne and Lancaster, they were enemies from then on. Five years ago matters came to a head when Earl Warenne encouraged one of his squires, Richard de Saint Martin, to abduct Lancaster's wife, Alice de Lacy and carry her off to Warenne's castle in Surrey. In reprisal Lancaster captured Warenne's castles of Sandal and Conisbrough and commandeered his land, the Manor of Wakefield.

'Over the following years Lancaster blamed the King for all the ills that befell England, whether they be famines, plague or raids by the Scots. And when King Edward took up with the Dispensers, a father and son, both of whom as you know are called Hugh le Dispenser, and made the younger his favourite, his 'next' Gaveston, the country became well nigh divided. And the rest you know.'

Hubert nodded. 'Aye my lord. We fought with the King at Boroughbridge and saw Earl Hereford die and heard that Earl of Lancaster was captured hours later. Then he was taken to Pontefract and executed in front of his own castle.'

'That is right. After being dragged before his cousin the King, in his own great hall. He was not allowed to defend himself, just as Gaveston had not been allowed to speak. He was found guilty by those nobles who were loyal to the king, including the Dispensers and his bitterest enemy, Earl Warenne of Surrey.'

'And has the king not given Earl Warenne his castle and lands back?'

'No. I suspect that he will in due course, but they are still held by the crown. I believe that it is his majesty's way of punishing Earl Warenne for his part in capturing Gaveston.'

Hubert shook his head. 'It is a sorry tale,

my lord. I do not think that I like this politics of yours.'

Richard laughed and remounted. 'Politics belong to no man, Hubert. Power is what it is all about, and I do believe that power and the pursuit of it is a great corrupting influence.' He shook his head. 'No, for me the most important thing is the law. That is what I believe in and that is what I make my guiding principle.'

Hubert bit his lip pensively for a moment then grinned. 'And so it is mine too, my lord. So shall we now go to Sandal Castle?'

'Aye, Hubert. We have been charged by the King to bring proper law back to the area. And we must begin by meeting the Deputy Steward of the Manor of Wakefield, who now holds the castle.'

'And mayhap we will get a bite at this castle, my lord?' Hubert asked hopefully.

★　★　★

They made their way passed the Sandal Magna village church of St Helens and started on the climb up towards the natural sandstone ridge upon which Sandal Castle stood; a natural stronghold with clear views over the surrounding countryside. By anyone's standards it was an impressive sight. Its ashlar stones glistened in the late afternoon light. A great keep with four circular towers crested an impressive motte, and a battlemented twenty-foot high curtain-wall with turrets at regular lengths along it surrounded a large bailey. The wall crossed the large moat on either side, ascended the slopes of the motte to abut upon the keep. Protruding above the walls, within the curtain-wall could be seen the roofs of spectacular halls and dwellings on the bailey and a great central barbican with nearby drum towers connecting to the keep.

As the road wound up to the top of the ridge they approached the outer defensive earthwork behind which was the large moat. Armed men were visible, looking down at them from the battlements.

'It looks to have had recent fortification, my lord,' said Hubert.

Richard pointed to a blackened scorched area on the outer casement of one of the towers. 'I suspect that area marks where Lancaster must have besieged it. And of course, in the five years that it was in his hands he strengthened it considerably.'

They rode along the side of the embankment and stopped in front of the gatehouse. The drawbridge was already down, bridging the moat but naturally, the portcullis on the castle side was down and locked in place.

'State your business!' challenged a gruff voice from behind the portcullis on the far side of the drawbridge.

'I am Sir Richard Lee and this is my assistant, Hubert of Loxley. I am the Circuit Judge of the King's Northern Realm and I am here to see Sir Thomas Deyville on His Majesty's business.'

There was silence for a moment, then the mumble of voices and the sound of a messenger's retreating feet. Then, 'You are expected, Sir Richard. Prepare to enter.'

The sound of cranking wheels was followed by a slow creaking as the portcullis began to rise and disappear behind the gatehouse wall, atop which could be seen defensive machicolations for pouring boiling oil and hurling missiles. When it had risen fully a porter and a man at arms with a pikestaff appeared from within. The porter made a clumsy bow and waved them in.

Once inside the castle the porter signalled to someone in the gatehouse and the portcullis began to descend.

An ostler appeared at a run and relieved them of their mounts, which he then led across the bailey courtyard to the stables block.

Sir Richard looked around and found

himself nodding agreeably at the structure of the castle. The keep was huge, rising four storeys from the base of the motte, which was already a considerable height above the level of the bailey. In itself it looked to be a good defensive structure, capable of defence should invaders manage to get past the outer moat and the great six to ten-foot thick wall. Yet clearly, the barbican, semi-circular in cross section, had been added to further defend the keep. It was protected by a ditch and inner moat of its own, so that it formed a stepping-stone between the bailey courtyard and the keep. Any attackers would then have to cross an internal drawbridge to reach the barbican, then pass through its gate with a portcullis and then fight their way along a right-angled passageway before coming to another gate and portcullis. From there they would have to traverse yet another drawbridge over the internal moat around the barbican to gain access to the large drum towers that protected an internal stairway leading up the motte to the keep.

'The architects of this castle were taking no chances of the keep being taken, were they, my lord?' Hubert asked, mirroring Sir Richard's own thoughts.

'And it is a castle with a goodly population,' returned Richard, pointing to the great semicircular bailey courtyard, which seemed to be thrumming with people, animals, chickens and activity. 'It is a fair-sized hamlet in its own right.'

At the far end of the courtyard, some men in aprons and smocks were hefting sacks into what seemed to be a bake-house, while next door smoke rose from the chimney of what was clearly a kitchen block. Dominating the courtyard though was a great hall, a manor house in itself with three storeys and a parapetted roof, with smaller, but no less grand apartments sweeping the curve of the bailey on its left. Hither and thither men and women criss-crossed the courtyard attending to the various tasks of running the castle, while above them on the battlemented walls half-a-dozen men at arms kept up a watch, on both the castle interior and the countryside without.

The porter had been standing respectfully in attendance and he now coughed. 'My master, Sir Thomas Deyville is come, Sir Richard.'

From a building to their left a door opened and a small stocky man in a knee-length purple robe and wearing a beaver hat came down the steps and stood facing Sir Richard and Hubert. He was of middle years with a pepper and salt beard and shrewd eyes which shifted from one to the other, as if appraising them as friends or foes.

'Welcome to Sandal Castle, Sir Richard,' he said gruffly, with the slightest of bows. 'I had expected you earlier.'

His slightly hostile tone did not go unmissed by Richard. From what he had heard about the Deputy Steward of the Manor of Wakefield, he had in fact expected no less. Indeed, it was because of his apparent harshness that King Edward had sent Richard to Wakefield. Richard smiled genially and returned the bow. A pace behind, Hubert followed suit.

'I am much impressed with the castle,' Richard said. 'We had intended arriving earlier, but we came through Wakefield and we became embroiled in an investigation. A criminal matter.'

Sir Thomas Deyville's eyes narrowed. 'A criminal matter? Is this something that should have been reported to me?' He nodded at the porter, who immediately turned on his heel and returned to the gatehouse. 'You had best come into my house, Sir Richard. We can talk there.' He pointed a stubby finger at Hubert. 'Your man can go over to the kitchens and have refreshment there. We shall dine later, since I have arranged a meal in your honour.' And turning he mounted the steps and held the door open for Sir Richard.

They entered an airy room that was plainly furnished with a couple of stout wooden stools, a table covered with scrolls, a map and several earthenware mugs. Sir Thomas rang a hand-bell and few moments later the door opened and a middle-aged woman in a shapeless grey gown and wimple limped in slowly, followed by a grimy boy bearing a flask and a fresh mug.

'This is my wife, Lady Alecia,' Sir Thomas announced.

Sir Richard bowed and took the lady's hand, noticing immediately the nodules of arthritis that explained her lameness. Yet, as he gazed at her face, he noted that she was still a handsome woman and must have been striking in her youth. He smiled. 'I was saying to your husband that it is a fine castle.'

Lady Alecia gave a wan smile. 'Thank you, Sir Richard. It is our hope that His Majesty King Edward will allow my husband the permanent stewardship. I feel that my daughter and I could settle here very well.' She unconsciously rubbed a marble-sized nodule on her wrist and winced with pain. 'I would hope that it would be good for my health.'

Sir Thomas snorted. 'Aye, well, there will be time for talking later, my love. Sir Richard will meet our daughter Lady Wilhelmina later at supper, when they all come.'

He snapped his fingers at the boy and pointed at an empty mug on the table. 'You will have some ale with me, Sir Richard?'

Sir Richard raised an eyebrow quizzically. 'When *they* come? I hope that you have not gone to trouble for me?'

'I said that I had arranged a meal in your honour. I have sent for some of the local people to come to meet my adviser,' Sir Thomas said glibly. He took a swig of his ale and added dismissively, 'It will be a small supper. Nothing elaborate.'

Richard nodded, secretly amused at Sir Thomas's description of him as his 'adviser'.

'Now we have important matters to discuss, my dear. Where have you arranged for Sir Richard to stay?'

'In the north tower of the keep, my husband. He will have a fine view towards the town and all comforts are close at hand.' She curtsied to Sir Richard and took her leave, preceded by the serving boy.

Sir Thomas drained half his mug straight away, wiped beer from his beard with the back of his hand then stood swirling the ale in his mug. 'I am a plain-spoken man, Sir Richard, and I will not beat about the bush. I do not see why his majesty has sent you here

71

to advise me. I am perfectly capable of running this — '

Richard laid his mug down on the table untouched. He held up his hand. 'You had better read the King's orders again, Sir Thomas. I am not here as an adviser. I am instructed as Circuit Judge of the King's Northern Realm to oversee the courts. Until I or his majesty deem it otherwise, I shall preside over the courts and you may watch and learn.'

Sir Thomas's eyes seemed to smoulder for a moment and his cheeks suffused beneath his beard. 'That is as maybe,' he said with a grunt. 'But tell me about this criminal case you talked about. Should it have been reported to me?'

'It already has been,' Richard returned unemotionally. 'A case of rape that has yet to have anything done about it. Apparently it was reported to the ward constable and then the manor clerk.'

'Ah, it is in hand then. I will get round to it.'

Richard shook his head and hummed, all the while fixing the other in his gaze. 'I hear that you have been getting round to a lot of things, Sir Thomas. Like two hangings, a few floggings and putting people in the stocks. I saw one such wretch in the stocks today.'

Sir Thomas's eyes narrowed for a moment. 'Did you now?' he asked, briskly. He drew himself up to his full height, which was a full head shorter than Sir Richard. 'I have dispensed law as I saw fit. The King's law.'

Richard smiled again. 'I am a Sergeant-at-Law, Sir Thomas, which is why his majesty has sent me here to the Manor of Wakefield. And from the sound of it you have actually dispensed with the law and have been dishing out punishments without proper precedent.'

'The Manor of Wakefield has the right to punish,' Sir Thomas said. 'I, as the Deputy Steward, have the right to do so.'

'I think you ought to consider that *Deputy* actually means *temporary*, as Lady Alecia just indicated, Sir Thomas! I shall be reviewing all cases that have been presented to the court since you arrived.'

Sir Thomas's eyes glared. 'By the — '

'And also I shall need to see a list of all those men from the manor who have been outlawed.'

'Contrariants, you mean! They are outlawed by the King's order. I hope you don't intend to try going against the King's instructions. Or do you intend to answer to him when he comes himself?'

'His majesty has no intention of coming to Wakefield, my lord.'

'Ha! Think you not!' Sir Thomas snarled triumphantly. 'Mayhap his majesty has not told you everything. Perhaps he intends checking up on you, too, Sir Richard. A messenger arrived the day before yesterday from him. He goes to stay at Rothwell Castle for a couple of days and then he plans to come here, to stay at Sandal and to see the Wakefield Mysteries at the festival of Corpus Christi.'

Richard picked up his mug and sipped. This was news that he had not expected. He wondered why his majesty had kept that to himself. 'And what mysteries are these, Sir Thomas?'

Sir Thomas began to guffaw. 'Oh Wakefield is the place for *Mysteries*, Sir Richard. We have the greatest of mysteries here. Mayhap you will learn more at supper.'

Richard was about to reply when the Deputy Steward raised his hand as if suddenly remembering a trifle. 'But talking of mysteries, did a messenger pass you on your way to Sandal?'

'He did. He was wearing the livery of the manor.'

'He brought me this,' Sir Thomas said, lifting the edge of the map that lay on the table. Underneath it lay an arrow with grey goose feathers. The arrowhead was sticky with recently congealed blood and with small slivers of strangely gelatinous tissue on it. 'This arrow was plucked from the body of a criminal this afternoon. You may even have seen him yourself.'

Richard raised his eyes quizzically. 'I saw no dead body in Wakefield.'

'No, he was probably alive if you saw him. He was in the stocks near the Tolbooth. The mystery is — why would anyone shoot such a villain as that through the eye?'

4

The Pardoner's Crime

Sir Richard looked out of the narrow window of his chamber on the third floor of the north tower of the keep. Down below he saw the village of Sandal Magna with its parish church of St Helen's and the road snaking its way through copses and fields towards Wakefield. There seemed to be a stream of travellers upon the highway.

'Late to be on the road to London,' he mused to himself. 'Or are they coming to the castle?'

And so thinking he crossed the chamber and pulled back the oiled goatskin shutter and looked out of the other window which faced due north. From it he saw the rest of the road and a clearer view of the travellers coming along the road, either walking, or riding upon horses or donkeys.

'Why, unless I am mistaken there comes Master Oldthorpe the apothecary and his good wife,' he said out loud.

There came a rap upon the door and he called out to enter. The stout oak door opened and Hubert entered. He stood on the threshold for a moment and admired the spacious chamber with its tapestries, a comfortable made-up bed, a chest, a cabinet and a table with a pitcher of water, a bowl and a flask of spiced wine. The floor was made of flat stone tiles and behind a curtained recess was a personal garderobe. A fire crackled in the hearth.

'This castle has a fine kitchen and an even finer cook, my lord,' he volunteered, as he advanced into the room, caressing his stomach. 'I have just eaten the best pigeon pie I have ever had in my life and washed it down with a great big — '

'Enough, good Hubert,' interrupted Richard, as he unbuckled his sword and laid it on the table. 'Unless you have forgotten, I have not eaten for hours and my stomach rumbles and I think it believes that my throat has been cut. I feel slightly sick as a result.' He sighed. 'And I have to await the meal this evening.'

'Are you sure that the sickness is not to do with your festering wound, my lord?' Hubert asked, concernedly.

Sir Richard gingerly rubbed his calf, and then shook his head with a look of delighted surprise. Both of them were well aware that such festering wounds could easily prove fatal in a short time. 'No, it has felt surprisingly good since the apothecary applied that leather poultice of his. It is possible that the potion that he gave me may have something to do with this nausea, but it is more likely to do with a sickening sight that Sir Thomas Deyville showed me.' And he told Hubert about the arrow that he had seen.

Hubert winced. 'Shot through the eye! I have seen men die from face wounds on the battlefield, but who would shoot some poor helpless sod who was locked in the stocks?'

'Sir Thomas has no idea. It is something that we shall investigate tomorrow before I open the court. The body has been locked in the Tolbooth and we shall view it in the morning.'

He snapped his fingers then pointed out of the window. 'Do you recognize that couple upon the road?'

Hubert peered down. 'Why, my lord, it is the apothecary and his lady.'

'That is what I thought. I think that they and those other travellers must be coming to a special meal that Sir Thomas has laid on. He said that he wanted me — *his adviser* — to meet with some of his locals. It looks as if half of the burgers and guilds folk of Wakefield are on their way.'

Hubert looked aghast. 'Did you say that he called you his adviser, my lord?' His hand went to the handle of his sword. 'The insolent dog!' he exclaimed indignantly. 'Shall I educate him, my lord?'

Richard grinned. 'I advised him otherwise myself. But he was neither amused nor put out, for he had another card up his sleeve. He had news that I was unaware of. Apparently the King is planning to come to Wakefield in three days.'

Hubert raised his eyebrows in surprise. 'But why would his majesty be coming without your knowledge, my lord, especially when he gave you this commission himself?'

'I do not understand it myself, Hubert. Sir Thomas was cagey about the whole thing. He said that Wakefield had the greatest of mysteries and that I would find out at supper. He would tell me no more, I think, because he was peeved that I had exposed the fact that he could not read — a handicap for someone who hopes to become the actual Steward of the Manor.'

Hubert held his hand to the window to see if there was a breeze. 'I am glad that you have been given this chamber, my lord. Had you been given one in the south tower you would have been prey to the winds from the south and the south-west. The cook and some of the others told me how those winds buffet the castle at times and get into your bones.'

'Where have they accommodated you?'

'I have been given a bed in the guard-room upstairs in the barbican, my lord. It is adequate for my needs.'

'And so what have you learned about the Deputy Steward from your conversation over your dinner?'

Hubert laughed. 'I was waiting for you to ask, my lord. Well, for one thing he has not been a popular replacement. He is gruff and curt to all, including his wife. Only his daughter, the Lady Wilhelmina escapes his ire, for he dotes on her. Apparently she is of unimaginable beauty and few can understand how Sir Thomas could have produced one so comely. I look forward to seeing if they are right.' He sighed, for thoughts of the fair sex were seldom far from Hubert's mind. 'He drinks heavily, though he is never drunk, and he is a stickler for orders. Apparently he has had handbells put all over the castle and trained the castle staff like dogs. They all know their own bell and must come running when he rings.'

'I have seen them already. He summoned his wife with one such bell.'

'And he is harsh, my lord. He carries a stick with a small leather lash on its end. He uses it regularly, on hands and on buttocks.' Hubert scowled distastefully. 'Especially on some of the serving girls' buttocks.'

Richard frowned. 'Is he a lecher, then?'

'That I do not know yet, my lord,' Hubert returned with a sly grin. 'There is a limit to the information I could glean from the cook, his lads and the ostlers. The pie did not take so long to eat.'

Richard stifled a yawn. 'Then I suggest that you work on it further. After you have brought my saddle-packs with my fresh clothes why don't you go for a stroll around the battlement walk. You may be able to get some further news from some of the guards.'

Once Hubert had taken his leave, Richard removed the king's document from his surcoat, then stripped the garment off, peeled off his hauberk and flung himself on the bed. Whether it was the effects of the apothecary's potion or his long ride and the events of the day, he did not know which, but he felt extremely sleepy. Within moments he had fallen fast asleep.

* * *

Richard was startled awake by the peal of six bells from somewhere within the castle. He woke and nodded with satisfaction to see that while he had slept Hubert had returned with his saddle-pack and noiselessly unpacked his

81

clothes and arranged his things on the chest and in the cabinet. He wiped sleep from his eyes then went behind the curtain and used the garderobe. Then he sluiced water from the pitcher into the large pottery bowl and freshened himself up. He dressed himself in fresh hose, a blue tunic and darker blue half-cape and pulled on a pair of calf leather boots. Then he picked up the burnished metal mirror that Hubert had laid out for him, ran his fingers through his hair, and attended to his teeth. Finally, he buckled on a belt with a stiletto and his personal food-knife, before letting himself out of the chamber.

The bailey courtyard was quiet and deserted except for two servants waiting on either side of the small stone staircase that led up to an upper porch supported on an ornate octagonal column. Above the door was a large, rather splendid sundial that indicated, if the deserted bailey had not already done so, that he was late. As Richard approached, one of the servants bowed then scurried up the stairs, opened the door and led the way into a semi-circular oriel gallery. He led the way across this into a Presence Chamber, the walls of which were covered in pikestaffs, swords and banners then stood at attention at another huge door that led into the Great

Hall. He waited until Richard reached the threshold, then he pushed open the door, entered and announced in a loud voice:

'Sir Richard Please, the new adviser to Sir Thomas Deyville.'

The Great Hall was full of people standing behind wooden chairs on either side of two rows of linen-covered trestle tables arranged along the length of the room. Sir Thomas Deyville, his family and a nun and a priest were also standing behind their chairs at the high table at the far end of the hall. Torches spluttered along the walls, each emitting an oily smoke, while a pink light shone through the greenish glazed glass of the three large mullioned windows which faced the bailey. A fire blazed in a great hearth beneath the arms of the de Warenne family, the owners of the castle for two centuries. Richard noted with interest that Earl Lancaster had not seen fit to have the arms replaced by his own.

Sir Thomas waved Richard forward, a thin sarcastic smile upon his lips. But Richard stood firm, hooked his arm through that of the servant who was about to depart. He drew him close and whispered firmly in his ear. The man coloured visibly, alarm written across his face.

'My apologies, my lord,' he said. 'I must have misheard from Sir Thomas.'

Then once more raising his voice to the assembled guests:

'*Sir Richard Lee*, Sergeant-at-Law and newly appointed by His Majesty King Edward the Second of Caernarvon as the Circuit Judge of the King's Northern Realm and Judge of the Manor of Wakefield Court.'

Richard nodded at the man and entered the hall, grinning inwardly, knowing full well that the servant had neither misheard his name nor misunderstood his position. He had successfully foiled Sir Thomas's attempt to diminish his status, as was clear from the cold, humourless stare he was receiving from the Deputy Steward as he walked along the hall between the two long tables. He nodded to the assembled guests who bowed and curtsied as he passed.

Halfway along he recognized Master Oldthorpe and his lovely wife. 'My thanks, Master Oldthorpe. My leg wound feels much improved and I am less fevered.'

The apothecary beamed and bowed again. Then Richard turned to Mistress Oldthorpe.

'How is the young patient?'

Mistress Oldthorpe inclined her head, two little points of colour forming on her cheeks. 'She is feeling improved, my lord. Before we came I arranged for her kinswoman Matilda to stay with her.'

Sir Richard nodded. 'Perhaps I can call and have this poultice looked at again tomorrow?'

The apothecary nodded readily and Richard walked on to the high table. 'My apologies for being late,' he said genially as he took the place indicated by Sir Thomas between Lady Alecia and the young Lady Wilhelmina. 'You seem to be always waiting for me, Sir Thomas.'

Sir Thomas waved his hand in dismissal. 'Sir Richard, you have already met my wife, Lady Alecia. This is my daughter, Lady Wilhelmina, and this is Lady Katherine, the Prioress of Kirklees and Father Daniel, the nun's priest of Kirklees Priory.' He patted the shoulder of the wiry priest with carrot red hair and a tonsure, adding, 'He is also the chaplain of the Manor of Wakefield and the parish priest of All Saints in Wakefield.'

'And also the finest playwright in England,' added the prioress, a small pretty lady of forty-odd years, who held herself erect and proud.

Bowing to the prioress, the nun's priest and the two ladies, Richard waited for them all to sit down before he too sat on the large carved chair that had been allocated to him. As he did so he was all too aware of the description that Hubert had been given of the Lady Wilhelmina, and he silently concurred, for she was indeed a rare beauty of some eighteen years or so. She wore a simple cap which complemented her long wavy, auburn hair and the gentle curves of her perfectly proportioned face. He found himself admiring her full lips and the intelligent blue eyes that met his.

Sir Thomas lifted a small bell from the table, rang it and then gestured for everyone on the long tables to sit. He remained standing while he spoke.

'Welcome Sir Richard, and welcome good people of the Manor of Wakefield. We shall eat and drink and then you shall have a chance to get to know our new — Sergeant-at-Law. And he shall get to know you and hear of our Wakefield Mysteries. And of our news.'

A chorus of polite laughter rang out around the hall and Richard frowned. Still the Deputy Steward was keeping things from him.

'But first, Father Daniel shall say grace,' Sir Thomas went on.

The nun's priest stood, clasped his hands together and with closed eyes recited a grace first in Latin then in English. When he had taken his seat, Sir Thomas picked up another bell, a larger one and rang it with three deliberate shakes. At the first bell a quartet of musicians in a minstrel's gallery at the far end of the hall above the entrance door began to play. Soon the air was filled with the music of harp, viele, olander and lute. At the second ring, the side doors opened and a team of servants filed in led by a butler who began directing his subordinates with almost military precision. A pantler and his assistants began serving trenchers for all, and finger bowls for every two people. A stream of serving women followed with salvers of cut meats, steaming pots and jugs of wine and ale. On the third ring, the castle cook himself entered, a merry-looking, round-faced fellow with a shock of ginger hair protruding from beneath a prodigious white cap. He walked with a marked limp, for one leg had clearly been broken and set badly in his youth. He carried a tray upon which was a roast boar's head surrounded by a ring of apples and with a crown of greenery. To his obvious delight the assembled guests applauded as he made his way towards the high table.

'I have heard that your cook is a rare artist,' Richard said. 'My assistant has tasted his pigeon pie and said it was delicious.'

The cook placed the tray in front of Sir Thomas and stood grinning at Richard. 'I have one great secret which I willingly tell all who would like to produce fresh meat,' he said, his voice booming and jolly, as if he was on the verge of laughter most of the time.

'Tell me your secret then, good master cook,' said Richard.

'Why, sir, it is simple. I only use the freshest of meat, fowl and fish, because I let them live until they are ready to be cooked. It is my mission on earth to cook and to feed all who will eat their fill,' he said.

'Aye, but not always at my expense,' growled Sir Thomas. 'You may have guessed, Sir Richard, that he is a man given to over-zealousness.' Then, turning his gruff eye on the cook, 'This looks adequate; you may go Gideon Kitchen.'

'May you all be blessed with an appetite to match this small repast,' said Gideon Kitchen as he retreated backwards, still grinning from ear to ear, despite his master's attempt to deflate him.

Richard felt his stomach juices go wild at the mixed aroma of roast chicken, venison and boar. He looked around the hall, his eye falling upon Emma Oldthorpe, the apothecary's wife. She smiled at him demurely and he felt strange warmth come over him. And in the corner of his vision he was all too aware of the pleasing perfume and charms of the Lady Wilhelmina sitting beside him.

'What think you of our little welcoming

feast, Sir Richard, Sergeant-at-Law?' asked Sir Thomas, leaning past his wife.

'Succulent!' Richard uttered without thinking. It was the word that was already in his mind, although he had not exactly been thinking of food.

★ ★ ★

After taking care of his master's belongings, Hubert had left Richard to slumber and made his way up to the battlements by an inner staircase on the far side of the bailey bakehouse. Evening was approaching and with it a glorious sunset had draped the sky with crimson and pink clouds. He strolled along and immediately engaged the first male-clad guard in conversation. He had recognized him straight away, since he had directed him to the kitchen that afternoon. They rapidly fell into the easy conversation of one soldier to another, for both Hubert of Loxley and Adam Crigg had done service as foot soldiers in wars; Hubert in England, Wales and Scotland and Adam in those as well as a time in Ireland, for he was a good ten years Hubert's senior.

'I remember how dull it is to patrol around a castle rampart,' said Hubert sympathetically. 'Especially when our masters are feasting and drinking until late in the evening.'

Adam's weather-beaten face creased into a wrinkled, lop-sided grin, on account of an old battle scar which prevented one side of his mouth from moving fully. 'I know that you have one master, so I hope that he is good to you. As for me, I have to be honest when I tell you that I don't rightly care much for any masters.'

Hubert clicked his tongue. 'I am fortunate and have a good one, but I understand what you mean. The likes of us can hardly choose, we have to do what we are told.'

Adam Crigg nodded sagely. 'Aye, our masters keep changing depending on their fortunes. I have been a soldier since I was eleven years of age, just as my old father was afore me. Don't misunderstand me, I have been loyal all my life to whoever has held Sandal Castle. That means that I was loyal to John de Warenne, the Earl of Surrey and fought wherever he dragged us. Then Thomas Plantagenet, the Earl of Lancaster besieged the castle and took it over, and I served him, God rest his soul. And now I am loyal to the King.'

Hubert grinned. 'True, Adam. We are all King's men now. And I expect all the other guards have a similar outlook on things.'

The old soldier's face contorted again and he looked sideways and spat through the nearest embrasure of the battlement wall. 'That makes me laugh. There are only a few proper soldiers here. That is me and about thirty of the original castle guard.' He leaned over conspiratorially and continued in a whisper. 'The rest of them — all sixty of them — are Sir Thomas Deyville's men. And I reckon they have sold their hearts and souls to the 'Deyville!' He grinned at his own wit.

'The trouble is, not one of them knows one end of a pikestaff from the other, so if we ever had a proper attack, they would be as much use as a bunch of milkmaids.'

He looked along the wall at another guard who was watching over another segment of the wall, between the next two turrets. 'We had best keep walking, Hubert, lest that young jackanapes reports me and I get my knuckles rapped.'

They walked on and Hubert shrugged his shoulders. 'Still, I suppose they will just have to learn, like we did, eh, Adam?'

Adam snorted derisively. 'They have learned a lot of things already, if you ask me, and not a lot of it is good. Like I said, they are the Deputy Steward's men and they behave just like him. Not a spark of human kindness among them. They'll all beat a serf or a bondsman as soon as look at him. I don't like it. These are my people. I am born and bred around here and I — '

He was stopped by a sudden shouted stream of profanity from behind them.

'What is going on here? What is that man doing up here?'

Hubert and Adam had spun round to see a furious mail-clad sergeant of the guard advancing upon them. 'Who let this man up here?'

Hubert had taken an instant dislike to the fellow and he stood his ground. 'I climbed the stairs myself! And *you* didn't stop me!' Then, before the burly sergeant could say anything further, he went on, his voice cutting and aggressive, 'And nor should — or *could* you have! I am Hubert of Loxley, assistant to Sir Richard Lee, the Circuit Judge of the King's Northern Realm who is eating with your master right now.' His voice had risen in volume with each word. After glaring at the sergeant he dropped his volume again. 'Or would you like to explain your attitude to him yourself?'

Hubert saw the other's hesitation. He recognized the pattern. A bully boy who was unable to stand up to bullying himself. He sneered contemptuously. 'I suggest you don't interfere with King's officers in the future.'

The sergeant glowered at Hubert and then at Adam. Then without a word he walked past them towards the other guard.

'The bastard will have harsh words with me later,' Adam whispered, unable to keep the humour from his voice. 'But it was bloody worth it!'

★ ★ ★

Despite himself, Richard enjoyed the meal. He found that after satiating his ravenous appetite with his trencher, heaped with roast boar, venison and the most delicious vegetable concoctions, and slaked his thirst with a couple of goblets of fine spiced Bordeaux wine, he was able to settle back and enjoy the conversation along the table. He nibbled cheese and sliced apples and listened to Lady Katherine discourse upon the concept of original sin and the need to resist temptation. He smiled as she pushed her goblet forward in the direction of the butler in the expectation that it would be replenished.

Then while Lady Alecia enquired of the prioress about some priory matter he took the opportunity to talk with the beautiful Lady Wilhelmina. To his delight he discovered that she was knowledgeable about many things, including art, music and falconry. He was surprised to learn that she was well-schooled in writing and that she could read both Latin and Greek, as well as speak French.

'My mother taught me,' she explained, catching Richard's look of surprise and his fleeting glance in her father's direction. 'She has a wonderful mind, Sir Richard. It is a pity that in this day a woman is only permitted to develop accomplishments in the homely arts, or in making babies!'

He looked at her in wonder, scarce knowing how to reply.

'Or rather, in making male babies!' she went on, with some spirit. She sipped some wine. 'If things were different I would like to study the law.'

Despite himself an indulgent smile formed on his lips and he saw a spark of ire flash in her eyes. He immediately regretted having drunk more wine than he should, for he had let his guard down.

'Do you not think that a woman has the wit for law, Sir Richard?' she challenged.

'Oh many women most assuredly would,' he returned, sympathetically. 'It is a shame that men have not the wit to let them.'

She smiled up at him, her eyes fixing his keenly. 'And you, Sir Richard. Do you have the wit? Would you be prepared to do a battle of wits with a — mere woman?'

He found the way that her lips curled into a smile utterly beguiling. He was about to reply when Sir Thomas clapped the nun's priest upon the back and immediately reached for one of his bells. As it rang out the chatter from the other tables abruptly halted, as did the music from the minstrel's gallery and the room went quiet.

Sir Thomas heaved himself to his feet. 'My guests, I trust that you have enjoyed your meal, your wine and the company. You will all, of course, enjoy the hospitality of the Hall, the Great Chamber next door and the rooms below this for the night.' He grinned affably. 'I would not wish you all to get in trouble by trying to get back into Wakefield after the eight o'clock curfew.'

Laughter echoed to the high rafters.

'My purpose in inviting you all here this evening was twofold. First to let you see and perhaps afterwards talk with Sir Richard Lee, who will be advising me in legal matters at the Manor Court in the next few days. And second, I wanted to bring all of the main people involved in the Wakefield Mysteries.'

Richard pricked up his ears. At last, he thought.

'Representatives from the burgers, all of the guilds, the clergy and the constables of three

95

of the town wards are here tonight.' He spread his hands to indicate the Prioress and the nun's priest at either end of the high table. 'And Lady Katherine the prioress of Kirklees Priory and Father Daniel, the playmaker are here to tell us about the final preparations for the Wakefield Mystery plays that are being performed on Corpus Christi Day itself.'

Richard listened and silently cursed himself for a fool for not realizing what the Deputy Steward had been referring to by 'the Mysteries'. He listened as first the prioress, then Father Daniel explained how each guild would be responsible for the putting on of various scenes of the Biblical story, plays and tableaux of which he had written the directions and dialogue of at least half.

'This man is a genius with words,' Lady Wilhelmina whispered. 'They already call him the Wakefield Master. My mother and the prioress say that he will be famous long after he is dead.'

'Rather be famous while he is alive,' Richard whispered back.

Sir Thomas took to his feet again once they had completed their speeches and deliberations. 'And I have one final piece of information to impart to you all. On the day of the Mysteries, we shall be joined by His

Majesty King Edward the Second, himself.'
He beamed about the hall as the good people
of the Manor of Wakefield gasped in surprise
and wonder. Finally, he looked at Richard.
'What say you to that, Sir Richard?'

Richard put down his goblet and wiped his
lips with a towel. He inclined his head and
stood up to address the hall. 'I say that this is
an undoubted honour for the Manor of
Wakefield and for the town itself. It is good to
see that it is so well organized, and that you
have such knowledgeable people to direct the
performances.'

People applauded his words and tapped
their goblets and beakers in approval on the
tables. When the tumult settled down again
Richard went on, 'Yet if his majesty is coming
to the manor so soon, it is beholden to us to
have all judicial matters taken care of. The
King's Law must be seen to be working.'

Another round of approval echoed about
the hall.

'As the Circuit Judge of the King's
Northern Realm and the Judge of the Manor
Court I am letting you all know that the first
session of the court will take place tomorrow
morning.' His eyes sought out the trestle table
upon which the constables of the town wards
were sitting. 'Tomorrow morning a jury will
be selected and sworn in and we shall begin

the investigation of two crimes that I already know have been committed. One is of a rape.'

There were gasps and exclamations of outrage.

'And one of cold-blooded murder of a felon in the custody of the township. Both are extremely serious and could have dire repercussions for the town.'

The hall mostly fell silent. 'Tomorrow all residents of Wakefield and the surrounding hamlets and villages of the manor will attend at eleven o'clock and the jury shall begin by viewing the body.'

He bowed and took his seat; all too aware that he was attracting looks and stares from all over the hall. He was also aware that Lady Wilhelmina's eyes seemed to register a sort of fascination.

After a signal from Sir Thomas the quartet began to play again and Richard nodded his head approvingly. 'You have a fine band of musicians there. Especially the lute player.'

Lady Alecia's eyes sparkled and she smiled, almost wistfully. 'Ah, that is Alan-a-Dale, my protégé. His fingers pluck those strings just as I used to be able to do myself. He is a beautiful artist.'

Richard nodded and sipped his wine. 'Indeed he is. And a most handsome young man, too.'

He felt the touch of a dainty foot touch his leg and in the corner of his eye he saw Lady Wilhelmina's lips give a half-smile. Despite himself he felt the colour rise to his cheeks.

★ ★ ★

Albin of Rouncivale had gone to his lodgings behind the shambles after finishing his day's work, his purse considerably swelled and his bag of pardons proportionately reduced. His assorted relics had worked well for him, especially his latest acquisitions. After exchanging his pardoner's clothes for a nondescript brown doublet and broad-brimmed hat he had gone for some supper and a mug of ale. But the Wakefield ale was too tempting, he found, and instead of visiting one tavern, he found himself visiting all six within the town, ending up in the Bucket Inn near to the Jacob's Well near the Warrengate.

Sitting in an inglenook by the blazing fire, he sat nursing his eighth mug of ale as he watched a group of Bucket Inn regulars playing dice at a nearby table. Through his haze he listened as they discussed the news that had already spread to every household and inn in the township.

'William Scathelocke was a decent pinder,' said one.

'But not as good as you, eh, George-a-Green?'

George-a-Green playfully cuffed his fellow on the side of the head and collected the dice with a sweep of his hand. 'He did a good enough job and he didn't deserve to be in the stocks in the first place.'

A greybeard with a bald pate nodded in agreement. 'Aye and he certainly didn't deserve to be murdered by a bowman.'

'Aye, but who could shoot a bow with that accuracy?' said the first speaker, a surly-looking fellow with a cloth over one eyeless socket 'There is only one real archer around here who could make such a shot and that would be the Hood himself.'

George-a-Green scowled at him. 'The Hood is no murderer. Take care of that tongue of yours, Hector, or you may lose it some day.'

The man called Hector shook his head with a grin. 'That I won't, George-a-Green. I am only saying what I expect a lot of people are thinking. And I am not afraid to speak my mind. I have' — he stopped and grinned slyly — 'faith in the Lord.'

'Aye and we have faith in the fact that you are a one-eyed drunken fool!' returned George-a-Green. And he and his fellows burst into laughter as Hector began to look even surlier.

Albin of Rouncivale had pricked up his ears, for something about the villain's death and the talk at the table had suddenly caused him to sweat. He wiped his eyes with his forefinger and thumb and looked blearily about the room of the inn. It was a lively, busy place, full of men taking their ease after the work of the day and before they headed home at curfew time.

As he blinked away his tiredness he was aware of a pair of eyes staring directly at him from the shadows of an alcove. He thought that in that glance he recognized the shadowy face. Was this the real cause of the perspiration and the anxiety that had descended upon him, he wondered? He averted his eyes and pretended to study the dregs in his mug. Surely no one would recognize him here, he thought. And if he was correct, why would *he* be sitting in the inn spying on him? He didn't like the first couple of answers that came to his mind. Warning bells were ringing in his mind and he decided to make his way home stealthily.

But, as he raised the mug to his lips and tilted it back he was aware that the other was still watching him. He needed to leave unseen. And, as usual, when he perceived himself to be in a tight spot, his mind saw a solution. The pinder, George-a-Green was a large fellow in a horsehair mantle with a long cloak. Pretending to bend to examine his foot, Albin picked up a burning twig from the edge of the hearth and surreptitiously tossed it upon the hem of the pinder's cloak. It took but a few moments for it to catch fire. Then a few more for his friends to notice the smell, then the smoke and finally the flames. And then there was chaos. There was jumping up, scraping back of stools, jostling and bumping, spilling of ale and fanning of tempers. Hands slapped, fists clenched and punches were traded. Within seconds a goodly fight had broken out, despite the remonstrances of the potman and a couple of serving girls.

But in the mêlée, Albin of Rouncivale disappeared.

Once outside he took to his heels, keeping into the shadows as he made his way to his lodgings by a circuitous route. As he left, his quick eye and quick wits perceived that there were two of them who had shown an interest in him. Whether they were common footpads or worse, he knew not. But their interest prompted him to decide that it was time to quit the town and move on at dawn.

When he finally made it to his room and had thought himself safe in bed, he heard them outside his room. He heard the footsteps in the corridor and elected to bring his planned escape forward. Gathering his clothes, his sack and his cross, for at times it doubled as a good cudgel, he let himself out of the window.

But as he ran, deciding to leave his donkey, he heard them come out through the same window. Damn this curfew! he cursed to himself. And all too clearly did he realize that they were gaining on him.

Ahead of him he saw a party of men and recognized them for the Warrengate constable and his men, about to do their round after curfew. He did not hesitate, but charged into them and was immediately held, buffeted and cursed for being a clumsy rogue.

'My lord, take me,' he gasped. 'I am a sinner, a criminal and I would confess to a crime.'

'Methinks he is a puddle-headed fool,' said a gangly youth with a stout cudgel upon his shoulder. Then he peered at Albin, his eyes registering recognition. 'Yet I recognize his yellow hair. I saw this man, this Pardoner today.'

Constable Ned Burkin hiccupped, for he had supped well on ale himself that night. 'And what is your crime, Pardoner?'

'That girl the other night. Lillian her name was. I did rape her in the cemetery!'

Ned Burkin reacted swiftly and struck

Albin about his ears. 'Take him, men. I never heard the like of this Pardoner's crime!' A slow grin spread across his face and he added, 'Hold him well, for this will look good on our watch.'

5

The Manor Court

Sir Richard awoke from a troubled slumber at cock-crow. As he performed his ablutions he could hear the castle swiftly come to life as servants tumbled off their pallets in attics and cellars to begin preparations to feed the guests and the Deputy Steward's household.

'Are you awake, my lord?' came Hubert's call through the door. Then at Richard's reply he came in bearing a basket containing cheese, a freshly baked loaf and a flask of ale. 'Gideon Kitchen had this ready just as you ordered last night,' he said, depositing the basket on the table and helping Richard on with his sword belt.

'Fine, then we shall be off straight away. I want to see that body as soon as possible before it gets too ripe. Have any of last night's guests left?'

'The town constables left before the sun came up, my lord.'

A bell tolled from somewhere within the keep.

'What is that?' Richard asked.

'The bell for the Earl's Chapel,' Hubert replied. 'My friend Adam Crigg, the guard I told you about last night, told me all about the castle. Earl Lancaster had the west tower strengthened and virtually rebuilt. He had his own private chapel constructed on the fourth level. I understand that whenever Father Daniel, the chaplain, is here, he holds a service in the Earl's Chapel for the household, before he goes to the main chapel for the castle staff and whoever may be staying as guests.'

'We shall have a look at this Earl's Chapel and say prayers before we leave then. It would make sense to ask our Lord for guidance before we start this day's work.'

★ ★ ★

Father Daniel and Lady Katherine, the Prioress of Kirklees Priory were both kneeling in front of the altar in the Earl's Chapel atop the west tower. Richard and Hubert stood at the open door looking in. The altar was carved from oak and covered with a fine linen cloth. On top of it was a large plain wooden cross with a plain white candle on each side. Behind the altar was an arched window with glazed green glass, and upon the smoothly plastered walls were painted scenes of the flagellation, the crucifixion and the resurrection of Christ. The ceiling was actually domed and a bell could be seen hanging within it; the bell-rope hanging down just to the side of the altar. On top of all of the walls clouds had been painted, with depictions of the feet of the Lord disappearing into them as he ascended to heaven.

Richard and Hubert genuflected and entered. At the sound of their feet the priest started and looked round, an expression of surprise upon his face.

'Good morning, Sir Richard,' he said, standing swiftly. 'Will you join us? I had not expected anyone else at this hour. The Deputy Steward and his good lady do not rise so early. I usually come back when — '

Richard raised an apologetic hand. 'We must away soon, Father Daniel, and a blessing for our work would be welcomed.'

The priest bowed his tonsured head. 'Lady Katherine and I were actually saying prayers to that very effect just now, Sir Richard. Murder is abhorrent and there has been too much bloodshed already. Earl Lancaster was — '

'What, he was murdered, too?' Richard asked.

The prioress was swiftly on her feet and laid a hand on Father Daniel's arm. 'He did not say that, Sir Richard. He meant to say that Earl Lancaster was a devout man himself. That is why he built this lovely chapel.' She shook her head sadly. 'Whatever his crimes against the King, he is with the Almighty now.'

Father Daniel placed his hands together. 'As we shall all be one day. And knowing that you are going to see that poor murdered wretch, before the blessing for your work, let us say a prayer for his soul.'

★ ★ ★

A small group was standing chatting in front of the Tolbooth on the Birch Hill when Richard and Hubert rode up. The Tolbooth was a squat single-storeyed stone building with barred windows and a stout iron-studded wooden door. In the empty square before it was an empty stocks and a pillory, the area round them being covered in rotten vegetables and cow dung. Richard dismounted and eyed it distastefully, having noticed the bloodstains upon the stocks and the ground behind it.

'Welcome to the Tolbooth, Sir Richard,' said one of the men, a well-fed man in his mid-thirties with a square-cut beard and porcine eyes. Richard recognized him as John of Flanshaw, the town bailiff and therefore, the main officer of the court. 'The body is inside in one of the cells below ground.' He pointed to the bloodstained stocks. 'I had everything left just as it was, so that you could inspect it if you wished.'

Richard nodded approvingly. 'I will, before we go to the Moot Hall to inspect the court rolls. First, let me see the body.'

The other four men had spread out to allow the bailiff to get to the door. Richard recognized three of them as the constables for three of the town wards. They all looked fresh after a good night's rest, but another, whom he presumed to be the fourth constable looked as though he had yet to go to bed.

'This is Ned Burkin, the Warrengate constable, Sir Richard,' the bailiff volunteered. 'He has important news to give you. He — '

'I will tell the judge,' Ned Burkin interrupted gruffly, as if keen to deliver his information personally. He turned to Richard, who winced at the smell of stale ale and bad breath that emanated from him. 'I arrested a man last night. A Pardoner.'

Sir Richard heard Hubert grunt behind him. 'Looks as if you were right, my lord,' he whispered. 'A charlatan after all.'

'That is as may be,' said Burkin, scowling

at Hubert. 'But his crime was more serious. He confessed to a rape, sir.'

Richard looked round at Hubert and raised a quizzical eyebrow. Then to Burkin, 'And whom did he rape?'

'I think it was that girl Lillian Fenton, sir.' He pointed at the door of the Tolbooth. 'He is locked up down there, in the cell next to the corpse.'

'Then we shall have a look at him after I have seen the body, then he shall have his say in court later today.'

The bailiff thumped his fist upon the Tolbooth door and a metal shutter slid back behind an iron grille. He barked an order to the turnkey and after some clanking of locks and shifting of bolts the door was pulled open and they entered.

'This is strange luck, sir,' said Hubert, as they descended the dark stone steps to the underground cells, led by the turnkey who preceded them with a candle. 'We come to investigate one case and another is solved in the process.'

Richard merely clicked his tongue and waited while the turnkey unlocked one cell and pushed the door open for the group to enter.

The body had been laid upon a pallet bed. By the light of the candle it made a grisly sight. He had been a young man in his mid-twenties, lean but yet well-muscled as if he had done physical work. His clothing reeked of cow dung and decayed vegetables, evidence of which stained his clothes. His face, Richard judged to himself as he looked at the unspoiled left side, would have attracted some women. Yet his brown hair was matted with blood from the dreadful wound on the right side. His whole eye socket had been destroyed where an arrow had entered and subsequently been yanked free. Congealed blood and grey-pink brain matter was visible around the gaping hole of the socket.

John of Flanshaw, the bailiff, retched and rushed from the cell and could be heard emptying his breakfast in the corridor.

'We shall have the opinion of the apothecary, Master Oldthorpe later on, I think,' Richard mused, straightening up, and turning to the constables. 'Have the body wrapped and be ready to bring it to the Moot Hall when I call for it. The session of the Manor Court will begin at eleven o'clock.'

In the corridor, John of Flanshaw was recovering himself.

'Have you made sure that the township knows to attend the court?'

The bailiff nodded. 'I had a proclamation made at cock-crow, Sir Richard. And the constables and their men will ensure that the reaves have everyone there.'

Ned Burkin had pushed himself to the front of the group. 'Will you question this Pardoner now, Sir Richard?'

To their surprise Richard shook his head. 'I shall look through the bars of his cell, but I shall not talk to him, for that could prejudice his case.'

They were about to protest, but Hubert silenced them immediately. 'Sir Richard is the Circuit Judge of the King's Northern Realm and is a Sergeant-at-Law. What he doesn't know of the law is not yet written. It is not your place — any of you — to question him.'

Richard had taken the opportunity while Hubert berated the bailiff and constables to look through the bars at the Pardoner. He recognized the man's lank hair and beardless face. And he noticed his sack and the cross which had been tossed in a corner of the cell with him. The Pardoner was on his knees, mumbling a prayer, his eyes tightly closed and his hands fervently clasped together.

Richard led the way up the steps and left the building. He walked across to the stocks and knelt down beside them. Blood had stained the wooden leg clamps, and a puddle of it had collected and congealed on the ground behind. In his mind's eye he tried to picture the man sitting upright with his legs outstretched, clamped in the stocks. Then the arrow hitting him in the right eye, tossing him backwards onto the ground, and blood pouring all over the place.

Hubert knelt behind him. 'A goodly shot to hit a man in the eye, sir,' he commented.

'If that was meant, yes,' Richard returned. He stood and turned round, trying to plot the trajectory of a shot. It was possible that it had come from several directions, yet the only clear point, and one which would have given the bowman cover of sorts, was an alley some fifty feet away. 'What is down that alley?' he asked.

'It leads to the bread-booths and the manor bakehouse, sir,' replied the bailiff.

'We will have a look over there, then we shall go to the Moot Hall and you can show me the court rolls, Master Bailiff. I take it that you can read?'

John of Flanshaw beamed proudly, his face recovering colour now. 'I can, Sir Richard. And it is my own hand that writes the rolls. You will not read a clearer hand than mine.'

Hubert snorted, for there was a part of him that considered reading and writing no fit task for a man, despite the fact that Sir Richard had taught him the basics.

★ ★ ★

The Wodehalle, as the Moot Hall was known locally, was a large timber-framed building capable of holding up to 200 people. Above its doors was the emblem of the de Warenne family, and above that was a small sundial. A long corridor led down one side of the building to a locked room called the Roll's Office, in which either the lord of the manor, or his steward or the steward's representative could consult with the bailiff. It was furnished with a desk and chair and several stools. Taking up a corner of the room was a large locked chest with numerous pigeon holes, containing the Manor of Wakefield court rolls. Dating back to 1274 and written in a mix of English and Latin on fine vellum scrolls, they recorded all of the dealings of the Manor Court.

Richard had spent an hour with the bailiff in order to familiarize himself with the latest rolls. He sat at the table with a vellum scroll unfurled on the table in front of him. From time to time he asked the bailiff for clarification of a point, but in the main he was much impressed by the standard of the entries.

'You have done well, Master John,' he said at last. 'And you seem to know the correct wording of the law.'

The bailiff beamed. 'We are proud of our law in Wakefield, Sir Richard,' he said, eagerly.

Hubert had been rocking back and forth on a stool and now, at the bailiff's words he snapped the legs down on the floor. 'Proud? A man has just been shot in your stocks! What is there to be proud of there?'

John of Flanshaw coloured and his jaw trembled as he sought a suitable retort. But he was stopped by Richard.

'Hubert is right, Master John. This heinous crime has left a dark stain upon the honour of Wakefield. But I cannot say that I am entirely happy about his punishment in the first place.' He jabbed the court roll with his forefinger and read out:

'*William Scathelocke, pinder of Wakefield did neglect his duty and failed on three days in May to clearing cattle out of the cornfields. Let him be put in the stocks for three days, receiving only bread from the manor bakehouse and water.*'

Richard shook his head. 'That is not justice; that is oppression and maltreatment. Nothing to be proud of there.'

'I do not pass sentence, Sir Richard,' the bailiff pleaded. 'I only carry out the court's orders and scribe them down.'

'And who did pass this sentence?'

There was a heavy tread at the door of the office, then a gruff voice.

'I sentenced that man, as you know well enough,' said Sir Thomas Deyville. He paced into the room and stood looking down at Richard, his thumbs hooked behind his belt. 'It was a fitting punishment for a lazy villain who caused loss to the manor.'

'The greatest loss was the poor wretch's life,' retorted Richard. 'It was a harsh and unjust sentence and should make all Englishmen ashamed. You have much to learn of justice and the law, I think, Sir Thomas.'

Sir Thomas's eyes seemed full of anger. 'I am not so sure that I agree, since his majesty set us a firm example when he settled with the Earl of Lancaster and half-a-dozen other rebel barons at Pontefract.' He sniffed. 'Still, I am keen to learn from you, Sergeant-at-Law,' he said sarcastically. 'I shall be back to sit with you when the court opens. My daughter follows and will also sit with us. But first, I am going to slake my thirst with some ale.'

Richard watched the Deputy Steward depart and noticed that Hubert was having a hard job of keeping his mirth from showing. 'I fear that you are not making the Deputy Steward a friend, my lord.'

'The law must be seen to be fair, Hubert,'

was all Richard vouchsafed in return.

The bailiff nodded. 'I echo that, Sir Richard. We want to be proud of our law again.'

★ ★ ★

On the other side of the screen was the dais of the main hall, upon which was a large oak table with four chairs for the court officials. There were no chairs or stools in the main body of the hall since all except the officials were expected to stand in attendance. A three-sided wooden pen faced the table for whoever was addressing the court or being addressed by it. To the left of the dais there was a line of twelve stools for the twelve elected members of the jury to sit and consider each case, and to vote when they were expected to by the court president.

After Richard had interviewed and instructed the four constables, he and Hubert had stayed in the Roll's Office until the crowd began to file into the hall just before eleven o'clock. The cacophony of over 200 people muttering and conversing was quite considerable, but the hush that replaced it in a matter of a few moments told him that Sir Thomas and his daughter, Lady Wilhelmina, had entered and taken their seats at the official's table. A moment later there was a respectful tap at the door and John of Flanshaw put his head round and informed him that the court was ready. Richard nodded and the bailiff retreated.

Hubert had stood up instantly, but watched with some amusement as Richard closed his eyes as if contemplating taking a quick sleep.

'Did you hear the bailiff, sir?' he asked, uncertainly. 'The court is — '

Richard opened his eyes and smiled. 'Waiting! I know, Hubert. And that is as it should be. It will do Sir Thomas some good to wait a while, too.' And he sat for another minute, then he leaned forward and opened a box that lay upon the table. From it he pulled out his iron-grey coif, the close cap that was his badge of office as a Sergeant-at-Law. He donned and straightened it upon his head, then stood and signalled for Hubert to open the door.

The hall was packed. Burghers, guildsmen, tradesmen, yeomen, bondsmen, villains, all were standing waiting expectantly. Twelve assorted individuals stood by the jury stools. The four constables with their men of the watch stood to the side of the table, while behind it, drumming his fingers impatiently, sat Sir Thomas Deyville with his daughter, Lady Wilhelmina. In contrast to Sir Thomas's scowling demeanour, she sat demurely, dressed in a splendid lilac cote-hardie that emphasized her female form and with a circlet and veil of gossamer thinness that did not hide, but simply made her beauty more alluring.

Hubert took a stance at the left side of the table and Richard took his seat beside Sir Thomas. As he passed Lady Wilhelmina he bowed and received in return a delicate inclination of the head and what he was sure was a smile from behind the veil.

He wasted no time in opening the proceedings. He introduced himself to the assembly, holding up the King's seal giving him full judicial powers in the Manor Court. Then he went on, 'And as the Circuit Judge of the King's Northern Realm, and a Sergeant-at-Law, it is my intention to demonstrate that English law is fair to everyone. The jury system is the bastion of our great legal system and we shall appoint these twelve men as jurors, to hear and where appropriate come to a decision, to help me the judge. All judgements will be carefully considered and given according to precedent of law. No person should be afraid of the law if he or she is innocent, but if guilty, then he or she can expect appropriate punishment.

'Master John of Flanshaw, the bailiff, will

record the events of this court in the Manor Court rolls.' He nodded to the bailiff and gestured for him to take his stool at the end of the table where his inkpot, quills and vellum scrolls were laid out in readiness.

'And he has already made out a list for me of the cases that we need to consider on this first sitting. So we shall begin.'

There were murmurs of irritation and a few exclamations of discontent from around the hall.

'Silence!' Richard snapped, thumping the table with a gavel. 'The court will behave with dignity and the authority of the court will be respected.'

Hubert suppressed a smile as he watched his master, all too aware that he was deliberately stamping his authority upon the court. He was also sure that he was doing so to impress the same thing upon Sir Thomas, the Deputy Steward.

'Master Bailiff, swear the jurors in.'

And while the bailiff did so Richard surveyed the gathering, recognizing various faces that he had seen the previous evening at Sandal Castle. He nodded to Master Oldthorpe and his wife, Emma. By their side was the bent, hunched figure of their simple servant, the hunchbacked Gilbert. Near the back of the court he saw Beatrice Quigley and her friend Matilda Oxley. He saw Father Daniel and Lady Katherine, the prioress. He knew that they and the rest of the assembly had high expectations.

He rapped the gavel again. 'The court is now in session.'

To the disappointment of the spectators he did not mention the murder of William Scathelocke, but instead read out a list of cases, complaints and assorted matters which had been reported to the bailiff of the court. The first few he dealt with and disposed of in a leisurely manner. Complainants and witnesses were instructed to stand in the court pen where they were directly questioned by Richard.

Sir Thomas sat and listened, from time to time growling or volunteering what he believed to be appropriate sentences. It was clear to all that Sir Thomas would have every scolding wife clamped in a scold's bridle, every thief parted with some part or other of their hands, and in the main seemed to favour public humiliation, beating and occasionally termination of life. But not so, Sir Richard. He questioned each complainant and counter-complainant. He summarized for the jury, awaited their opinion, then passed judgement. Warnings and fines were the result in the majority of cases. Yet in some cases that involved town burghers he instructed the bailiff to hand the proceeding over to the Burgher's Court, for them to investigate in their own court at a later date.

'And now we come to the case of the murder of William Scathelocke.'

There was much shuffling of feet, clearing of throats and muttering. And from the back of the crowd someone called out, 'About time!'

Some of the crowd began to laugh, but immediately stopped as Richard rapped his gavel on the table.

Hubert had the eyes of a hawk and spotted the caller. At a nod from Richard he dashed into the crowd and pushed his way through to collar the man, a large fellow with a cauliflower ear. Unceremoniously shoving one of his arms up his back he half pushed him back through the crowd to deposit him in the court pen.

'Your name, fellow?' Richard snapped.

'Simon the Fletcher — sir,' he replied in a surly tone.

Hubert lifted his hand to cuff his ear, but Richard stayed him with a raised finger.

'Well Simon the Fletcher, and everyone else for that matter, mark my words well. This is a court of law. A fair court, but it will not be viewed as a place of amusement. You will observe the dignity of the court. You may return to the audience.'

Sir Thomas leaned forward and slapped his hand on the table. 'Are you not going to deal with the oaf's impudence? A few strokes of the lash would serve him well.' He leaned back with an ill-disguised sarcastic sneer, 'Or one of your little fines, perhaps?'

'I thank you for all of your suggestions this morning, Sir Thomas, but I suggest you continue to observe and hold your counsel until we are in private.'

Then as Simon the Fletcher turned, his brow covered in a patina of perspiration at the thought of a flogging, Richard called him back.

'Stay close to the front, Simon the Fletcher. The court may yet have use of you.' He turned then to the constables. 'Go now and bring the body of the murder victim.'

An eerie hush fell over the crowd for several minutes until two of the constables and two men of the watch returned with the grisly bundle wrapped in an old horsehair blanket. At Sir Richard's direction they laid it on the floor in front of the table.

'Lady Wilhelmina, this will be an unpleasant sight. Would you care to withdraw?' When she shook her head, Richard raised his voice to the crowd. 'I make the same offer to any female here. This man's death was brutal and it is an ugly sight. If you wish to leave, you may do so until we have finished viewing the corpse.'

Several ashen-faced women and girls accepted the offer and made their way out. When the hall was ready Richard gestured to Constable Ned Burkin who drew back the blanket to reveal the body. Despite herself, Lady Wilhelmina uttered a small gasp from behind her veil. Several of the jurymen uttered exclamations and there was a surge in the crowd as many tried to gain a clearer view.

'First of all, I need to have this body formally identified. Are there any of his kin present?'

John of Flanshaw coughed to draw Richard's attention. 'He had no kin, Sir Richard. He was one of the pinders and he lived by the pinder fields. If it is helpful, I can identify him.'

Richard nodded. His eye fell on the apothecary. 'Master Oldthorpe, step forward please.'

The apothecary's eyes opened wide with surprise and he made his way through the crowd.

'I need your medical opinion. How did this man die?'

With a look of relief the apothecary

acquiesced. He pulled up his knee-length mantle and crouched beside the body. He put his hand over his nose and bent over the head to look into the gory eye socket. He reached into a pouch at his side and drew out a long metal probe. The crowd watched distastefully as he put it into the empty eye cavity and moved it hither and thither to examine the extent and the depth of the wound. Then he ran his hands over the abdomen, which had swollen with gas and lifted each of the limbs in turn. At last he pushed himself up to his feet and wiped the probe on the hem of his mantle.

'This man has been dead for a short time, I think. Less than a day, but long enough for *rigor mortis*, the corpse stiffness to set in. The skin has gone purple where the blood has stagnated. There is no putrefaction, just the beginning of bloating. The cause of death is clearly this wound to his head. An arrow wound, I would say. It almost went right through his head, and it certainly made a mess of his brain. Whoever pulled the arrow out removed his eye, or what was left of it, and a goodly amount of his brain. He would have died instantly, my lord.'

'I thank you, Master Oldthorpe. You may step back.' He looked aside and nodded approvingly to see the bailiff busily recording events on a scroll. 'Now step back into the pen, Simon the Fletcher.'

The large man looked uncomfortable as he took his place in the three-sided enclosure, his eyes staring aghast at the dead body lying in front of it.

'What do you make of this arrow?' Richard asked, snapping his fingers at Hubert who unwrapped the murder weapon that had been lying on the table throughout the proceedings and handed it to the arrowsmith.

The fletcher picked it up gingerly. 'It is well made, sir.' He held it up and looked down its shaft. 'It has a poplar shaft, which makes it light. The flights are made of grey goose feathers and trimmed most particularly.' He touched the tip of the arrowhead and hefted it. 'It is a narrow broadhead arrowhead, well weighted and as good an arrow as you could find.'

Richard had watched the large man with interest. 'How long have you been a fletcher?'

'All my life, sir. As my father was and his afore him.'

'Is this arrow one of yours?'

Simon shook his head. 'It isn't locally made, sir. I tend to use ash for the shafts. Most of my fletching is simple design, for that is what most folk want. This is an arrow built for accuracy.'

'A hunting arrow?'

'Maybe, sir, but I would say it was shot by a marksman.'

'And are there any *marksmen* about this town.'

The large fletcher shifted from foot to foot. 'Like all towns we have regular archery training, sir. It is demanded by law. If you go down to the archery butts on the Ings fields on Thursday afternoon you will find a number of fair shots.' He looked at Sir Thomas nervously. 'Although the best of them is no longer with us.'

'Is he dead?'

'No, sir, he is outlawed. His name is Robert Hood.'

Sir Thomas thumped his fist on the table. 'Damn that name. He is a wolfshead! A traitor to the King and he has had the nerve to demand tolls from travellers in the woods.'

Richard realized that he had not told the Deputy Steward about his own meeting with the man called Hood. He rapped his gavel.

'One more question, Simon the Fletcher: did this Robert Hood buy his arrows from you?'

'No, sir. He was a forester. He always made his own.'

Richard nodded pensively, his eye roving around the assembly and catching sight of

Matilda and Beatrice. They were both looking very anxious. He leaned forward. 'You may stand down, Simon the Fletcher.'

Then he indicated to the bailiff, 'Please record that William Scathelocke was murdered while in the town stocks by an unknown assailant. The whereabouts of an outlaw named Robert Hood needs to be ascertained. He is not to be killed, but must be taken alive.'

'That is outrageous!' growled Sir Thomas. 'He is an outlaw and any man may take his life. That is the law — or did you not know?'

Richard inclined his head politely. 'I know the law, Sir Thomas. But I am in charge of this court. It is my duty to investigate all unlawful killings. A man has been murdered here and I mean to know why. I need to talk to this outlaw Robert Hood, to ascertain if he is the killer. If he is not, then there is a killer abroad in this town and no one is safe.'

'Then I shall make it my business to have the wolfshead captured and brought before this court in chains!'

Richard had a suspicion that the task Sir Thomas had set himself would not be so easy, but he said nothing in direct reply. Instead, he addressed John of Flanshaw.

'Enter in the rolls that the Deputy Steward, Sir Thomas Deyville undertakes to apprehend

Robert Hood the outlaw, and bring him before this court — alive and well.'

He rapped the gavel and addressed Ned Burkin. 'Have the body taken back to the Tolbooth and bring the prisoner before us.'

6

Benefit of Clergy

There were angry mutterings and threatening movements within the crowd as Constable Ned Burkin and one of the other constables marched the Pardoner through to the court pen.

Sir Richard rapped the table with his gavel. 'This court will now try the case of the rape of Lillian Fenton, a maid of this town. She is as I understand it, not yet well, so who will stand in her stead as accuser?'

Beatrice and Matilda pushed through. 'We will, Sir Richard,' said Beatrice. 'I am Beatrice Quigley, the owner of the Bucket Inn.'

'And I am Matilda Oxley, cousin of Lillian Fenton.'

'Mark this, members of the jury,' Richard counselled. Then he asked the Pardoner, 'Your name?'

The Pardoner had been standing with his hands clasped together and his head bowed. He seemed to tremble with fear. 'I am Albin of Rouncivale.'

'Well, Albin of Rouncivale, I am told that

you have confessed to the rape of Lillian Fenton, a maid of this town. Is this true?'

The Pardoner swallowed hard, his Adam's apple rising and falling slowly, as if his mouth was devoid of saliva. 'It is true that I confessed to the watch last night, but, my lord, I am a Pardoner and I claim the benefit of clergy.'

'What is this?' snapped Sir Thomas.

Richard pursed his lips. 'A Pardoner, eh! And can you read and write, Albin of Rouncivale?'

'I can, my lord. In both English and Latin.'

Richard signalled to the bailiff. 'Bring a fresh scroll and a quill.'

When they were placed on the table in front of Richard he directed the Pardoner to approach the bench and pick up the quill. 'Now write this in Latin: *O God, have mercy upon me, according to Thine heartfelt mercifulness.*'

The Pardoner's hand shook and he genuflected and thought for a moment, then wrote in an unsteady hand:

Miserere mei, dues, secundum misericordium tuam.

Richard spun the scroll round and inspected it. Then he nodded his head. 'It is so. He can write in Latin, so is granted by law the benefit of clergy. This case will be heard by an ecclesiastical court.'

The Pardoner again made the sign of a cross over his heart and hung his head in silent prayer.

The crowd muttered angrily and threatened to move forward towards the Pardoner.

'That is unjust, my lord!' gasped Matilda.

'If he raped Lillian, he deserves — ' began Beatrice.

Richard rapped his gavel. 'Enough! My decision shall be recorded. Albin of Rouncivale shall be tried by an ecclesiastical consistory court in York. Until then he shall be taken and held in land belonging to the Church.'

'There is nowhere here in Wakefield, Sir Richard,' John of Flanshaw volunteered.

'And what of Nostell Priory? I hear that is close by.'

'It is, my lord. Yet it has only a prior and five monks. They are White monks of the Cistercian Order, all of whom have taken the vow of silence. I fear that they would not be able to hold someone against their will.'

Richard frowned and stroked his upper lip thoughtfully. Then his attention was caught by a wave of the hand from Father Daniel.

'Lady Katherine says that he may be

quartered at the Priory of Kirklees, Sir Richard. She and I shall be returning there today.'

Richard bowed to them. 'I thank you for that. Two of the Wakefield constables and two men of the watch will accompany you and guard him on the journey.' He nodded to Constable Burkin. 'Take the prisoner back to the Tolbooth until then.'

He rapped his gavel. 'I declare that this session of the Manor Court is now over. You may all leave.'

As the people started filing out, Sir Thomas shook his head angrily. 'Sir Richard, if that is an example of your law-giving, then I have no time for this 'fair law' of yours. These people need strong law, examples must be made. Instead of that you give them fines, warnings and tricks with Latin. That Pardoner should be castrated and have his eyes put out, at the least.' And with a final shrug he rose and departed. 'Come, Daughter,' he called over his shoulder.

Lady Wilhelmina rose and placed a hand on Richard's sleeve. 'I hope that my father's harshness will not sour our relationship,' she said. 'I myself found this law session of great interest and I would talk to you later, if I may.'

Richard inclined his head and watched as

she left. He was conscious that his cheeks burned, but which emotion was responsible for it he was unsure. Certainly, he had to admit that he found the Lady Wilhelmina quite captivating.

★ ★ ★

For some time later Richard, Hubert and John of Flanshaw sat in the office going over more of the court rolls.

'I cannot make head nor tail of them, my lord,' said Hubert, scratching his head. 'Latin is more schooling than I ever had, despite your kind teaching. Not like that Pardoner. What was it you said he could have again?'

'The benefit of clergy,' Richard returned. 'In the old days all clergymen were exempt from common law and could only be tried under canon law in an ecclesiastical court. When King Henry the Second came to the throne he changed all that and said that everyone would be tried under Royal Law. Thomas Becket, the Archbishop of Canterbury argued with the King and was murdered for his pains.'

'Blessed Thomas, the Martyr?' Hubert asked.

'The very same. King Henry was forced to make amends to the Church and agreed that the courts would have no jurisdiction over the clergy.'

'But a pardoner is not a proper clergyman, is he?'

Richard rubbed his chin and smiled ruefully. 'He lives by selling pardons given by the church. In this day that entitles him to claim clerical status. And he passed the test, which was to be able to read and write in Latin.'

'And so even if he is guilty of this rape, he will probably go free?'

'If he can get twelve compurgators, that means people prepared to swear an oath as to his innocence, then, yes, he will go free.'

Hubert blew air through his lips. 'Then I am not sure that I like this law. And I don't think many of the folk in court today liked it either, my lord.'

'That is as maybe,' Richard replied, scanning the vellum scroll in front of him. 'Yet it is the law.' He turned to the bailiff. 'Have you found that document yet, Master John?'

The bailiff turned with a smile. He was holding a roll of parchment. He blew a thin layer of dust from it and handed it to Richard. 'This is for the years 1316 and 1317.'

Sir Richard unrolled it on the table and

they both pored over it.

'This looks like it!' John of Flanshaw exclaimed with delight.

Richard ran his finger along the entry, translating the Latin from the spidery writing.

'On 25 January 1316, Robert Hood paid two shillings in return for a piece of the Earl's waste ground on Birch Hill between the houses of Phillip Damyson and Thomas Alayn. This land was 30 feet long and 16 feet wide, enough to hold the aforesaid Robert and any family, rendering yearly sixpence at the three terms of the year to the lord.'

He ran his finger further down the scroll.

'In the summer of 1316 Robert Hood was fined twenty pence for not obeying the Earl de Warenne's summons to join his army to aid the King in his campaign against the Scots.'

'That is right, Sir Richard,' the bailiff volunteered. 'He would have been busy building the house. It is a large five-roomed home now. He would rather have paid the fine than lose the building time in summer.'

Richard sighed. 'But he did join with Earl

Lancaster and lost it all. He surely cannot be a King's man.'

'But my lord, you know that he — ' Hubert began, but was cut off in mid-sentence by Richard's shake of the head and gesture with his head in the bailiff's direction. Hubert gave a slight nod, realizing that Richard had not told Sir Thomas that they had met the Hood, and that for some reason of his own he did not intend the bailiff to know either.

Yet John of Flanshaw did not seem to have picked up on the exchange. 'I think that like most men of his station he does what he is told, Sir Richard. But you are probably correct. He is unlikely to be well-disposed to his majesty.'

Richard nodded and stood up abruptly. 'Thank you Master John. You may clear these records away. I will call on you soon.' And with a gesture to Hubert they left the Roll's Office and the Moot Hall.

'Where to now, my lord?' Hubert asked.

Richard smiled. 'We go our separate ways now. I am going to the apothecary's and you are going for a mug of ale at the Bucket Inn.'

Hubert's eyes brightened. 'I am? And I take it that I am going to ask questions?'

'You are. I want you to find out what you can about William Scathelocke, the pinder.'

Richard was conscious of the scrutiny of the townsfolk as he rode to the apothecary's premises on the Westgate. He entered and found Emma Oldthorpe behind the counter crushing herbs in a large pestle and mortar.

'Is Master Oldthorpe in, Mistress Old-thorpe?'

Emma Oldthorpe had smiled upon his entry and Richard fancied that he had seen a touch of colour appear on each cheek.

'I am afraid that he has gone to Pontefract this afternoon, Sir Richard. We both normally go, for he rents a small room at the back of a fellow grocer's shop and consults. I have had to stay today, since we still have to look after young Miss Lillian Fenton. My husband wants her blood to be built up to chase away the excess of black bile that had made her so melancholic. I am just preparing a stock of medicine for her.'

Richard nodded. As an educated man he had some understanding of medicine and of the Doctrine of the Humours, as the four vital fluids were known. Blood, phlegm, yellow and black bile, excess of any of them being regarded as the cause of illness.

'And what will you be using to build her blood?' he asked, with genuine interest.

She pointed at the mortar with the pestle. 'I am mixing herbs from our own physic garden. Fenugreek, parsley, celery and yarrow.' She laid the pestle aside and lifted and poured the powdered herbs into a bowl containing a bloody pulp. 'We mix this with some good cow's liver and then mix that with bosh water.'

'Bosh water?' Richard queried.

'Yes, sir. Bosh water from the blacksmith's trough. He quenches hot iron in it and it is a good tonic for the blood.'

And so saying, she stirred the mix with a wooden spirtle and then poured a good pint of dark liquid into the bowl and then stirred again. 'Normally our Gilbert would help me do this, but he is out delivering potions to some of my husband's sickest patients.'

'Is Lillian still with you then?'

'Yes, sir, we have put her upstairs. Her kinswoman Matilda comes and looks after her and she is hoping to take her back home to the Bucket Inn later today. My husband says that he will decide upon his return from Pontefract this evening.' She tapped the spirtle on the side of the bowl. 'It just needs to settle for a while then I will pour it into a flask ready for her next treatment.' She wiped her hands on her apron and smiled again. 'Now, Sir Richard, was there any message for me to give to my husband?'

'Actually, I was going to let him look at my wound and the dressing.'

Emma Oldthorpe put a hand to her mouth. 'Goodness! He must have forgotten. Yet I can look at it if you wish?' And gesturing towards the door she led him through to the room where they had cauterized Lillian's wrists the day before. Emma pointed to the couch and Richard lay down.

'I understand that you help your husband a lot, Mistress Oldthorpe.'

'Please, Sir Richard; my name is Emma if you would prefer to use that.' She pulled his boot off and eased his hose up over his knee. Then she began to undo the bandaging on his leg. 'How is it feeling, sir?'

'It is much improved. I no longer have the ague or the fever and sweating. The potion and the dressing seem to have had a near miraculous effect.'

Emma gently peeled the mouldy leather pad from the arrow-wound and dabbed pus away from the margins of the gash.

'Arrows make a nasty mess of flesh,' she said, looking up at him with her large green eyes.

'I got this at the battle of Boroughbridge,' he said. 'It has been most slow to heal. And I agree, arrows make a mess.'

'I did not enjoy seeing the body of that poor man at the court this morning,' Emma added with a wince of disdain. 'Who would do such a thing, Sir Richard?'

'That is yet to be found out, although suspicion falls on one man.'

'On Robert Hood?'

'It is only suspicion. There is no proof as yet.'

Emma rose and folded the leather pad. 'I will replace it with another piece then I will rebind it.' And she went back into the shop, returning after a few moments with another mouldy square of leather. She closed the door after her, bent down beside the couch and redressed the wound.

'You do not have an accent from these parts, Emma,' Richard commented. 'Where are you from?'

'From the West Country, sir. I met my husband there and we have moved many times. We lived in Warwick for a while and then moved to Pontefract before settling in Wakefield. My husband is a good man. He even took my poor cousin Gilbert in and gave him a home.' She sighed. 'Gilbert is hunchbacked and somewhat simple-witted, Sir Richard.'

Richard nodded. 'Your husband certainly seems to know his work. I was impressed with his examination of the body this morning. And his treatment of the girl Lillian and of my own wound. Yet he is . . . ' he hesitated, 'considerably older than you.'

Emma averted her eyes. 'But as I say, sir, he is a good man. He has taught me many things. About grocery and spicing, and his apothecary work. And he taught me much of midwifery.' She finished binding his bandage. 'The leg is still somewhat swollen, Sir Richard. If you would permit me, I will rub it a little. That will help to dispel some of the fluid that accumulates after a wound.'

Richard nodded his head and rested back, finding Emma's gentle manipulation on his calf very relaxing. 'Did you know the man in the stocks, William Scathelocke?'

'Of course, Sir Richard. He was a pinder and one of the best slaughtermen in the area.'

'And did he work for any particular butcher?'

Emma pursed her lips as she kneaded his lower leg. 'I think not, Sir Richard. You would have to ask around in the shambles where all the butchers' shops are. Or ask at the guildhall.'

'I shall do that. And in fact I must pay a visit to the guildhall sometime. I must learn more of the Wakefield Mysteries.'

'Ah yes, the plays. My husband and I are

involved, since he is the master of the spicer and grocer's guild.'

Her skilful fingers had begun rubbing the back of his knee, gently working on the lymph nodes that had swollen there.

'Will you be acting in these plays, Emma?'

She laughed, a sweet trill of a laugh that seemed to bubble up with pleasure. 'Oh I could not act, Sir Richard. But I help some of the other wives and seamstresses with costumes.'

Richard was feeling extremely relaxed. Yet he was also aware as Emma's hands moved above the knee to work on his thigh muscles that he was feeling something else. Something he had not felt since his wife had died. He felt himself becoming aroused by this green-eyed wife of the local apothecary. His manhood had begun to enlarge, producing a bulge that he was both conscious of and embarrassed by.

'That is good, Emma,' he said, abruptly sitting up and swinging his legs off the couch. 'I . . . I must away on business.'

Emma's cheeks had developed two patches of crimson, and she had snatched her hands away and put them behind her back. She rose quickly, her eyes fixed on the floor. 'I would suggest that you return tomorrow, sir. I . . . I could redress the wound.'

Richard pulled on his boot, stamped the heel on the reed-covered floor to get it in place. 'And I shall settle with your husband then, if that is all right?'

He left quickly, embarrassed that Emma Oldthorpe had seen that she had aroused him as a woman may arouse her husband. Yet as he mounted his horse he could not help the smile that had crept to his lips.

★ ★ ★

Hubert usually performed tasks that Sir Richard set him with vigour and zeal. When his mission involved indulging himself in food and a mug or two of ale, his enthusiasm soared. And when it might involve spending time with a buxom wench such as Mistress Beatrice Quigley of the Bucket Inn, he moved with the verve of a stallion given the run of a paddock.

The inn was only half full after the usual midday rush. It smelled agreeably of rabbit stew and freshly baked bread. Hubert ordered a mug of ale, a plate of stew and a hunk of bread from one of the serving girls and ate with gusto. In answer to his query about the whereabouts of the landlady the girl answered that she was busy with the ale-taster, who was checking the strength of her beer in the Bucket Inn brewhouse. Accordingly, after wolfing his food down Hubert ordered another mug of ale and moved to an inglenook where he sat watching the rest of the clientele.

His spirits rose when Beatrice came in, shaking her head and cursing the incompetence and impudence of the town ale-taster. The girl who had served Hubert whispered to her and she turned and spied Hubert.

'Good day, Master Hubert,' she greeted, her voluptuous lips forming into a smile that revealed her strong white teeth and the appealing gap between the two front ones. 'Is your master Sir Richard not with you this afternoon?'

'He has gone to the apothecary's,' Hubert replied, standing and gesturing to the seat beside him. 'But I would be grateful for some of your time and the answer to a question or two.'

Beatrice's eyes sparkled and she winked. 'Questions about the law, or did you want to ask me questions of a more personal nature?'

Hubert laughed. He certainly found Beatrice Quigley an attractive woman and he was pretty sure that she had felt the same force. A handsome couple they would make, he felt. And a handsome coupling, a little demon in his mind urged. 'A few of both,' he

145

grinned. 'Will you drink some ale with me?'

'I will have a little mead,' she returned, signalling to the serving girl.

'A sweet drink for a sweet lass,' Hubert said, raising his mug to her.

In return she smiled coquettishly and gave him a playful prod in the ribs with an elbow. Her drink arrived and they politely clinked pots. As they drank they naturally fell into conversation. He told her of himself and she told him of how she had inherited the Bucket Inn when her husband had died of apoplexy.

'That was after a night of excessive passion, Master Hubert,' she confided.

'Enough of the 'Master,' Beatrice. I am plain Hubert to you.' And already his mind was thinking of the coupling that he hoped would be not long in coming, especially as she was being so candid. 'But to business, now,' he said tweaking her knee through her dress. 'Mayhap we shall have time for further chat later.'

'I am all attention, Hubert. Ask what you will.'

'Sir Richard is concerned about the murder of the man William Scathelocke. Do you know anything of him?'

Beatrice coloured and took a sip of her mead. 'Of course. He was one of the pinders and an excellent slaughterman. He could dispatch an ox, pig or horse as quickly as that,' she said, snapping her fingers in front of her. 'His main problem was that he drank too much. Of late he was always drunk.'

'Why did he drink?'

Beatrice bit her lower lip. 'A woman, of course.'

'Which woman?'

'Matilda Oxley.'

Hubert's jaw dropped. 'You mean — '

'Lillian's cousin. That is right.'

'But she is betrothed to the outlaw Robert Hood, isn't she?'

'She is now. He and William Scathelocke were friends once, then they became rivals for Matilda's affections.' Beatrice sighed. 'And she chose Robin.

'And then he began drinking. He was always drunk. It made him ill and he became incompetent and stopped doing his job properly. That is how he ended up in the stocks, although in everyone's opinion the punishment was too harsh.'

'Did he drink here?'

'He used to, until he was spurned by Matilda. From then on he hated her, Robin and everything to do with them.'

Hubert contemplated taking another sip of his ale, but laid the mug down instead. He leaned closer to Beatrice and whispered,

'Could he have been the one who raped Lillian?'

Beatrice's eyes opened wide in first alarm, then in shock. 'So that's it! You want to tidy this case away and have it pinned on poor William Scathelocke?' She shot to her feet, her eyes blazing. 'You know full well that a Pardoner confessed to the crime this morning. Why are you trying to say such a . . . a horrible thing?'

A trio of men drinking at a neighbouring table looked round to see what all the commotion was. As one they stood up and advanced towards Hubert.

'Is this bumpkin causing you grief, Beatrice?' asked one, a big man in a horsehair mantle. 'Shall we show him the dust of the lane?'

'It looks like that judge's man,' said another, with a cloth over one eye socket.

'That's no excuse for upsetting Beatrice,' said the third, a bald older man with a grey beard. 'Just say the word, Beatrice.'

Hubert eyed them all, but without fear. With the possible exception of the big man he felt sure that he could give a good account of himself against all three if needs be.

But Beatrice shook her head. 'He is just leaving, thank you, lads. I don't want you or your gang breaking any more of my chairs like last night.'

George-a-Green was contrite. 'That wasn't my fault, mistress. That was all because some jackanapes set fire to my cloak.'

The others chorused support for the pinder.

'Beatrice, I did not mean — ' Hubert began.

But the look in her eye told him that remonstration would be useless. He stood and bowed before taking his leave.

Once outside he chided himself for being so unsubtle. Then he grinned as the image of her standing over him with her flashing eyes and heaving breast came into his mind. She was certainly a woman of spirit. Taming that spirit was going to be a challenge that he would relish.

* * *

Neither Sir Richard nor Hubert made any mention to each other of the emotional meetings that they had both had since leaving the Moot Hall. Together they made their way back to Sandal Castle.

After visiting the guildhall and finding it closed and locked Richard had paid a visit to the shambles and talked with several of the butchers there. All had known and used William Scathelocke and confirmed that he had been a good and useful slaughterman. They had all mentioned his drinking and his rowdy behaviour, but none had known why he had started drinking so much. The news of him being a rival for the affections of Matilda Oxley had come as a surprise to Richard.

'Could that be another link with the Hood then?' Richard mused. 'Perhaps the Hood could have been getting rid of an old enemy when he found him there like a sitting duck? Or perhaps he could have been ensuring his silence.'

'How so, my lord?'

'Suppose that the Hood had been the rapist? The stocks are not far from the cemetery. It is possible that Scathelocke had seen something.'

Hubert chewed his lip. 'I asked Beatrice Quigley if she thought that Scathelocke could have raped the girl. She went half mad and virtually threw me out of the Bucket Inn. She went on about the Pardoner having confessed.'

Richard nodded. 'And, of course, there is nothing to suggest that the two crimes are in any way linked. Unless the Hood is involved.' He patted his mount's neck and it snickered back at him. 'But the more one thinks about it, the more likely that seems. One thing is a pity though.'

'What is that, sir?'

'That we don't have one of the Hood's arrows. And we were so close to them only yesterday morning.'

* * *

It was late afternoon by the time the little procession left Wakefield and took the road towards Kirklees Priory, some ten miles distant. Lady Katherine and Father Daniel went first in a horse-drawn common cart, followed by Ned Burkin and the Pardoner, then by Owen Kidd, the Northgate constable and two other men of the watch.

The prioress and the nun's priest were busily discussing a priory matter, Ned Burkin was slurping from a skin of ale, and the Pardoner was hunched over his donkey, mumbling in Latin.

Owen Kidd prodded the Pardoner with the staff and cross that he was carrying along with the Pardoner's other belongings. 'You are a lucky dog, Pardoner,' he said. 'Sir Thomas would have had your balls cut off and your eyes fed to the crows by this afternoon if he had his way. The new judge seems a much more . . . mealy-mouthed type.'

Albin of Rouncivale mumbled obsequiously and seemed to hunch up further, as if in attempting to do so he would disappear and escape further taunts. He was feeling totally wretched and more than a little scared. So far no one had shown him any shred of kindness. He knew that everyone would consider him an outcast, guilty and worthy of nothing except castration, blinding and even death. He knew that he would have to bide his time and try to gain the support of the prioress and the nun's priest and then perhaps he would have a chance at the consistory court in York.

The two men of the watch chuckled away to each other.

'Come on, Ned, let us have some of that ale,' one of the men complained.

In answer Constable Burkin made a sign, took another swig, then said, 'You men just keep your eyes peeled. I will watch the prisoner; you just look out for robbers and outlaws as we pass through these woods.' He turned and blinked at the Pardoner. 'I must say though, you don't actually look like the sort of a man who would rape a young girl.'

Albin of Rouncivale looked up at the constable. He shook his head. 'I didn't rape her.'

Ned Burkin stared at him as though he was talking to a madman. 'What are you saying to me, you dog? You said yourself that you raped her. And you stood before the judge this morning and — '

'I admitted no crime this morning. I just claimed benefit of clergy. I was fleeing for my life last night and I had to get away from two men. That is why I confessed and let you arrest me. I think they were going to kill me.'

'What foolery is this?'

'I needed to have my case tried by a consistory court. Once we get to Kirklees Priory I will talk to the prioress and the nun's priest.'

Ned Burkin scowled. 'I think that you should be talking to them now, you villain.' And he called out to Father Daniel.

The nun's priest pulled on the reins and stopped the cart and turned round as the constable and his prisoner drew near.

'Gad, we're stopping now!' exclaimed one of the men of the watch. 'It will be nightfall before we reach Kirkless Priory at this rate.'

'I can't say I like these woods,' groaned the other man of the watch, a gangly fellow with yellow teeth. 'These shadows make me feel uneasy.'

Constable Burkin touched his forelock. 'This Pardoner says he needs to talk to you both. He says that he only confessed to this rape to escape from two — '

A high-pitched whistle rang out, followed

by a call from behind them.

'Pardoner! Prepare to pay for your crime!'

They all turned round, but saw no one on the road.

Then there was a whooshing sound followed by a chunking noise and the Pardoner shrieked.

As they all turned at the sound, they saw him slowly tumble backwards off his donkey to lie fumbling helplessly at an arrow that had skewered him through the throat. Blood was gushing from the wound and he was making dreadful gurgling noises, his eyes rolled up so that only the whites showed. Then, before anyone could dismount and reach him, his body convulsed once then he lay flaccid, his arms thrown out in a macabre cruciform position.

The Pardoner, Albin of Rouncivale was dead.

7

Minstrelsy

Dinner at the castle was a wholly different occasion from the previous evening. Richard supped at the high table with Sir Thomas, Lady Alecia and Lady Wilhelmina, while Hubert ate at one of the long tables with the castle servants and their families. The food was less varied but of an agreeable standard, served with aplomb by Pringle the butler and his staff, while the minstrels played in the gallery above.

'You are a widower I believe, Sir Richard,' Lady Alecia stated, rather than asked.

'I am, Lady Alecia. My wife died in childbirth less than twelve months ago. My son lived for a few days. May the Lord bless their souls.'

Sir Thomas grunted. 'My wife lost two sons before we had Wilhelmina,' he said, sourly. 'Although she has a mind faster than most men.'

'Father, please!' Lady Wilhelmina protested.

'Oh but you have, my dear,' said her

155

mother. 'And you have so many accomplishments. You can sing, play the harp, and speak French and Latin. And you can read and write like — '

Sir Thomas thumped his fist on the table. 'Enough, Alecia! Are you trying to marry our daughter off to Sir Richard?'

Richard smiled inwardly. He knew that Lady Alecia had probably touched a raw nerve with her husband when she had alluded to her daughter's literacy. He suspected that Sir Thomas had somehow managed to keep his own illiteracy from her with his overbearing ways.

Lady Wilhelmina gave her own spirited reply. 'Father! Mother! You have embarrassed both Sir Richard and me. May I withdraw?'

Richard raised a hand to protest, but Lady Wilhelmina had already risen, studiously keeping her gaze averted from him.

'Lady Wilhelmina,' Richard pleaded, 'there is no need to feel — '

But it was too late. After curtsying to no one in particular she flounced out of the hall. As she did so, all of the other diners had either shot to their feet or were busily pushing back their stools in order to do so. Sir Thomas had said nothing to try to restrain her and he said nothing when his wife also retired after first giving her most profuse apologies to Richard. Once again the rest of the hall stood as the Deputy Steward's wife swept out of the hall.

Sir Thomas reached across the table for a jug and replenished his mug. 'Women, eh?' he chuckled. 'I fear that they do not understand much of the real world.'

Richard shook his head in disagreement. 'Yet your daughter attended the Manor Court today. That implies to me that she is very interested in what is happening in the real world.'

Sir Thomas quaffed his ale and pursed his lips pensively. 'She has a curious nature, Sir Richard,' he explained. 'It is no more than that.' He leaned forward on one elbow. 'Actually, I rather think she may have inherited that curiosity from me. I am very curious to know what you have learned about the murder of that villain Scathelocke?'

Richard was surprised by the question. 'And how do you know that I have learned anything, Sir Thomas?'

The Deputy Steward laughed. 'Perhaps you think that I am a complete simpleton, Sir Richard,' he said, fixing Richard with a less than friendly regard. 'Let me assure you that I am not. I mean to be the true steward of Sandal Castle very soon. Perhaps even Lord of the Manor of Wakefield in time. Suffice it to say that I know of all of your movements today.'

Richard felt his hackles rise, yet he restrained himself from showing any disquiet. 'So you have had spies watching me, Sir Thomas? I am not sure that his majesty would take too kindly to having one of his Sergeants-at-Law interfered with when he is investigating the murder of one of his subjects. Remember that I am here under his warrant.'

Sir Thomas merely grunted and gulped more ale. Then he belched slowly. 'Then if I were you I would be careful in your investigations. You don't want to discover a viper's nest. You know what an aversion his majesty has to snakes. Just think of what happened to Earl Lancaster.'

★ ★ ★

After supper Hubert had gone for another stroll round the battlement walk. As he expected, Adam Crigg was on duty on the same section of wall as the night before.

'Did that oaf grumble at you last night?' Hubert asked.

Adam gave a lop-sided grin. 'He yelled a bit and tried to belittle me in front of the guardroom, but quite honestly, I don't give a witch's wart for him.'

They walked on, Adam keeping a constant watch on the approach to the castle.

'What are the castle defences like?' Hubert asked.

Adam grinned again. 'If you weren't the judge's man and a fellow soldier I might take you for a spy,' he joked. He turned and spat. 'But the truth is that this castle would take a good siege now. It didn't before Earl Lancaster took it, but he shored it up and did a lot of reinforcements. With the drawbridge up it should be pretty damned impregnable. We've got an outer and an inner moat, machicolations above the main gate and on the barbican. And that barbican would defend the keep against an army. We've got three wells and plenty of food to last a few months.' He grinned again. 'And plenty of ale and wine.'

Hubert tapped Adam's pike. 'Your weapons seem to be well sharpened and in good condition. I suppose you've got an armourer to maintain everything.'

Adam clicked his tongue. 'We did have a good one. Old Jomo was the armourer and castle blacksmith for twenty years. What he didn't know about ballistas, onagars, axes and halberds just wasn't worth knowing. And he could mend anything from a ploughshare to a church bell. It was him that I told you about last night. Earl Lancaster had him make new bells for his chapel in the west tower and for the Church of St Helens in Sandal Magna. And the Earl had him make all those other little bells that the Deputy Steward is so fond of.'

'What happened? You talk as if he isn't here anymore.'

'He isn't anywhere, friend Hubert.' He crossed his heart. 'I just hope he's forging bells and angel arrows up in heaven, and not working on the Devil's forge down below. He died one afternoon about a year or so ago. He had a good breakfast, then just got ill straight afterwards. Master Oldthorpe was sent for by the Earl, but there was nothing he could do. By noon he had given up the ghost. Gideon Kitchen was bloody inconsolable for a week and thought that he must have poisoned him.'

Hubert shook his head sympathetically. 'These things happen sometimes. An Act of God, maybe?'

'Maybe. It was just fortunate that he had no family. Anyway, he's buried over the hill. I sometimes salute him when I hear the chapel bell ringing.'

Hubert patted the sword at his side. 'It is a pity, right enough. I would have liked to get this faithful old fellow of mine sharpened.'

Adam looked at it with the eye of a professional soldier. 'I'll take care of that for you, friend Hubert. For a mug of ale!'

'Right willingly will I buy you one, or several. A good drinking session would go down well with me,' Hubert replied with a laugh. He looked about the walls, where two other guards were watching their sections. 'Where is your sergeant this evening?'

'Sleeping! The dozy clod. He is taking a party out at first light. Sir Thomas came back this afternoon huffing and puffing about your master. He says that he is going to capture Robert Hood.'

'He does, does he?' Hubert mused.

'Aye. But I reckon we might see pigs fly over this wall afore that happens.'

★   ★   ★

Richard had retired to his room in the North Tower after supper to rest and to get his thoughts in order. The murder of William Scathelocke bothered him. It all seemed so messy. And Richard did not like mess.

He lay on his bed staring at the ring of light cast on the ceiling by his guttering candle.

'But damn me, I do like the look of that apothecary's wife,' he whispered to himself. Then he immediately felt guilty. Not so much

161

because thoughts of cuckolding the apothecary had gone through his mind, but because he was not yet over the loss of his own wife and child. He pummelled his temples to force the thought of Emma Oldthorpe from his head.

As he did so, he fancied that he heard a footstep in the corridor outside his door. 'Hubert? Is that you?'

There was no answer at first. Then he heard a feminine voice calling his name softly through the door.

He rose and threw it open. Despite himself he gasped at the sight of a cloaked and hooded figure standing in the shadows. His hand went to the dagger at his side, but he refrained from drawing it when the figure reached up and threw back the hood.

Lady Wilhelmina was standing there, a voluptuous smile upon her lips.

★ ★ ★

As a trained soldier Hubert had woken at the sound of the drawbridge being lowered and the portcullis being raised. A couple of candles illuminated the guardroom where he had been given a pallet bed, and by the darkness of the hour, the deep snores of the off-duty guards and the size of the candle stumps he gauged that it was at least two hours before cock-crow. The cadence of horses crossing the drawbridge brought back the image of Adam's face as he told him of Sir Thomas's plan to capture the Hood. He grinned, then turned over and within seconds had fallen fast asleep again.

When cockcrow did come he was instantly awake and immediately alert. And extremely hungry. After using the communal garderobe and making his ablutions in the trough at the back of the guardroom, he followed his nose over the inner moat from the barbican to the bailey, heading in the direction of the bakehouse. Already the castle was coming to life as the grooms swept out the stables and fed the animals in the undercroft and the domestic servants bustled about emptying chamber pots, sweeping flagstone floors and replenishing rushes on the floors of the various buildings. The inevitable guards kept up a watch on the battlement walls and the air hung with the smell of wood-smoke, baking bread and cooking meat.

As he approached the bakehouse, where he could hear the merry voice of Gideon Kitchen issuing orders amid peals of laughter, the melodic sound of a lute caught his attention. As he passed the stairs that led up to the oriel gallery and the Great Hall he saw the lute-player sitting cross-legged atop a barrel, seemingly blissfully unaware of all that went on around him. He was a young man in his early twenties, clean shaven and smartly clad in red tunic and hose. When Hubert stopped to listen to him he looked up and abruptly strummed his instrument then stopped the strings vibration with the flat of his hand.

'You play well, young Master — '

'Alan-a-Dale,' replied the youngster with a smile of delight. He made a circular roll of his hand and inclined his head in a little bow. 'Might I play you a song?'

Hubert grinned as he shook his head. 'I would love to hear more, but I fear that the rumbling of my stomach might drown out any music you play. Later, perhaps.'

'Of course, sir. I have had the honour of playing before your master Sir Richard.' He played a few notes, and then strummed again. '*A clever, clever knight,*' he sang. Then his fingers moved nimbly and he played a few more notes. '*And he will do well.*' He played another few notes. '*To show that he can do right.*'

Hubert was already striding off towards the bakehouse, but as the minstrel played another few notes, strummed loudly then stopped, he wondered whether Alan-a-Dale was being deliberately impertinent. If he was, he would box his ears. He wheeled round to demand what he meant.

But Alan-a-Dale had gone.

'Where on earth — ?' he began.

'Where is what, Hubert?' Richard asked, as he walked across towards him.

Hubert told him of the minstrel's little ditty. 'Should I go and find the fool, sir?'

But Richard shook his head and pointed towards the bake-house. 'It is no more than one can expect from a minstrel,' he said. 'Now come, we shall see what Gideon Kitchen can offer us to break our fast.'

Hubert fell into step beside Richard. He said nothing, but he wondered why his master had suddenly coloured.

Gideon Kitchen was true to his word, in that he fed them a sumptuous breakfast of gruel, newly caught fried trout, and hunks of bread, all washed down with mugs of ale. And as they ate, he regaled them with many a jest.

'I think that you have a jibe for every occasion, Gideon Kitchen,' said Richard.

'I have to, Sir Richard. A happy eater is a contented eater, and a contented eater is another rung on my ladder to heaven.'

'Well, no one will ever die from eating at your table, Master Kitchen,' said Hubert with a laugh.

The cook eyed him with a hint of suspicion for a moment, then burst out laughing again. 'Nay, not unless he wants to get plucked, roasted and served up with the capons and boars at my lord's table.'

Hubert wondered if he had inadvertently touched a raw spot with the cook, and remembered that Adam Crigg had told him how upset Gideon had been when the castle blacksmith had died. He made a mental note to tell his master about it later:

As it was, it was put out of his mind, for, as they left the bakehouse they saw Sir Thomas Deyville come striding across the bailey courtyard from his chambers beside the gatehouse. His face bore an expression of grim determination and in his hand he swung the wooden flail of which he was so fond.

'Sir Richard!' he barked. 'I need a word with you!'

Hubert said softly under his breath, 'He seems an angry bull this morning. Has something upset him, do you think, Sir Richard?'

Richard also replied under his breath, 'It looks like it. I think that it might be sensible if I meet with him on my own, good Hubert. Why don't you go and look to our horses in the stables?'

Hubert bowed and withdrew, although

there was something about his master's manner that had stirred his curiosity and he would rather have hovered about nearby.

'I am at your service, Sir Thomas,' Richard said, with a bow. Despite his apparent calm, he was inwardly dreading this meeting with the Deputy Steward.

But to his surprise, when Sir Thomas reached him, his bearded face broke into a grin. 'I think that it will be me who is doing you a service this day, Sir Richard. I am expecting before long to have apprehended that wolfshead, Robert Hood and his snivelling band of fellow outlaws. I had my men leave in the hours before cockcrow, to set a trap.'

They had started walking towards his private quarters when one of the sentries on the battlements called out, and a series of yells culminated in the bell in the gatehouse block being rung.

'A rider approaches, Sir Thomas!' the gatekeeper called.

Sir Thomas momentarily grinned triumphantly at Richard, and then he turned as the gatekeeper appeared from his post. 'Well let him in, man! Let him in!'

A few moments later the drawbridge was lowered and the portcullis clanked upwards. A rider galloped across the wooden bridge, entered the castle and reined to a halt in front of the two knights.

It was Ned Burkin, the Warrengate Constable. He looked to be a worried man.

'Your pardon, Sir Richard and Sir Thomas. I . . . I . . . bring news.'

'Out with it then!' barked Sir Thomas.

Ned Burkin dismounted and swallowed several times, as if he was having difficulty getting his tongue to articulate words. He directed his reply to Sir Richard.

'It is the Pardoner, sir. He was murdered last night. By a hidden archer.'

Both Sir Thomas and Sir Richard were taken aback at the news. As the Deputy Steward opened his mouth to bark a command, Richard put a restraining hand on his arm.

'I think it would be best if we were to listen to the constable's tale in the privacy of your chamber.'

And so, a few minutes later, in the office of Sir Thomas's chambers Ned Burkin recounted the death of Albin of Rouncivale.

'So we did not dare return to Wakefield last night,' he explained. 'The killer could have picked us all off at his leisure. We went on and stayed the night at Kirklees Priory as had already been arranged. This morning at first light I travelled here.'

Sir Thomas had been prowling the room like a caged animal. He stopped and abruptly thumped the table with a fist, scattering maps, bells and an empty mug. 'That wolfshead Hood! My men should have snared him by now. By thunder we shall have him hanged by sundown!'

Richard eyed him dispassionately. '*If* he committed a murder, and if it can be proven, then he will certainly be sentenced to death — but definitely not by sundown today. The law will move appropriately and not with undue haste.'

The Deputy Steward grunted, picked up one of his hand-bells and vigorously shook it. It was answered almost instantly by the serving boy Richard had seen when he arrived at the castle, who came in bearing a jug of ale.

'Where is the body?' Richard asked.

'Still at the priory, Sir Richard,' Ned Burkin replied nervously. 'I thought it best to obtain your instructions before I moved it to Wakefield.'

'Good thinking, Constable,' Richard replied. 'And are the prioress and the nun's priest still there?'

'They are awaiting your visit, Sir Richard.'

'Excellent. Then my man Hubert and I shall ride back with you straight away.' He turned to Sir Thomas. 'Will you come too, to see the body?'

Sir Thomas gulped a mouthful of ale and shook his head. 'I have no need to see the wretch. Besides, I have a live fish to catch. I will wait to see my men bring in the outlaw and his rabble.'

Ten minutes later, Sir Richard and Hubert were preparing to follow Constable Burkin across the drawbridge on their way to Kirklees, some ten miles west of the castle. But before they had actually mounted their horses the gatehouse bell rang out again, followed by a yell from the sentry on the battlements above.

'The men are back, Sir Thomas,' he hailed. 'But they . . . they . . . '

'They what?' bellowed Sir Thomas.

In answer a motley line of men on foot appeared as they crossed the drawbridge. They were not only horseless, but weaponless and devoid of their chain-mail and their helmets.

'What in the name of hell?' Sir Thomas cried, his face suffused with fury. 'Where? How? What? Explain yourselves!'

'We . . . we were ambushed my lord. There must have been a hundred or more of them,' the sergeant muttered, hanging his head in shame and quaking with fear, as he saw the

Deputy Steward's knuckles whiten on the wood flail in his hands. 'They took — everything. They said it was all part of their toll.'

'Toll?' Sir Tomas spluttered, his face almost apoplectic.

'Their toll for using their forest, sir.'

While Sir Thomas cursed and shook with rage, Richard mounted and signalled for Constable Burkin and Hubert to do likewise.

'I shall leave you to this, Sir Thomas,' he said. 'We shall go to investigate this murder.'

Lady Alecia and Lady Wilhelmina came out of the Deputy Steward's chambers as they were passing. Richard touched his forehead as he passed.

Hubert did not fail to notice the sparkle in Lady Wilhelmina's eyes and the instantaneous colour that appeared on her cheeks as they passed.

★ ★ ★

The journey to Kirklees Priory was uneventful and they did not meet anyone on the road except for a couple of drovers and a meagre herd of cattle, and a group of what seemed to be professional beggars. They were able to travel quickly on their fresh mounts, yet warily in case of outlaws.

Eventually they came to a small valley. It was a fair sized Priory of the Benedictine order, consisting of the usual buildings; a chapterhouse, church and bell tower, dormitory, hospital and cloisters. They were met at the gatehouse by a young novice, who immediately arranged for an ostler to take their horses while she scuttled ahead to take them to Lady Katherine's office, where she and Father Daniel were waiting.

'This is an evil business, Sir Richard,' the prioress said, wringing her hands, from which her rosary dangled. 'Can I offer you refreshments after your journey?'

Richard declined for all three of them. 'Murder is always evil, Lady Katherine. Pray let me see the body in the first instance, then we shall talk.'

Without further ado Father Daniel led the way out along the cloister towards the far end of the quadrangle where the hospital block was sited. He opened the door of an outhouse and stood aside for Richard to enter.

The body of Albin of Rouncivale had been laid on the floor and covered with a blanket. Richard knelt and gingerly lifted the blanket to reveal the corpse, lying on its side with a blood-stained arrow through the throat.

'We left the arrow in him,' Constable Burkin explained, as he took the blanket from

Richard. 'I thought you might want to see how he had been killed.'

Richard nodded approval. Ned Burkin had seemed to him a hard-drinking sot, yet he felt that he showed potential. He returned his attention to the body.

Hubert leaned closer and scrutinized the dead man's purple-mottled face. 'He almost seems to be smiling,' he observed drily.

'But the poor fellow hardly had anything to be happy about, did he?' Father Daniel queried.

'The *sardonic smile of death* is common enough,' Richard commented. 'The muscles go rigid after death and pull the mouth into this leering grin.'

'You don't think that he could have been smiling at the moment of death, do you, Sir Richard?' Hubert asked. 'Could he have recognized his killer?'

Richard shook his head and straightened up. He turned to Father Daniel.

'Why did you just say that he had nothing to be happy about?'

The nun's priest shuffled uncomfortably from one foot to the other. 'I . . . I merely meant that he was in a quandary. He was accused of rape and on his way to an ecclesiastical court. And now look at him. Murdered like that.'

'The constable here says that he claimed that he was innocent just moments before he was shot. He said that he called out to you and that he was explaining what the Pardoner had told him when it happened. Is that correct?'

'Just so. But I never heard him, for the killer struck at that moment.'

Hubert clicked his tongue. 'But surely it is not unexpected that he would claim to be innocent before the trial?'

'Except that he had already confessed to the crime when he surrendered himself to Constable Burkin,' Richard replied.

Constable Burkin held the blanket out, as if ready to recover the body. 'Have you seen enough, Sir Richard?'

Richard shook his head. 'I need to see the body unclothed.' He turned his head to Hubert, who bent down to help.

'Wait!' Richard said, as Hubert started to tug at the Pardoner's tunic. 'We shall cut the clothes off.' And, drawing a double-edged hunting knife, he inserted the blade under the neck of the garment and, while Hubert exerted traction, he cut all the way down. Then they peeled the clothing aside. Once the body was unclad, he ran his hands over the stone cold torso with its corrugated rib cage and over the limbs, testing for muscle rigidity and for any other abnormal signs.

'He looks a pitiful sight,' Father Daniel said. 'Not too well fed. And there is a vulnerable look about him. Something almost virginal, I think.'

Richard chewed his lip pensively. 'Indeed, I think that you are right, Father Daniel.' He ran his fingers over the dead man's face and jowls. 'No beard at all. I fancy that he has never shaved in his life, although he must be in his thirties.'

'And no hair on his body, except for that lank yellow stuff that hangs down over his shoulders like a girl's,' said Hubert.

Richard still had his knife in his hand. He pointed the tip at the Pardoner's small exposed penis. 'And this is like a young boy's member.' He slipped the blade under the penis and lifted it up so that he could feel the shrivelled scrotum. 'And there are no balls in his sac.'

'So what?' Hubert asked.

Richard stood up and sheathed his knife, before wiping his hands on his breaches. 'It makes it highly likely that he was telling the truth about one thing.'

'I am afraid that I do not follow you, Sir Richard,' said the nun's priest.

'It is simple enough,' Richard replied. 'This man is like a gelded horse, or like a mare. It is unlikely that he would have been able to rape a woman. Or that he would even have the desire to.'

Hubert snapped his fingers. 'Of course!' Then he frowned. 'But why did he confess to the crime?' He shook his head. 'And so the poor sod was murdered because the killer thought he was guilty.'

Richard frowned. 'If I had not given him the benefit of clergy then he would still be alive.'

The others could see by Richard's expression that he was troubled by this, as if he felt in some way responsible. But then he exhaled deeply and turned his attention again to the body.

'Which brings us to this arrow. Unless I am much mistaken it is the twin of the one that killed William Scathelocke.'

* * *

The bells tolled, calling the nuns to *Sext*, the fourth of the six services of the day. While Lady Katherine and Father Daniel went to take the service Richard and Hubert sat and ate bread and cheese and drank some of the watered-down ale that Lady Katherine permitted the fourteen nuns under her care to consume. Constable Ned Burkin and his two assistants had already started back with the Pardoner's body in a cart, with a message for the bailiff John of Flanshaw to alert the townsfolk about a special session of the court that Sir Richard intended to hold on the following morning. He impressed upon them that they were to tell only the bailiff about the murder of the Pardoner and that he was not to give anyone the reason for the court session. Further, they were to take the body directly to the Tolbooth and keep it concealed as they did so.

'Forgive me if I speak out of turn, Sir Richard,' Hubert said, as he munched a crust of bread, 'but do I detect a closeness between the prioress and the nun's priest? A closeness that is not quite — '

Richard nodded. 'I suspect so, too. Which is dangerous for them, since in 1315 the King's archbishop censured Kirklees Priory because the nuns were said to have been consorting with men. They had the threat of excommunication put upon them.'

'So I am guessing that if they have got a relationship they would do anything to keep it from the King's ears or that of the archbishop?' Hubert asked. He swigged some ale. 'Will they be coming back to Wakefield to attend the court tomorrow?'

Richard nodded. 'Aye, Father Daniel has to

return to meet with the guildmasters, and the prioress will be following with some of her nuns after dealing with some priory matters. We will go with Father Daniel after he has finished this service and he can show us where the Pardoner was killed.' He frowned. 'I have to say that there is much that bothers me about this Pardoner's death, Hubert. It bothers me a great deal.'

8

The Wakefield Master

Father Daniel, riding the Pardoner's donkey, led Sir Richard and Hubert along the trail towards Wakefield. He stopped at the spot where the murder had taken place.

Richard dismounted and tethered his reins to a nearby branch.

'The exact spot, Father Daniel — show me the exact spot where it happened.'

The nun's priest ran a hand through his mane of red hair and looked about to get his bearings. After a few moments' consideration he urged the donkey forward to a point in the middle of the dusty trail.

'It was here,' he said, pointing to a dark area on the ground. 'That is where he fell. You can still see where the blood soaked into the ground.'

'But the donkey would have been facing the other way,' Richard pointed out. 'Please turn the animal round, Father Daniel.'

As the nun's priest turned the donkey around, Richard looked up and down the trail and then scanned the bramble and bracken-dense woodland on either side. It was clearly an excellent place for an ambush.

'Where were you and the prioress?'

'Just ahead of us now. The constable had called to us and ridden up to us with the Pardoner.' He ran a soothing hand along the animal's neck as it began to fidget, as if it recalled the violent death of its master and recognized and smelled the spot where it all happened.

'The constable began telling us that the Pardoner wanted to speak to us, then we heard the whistle and the call.'

'And what was called?'

'I am not sure of the exact words, but it was something like 'Pardoner, die for your crime!''

'And where did the call come from?'

'From behind us. We all looked round, including the Pardoner, and the arrow caught him in the throat.'

Richard nodded. 'And he must have fallen backwards into the dirt there.' He bent down and closely examined the ground. And then as Father Daniel described the position of the body he drew a rough outline in the dirt of how the Pardoner had lain.

'Remember what this looks like, Hubert,' he directed. 'We shall make a drawing of this later for the court.'

He drew a line from the neck of the

outlined figure and added an arrow pointing towards the woodland to the left. 'Wait here,' he said, straightening up and walking steadily in the direction of the line.

'He is tracing the place where the arrow was fired,' Hubert explained.

They watched as Richard disappeared into the undergrowth. For several minutes he moved hither and hither, bending, moving on hands and knees, sniffing trees and minutely examining the ground. Then they heard him move off further into the woods, only to reappear after about another ten minutes a hundred yards or so distant.

'What have you learned, Sir Richard?' Father Daniel asked as he finally approached.

'Interesting things,' was all that Sir Richard would volunteer as he untied his horse and mounted. 'Let us proceed. After you, Father Daniel.'

They rode in silence for some time. Hubert knew his master only too well and was aware that he would be piecing things together in his mind and reconstructing the events leading up to the murder.

At length Richard seemed to come out of his reverie. 'Father Daniel, tell me more about these Wakefield Mystery plays.'

For about the first time the nun's priest seemed to smile, as if thinking about the thing close to his heart had cast a light into the dark mood that the murder of the Pardoner had plunged him.

'It is a cycle of miniature plays which the guilds perform to tell the story of the world from *The Creation* until *The Final Judgement.* We have many of the great stories of the Bible, such as *Noah and the Flood, The Flight into Egypt* and *The Hanging of Judas.*'

'So it is rather like the plays performed at York? I saw them once,' said Richard.

Father Daniel considered his answer. 'They are similar, but yet I — or rather *we* — have written several which are unique to our town. We have twenty-nine plays in all and since all of the guilds are involved in some way there will be almost three hundred people taking part as players, singers or involved in making costumes and so forth. There are parts for two hundred and forty-three players. All of them have to be guildsmen.'

'And how will they be performed? Have you a stage?'

'No stage, Sir Richard. Or rather, we will perform it with several pageants, or movable stages, each specially constructed by the guild of carpenters, then decorated by the guilds responsible for their plays.'

Hubert swatted at a fly. 'And where will this take place?'

'In the Bull Ring on Corpus Christi Day. We will start at nine bells in the morning and it will take several hours. First we will have a processional pageant from the Church of All Saints through the streets of the town, then the stages on the great wagons will be arranged around the Bull Ring and the plays will be performed in rotation.'

'How many guilds are there?' Richard asked. 'I learned from Mistress Oldthorpe, the apothecary's wife, that there is a Grocer's Guild, and I imagine that you represent a Religious Guild.'

'I do, Sir Richard. I and Lady Katherine represent the Guild of St Oswald and we are the directors. Then there are the trade guilds like the grocers, the butchers, the haberdashers, the glovers. The craft guilds like the carpenters, the fletchers, the barkers, the thatchers, the tanners, the dyers, the wheelwrights, the millers and the pinders. You probably know that in York they perform over fifty plays, so they are fortunate in having almost sixty guilds. In comparison we have seventeen guilds, so all but a few guilds have responsibility for two plays.'

Richard ducked a low hanging branch. 'William Scathelocke, the man who was murdered in the town stocks, must have belonged to the Guild of Pinders, is that correct?'

'He was, Sir Richard.'

'And he was also a good slaughterman? I take it that he would have been known to the Guild of Butchers as well?'

'Indeed he would sir. I could introduce you to George-a-Green, the master of the Wakefield Guild of Pinders if you wish?'

'I would appreciate that. And can you also introduce me to the master of the Butcher's Guild?'

Father Daniel nodded. 'Without doubt. I am going to a meeting at the Guildhall this very afternoon. It would be an honour if you would come with me.'

Richard smiled, almost distractedly. Then he seemed to drift into another of his contemplative reveries and conversed no more until they at last came within sight of Wakefield and began the slow climb to the town.

★ ★ ★

The Guildhall was a rather grand name for a building on one of the side-streets behind the Westgate. It had in the past been a tavern called the Fighting Cocks, for the single reason that its central feature was a cock-pit sunk into the ground, surrounded by a circular wooden wall. As such, when the original town guild fragmented into several craft guilds, then into a combination of trade and craft guilds, it seemed admirably suited for the badinage that was inevitable between the masters of the respective guilds. In other towns the guilds met in the Moot Hall, but in Wakefield such was the pride in the fact that there were so many freemen and burghers, all of whom were eligible to become guildsmen and thereby guild-masters, that they decided that they needed a separate guildhall. And since the Fighting Cocks Tavern had a ready made ring which could be partitioned off into small cubicles for each guild, no guild could claim dominance in status by virtue of position. Hence it was bought by common purchase and duly commissioned as the Guildhall. It was there that the town burghers held their Burghers' Court to deal with all matters appertaining to the burghers of the town, and where the guilds came together to decide on matters that affected all of the guilds, including the production of the Corpus Christi plays.

One of the first by-laws passed by the burghers was the continuation of the license of the Fighting Cocks as a private premise, so that meetings of the guilds could be held with suitable refreshments, yet without the encumbrance of having to deal with non-guildsmen.

Hubert immediately appreciated the hostelry-like atmosphere of the Guildhall when they entered. There was a satisfying smell of ale, stale sweat and the distinctive odour of working men and a hubbub from conversations around the central ring, where a mix of characters seemed to be socializing and gossiping rather than settling the affairs of the guilds. There were neat haberdashers and their assistants, nimble-fingered tailors and cobblers, flour-dust-covered millers and rustic fullers and cordwainers. Mugs clinked, men spat on the rush covered dirt floor and, as expected, there were some raised voices and a bit of pushing and shoving as points were made.

An apprentice appeared bearing mugs of ale and offered them to Father Daniel, Richard and Hubert.

'There is usually some social exchange like this before the business is brokered,' Father Daniel explained.

Richard nodded non-committally. He felt that allowing alcohol was potentially hazardous and he sensed that Father Daniel felt likewise.

'A little ale helps to calm folk,' Father Daniel went on. 'But a lot makes most men disagreeable.' He gave one of his rare smiles. 'That is why I always try to get my business done early on in the proceedings.'

Richard laughed and sipped his mug of ale, noticing that Hubert had taken two mugs and seemed to be finishing off the first already.

'Ah, there is George-a-Green,' said Father Daniel. 'He is the Master of the Guild of Pinders.' He edged between a couple of men in aprons who smelled strongly of a tannery works and tapped a big fellow in a horsehair mantle on the shoulder. He said a few words then returned with him.

Hubert was wiping ale from his lips and immediately recognized the pinder as one of three men who had been prepared to eject him from the Bucket Inn the day before.

George-a-Green nodded peremptorily to Richard and ignored Hubert. 'Father Daniel says you wanted to talk to me, Judge?' he asked, with less than enthusiasm. 'What do you want?'

Hubert squared up to the large pinder. 'Some manners first, or perhaps you need to be shown some?'

Anger flashed in the pinder's eyes, to be replaced by a disdainful smile. 'And do you think that you are the man to show me, Master Jackanapes.'

Richard put a restraining hand upon Hubert's arm. 'Enough!' he commanded. 'There will be no brawling. I have his majesty's authority and the town has a vacant pillory which can be filled if needs.'

The pinder eyed Richard with a look of ill-concealed contempt. 'Aye, Judge. An empty pillory and an empty stocks. William Scathelocke was murdered in them, didn't you know.'

'Take care with that brusque attitude of yours, Master George-a-Green,' Richard warned. 'It is precisely about William Scathelocke that I wanted to talk to you.'

The pinder's eyes narrowed suspiciously. 'Why me?'

'You are the Master of the Guild of Pinders, are you not?'

'Aye.'

'And William Scathelocke was a member of your guild?'

'He was. And he was a decent pinder. He knew all about his animals and he didn't deserve to be in the stocks in the first place.' He spat on the floor by Hubert's foot. 'If he hadn't been put there, he wouldn't have been shot dead.'

'How do you know that?' Richard queried. 'Whoever shot him might have had many other opportunities to kill him.'

The pinder scowled. 'Maybe. Maybe not.'

'I hear he was also a good slaughterman.'

'He was, but why don't you ask one of the butchers?'

'I will. Where are they?'

'Father Daniel will show you. That all, Judge?'

Hubert gritted his teeth. 'I told you — '

But again Richard stayed his hand. 'That is all for now, George-a-Green. But tomorrow be prepared to answer questions in the Manor Court.'

The pinder had been on the verge of going, but at this he eyed Richard with narrowed eyes again. 'We all heard about another court, but why is it being held so soon?'

'Because there has been another murder.'

The effect of this news was spectacular. The room had been filled with conversation, yet it suddenly went quiet. Clearly, everyone had been eavesdropping on Richard's conversation. That was as he had suspected, and he smiled inwardly at the effect.

'You may go now, Master Pinder,' he said. Then, turning to Father Daniel, he said, 'Now please, take me to the Butcher's Guild.'

Hubert caught George-a-Green's eye and smiled. 'Didn't you hear my master, pinder? You may go. Be a good fellow and run along now.'

He grinned as the pinder clenched and unclenched his fists then flounced off.

* * *

After talking with Rufus Radstick the Butchers' Guild-master Richard had sent Hubert on a mission to the Bucket Inn while he made his way to the apothecary's to have his leg redressed.

'My husband is out visiting patients, Sir Richard,' Emma Oldthorpe told him, her eyes darting hither and thither as if fearful of making contact with his.

'Ah, I had wondered why he was not at the meeting of the guilds,' Richard returned.

Emma put a hand to her mouth and gave a small gasp. 'Oh, he will be so disappointed. He hates being late or missing appointments. He must be held up with a difficult case. He said he thought that one of his charges was on the point of death.'

'Shall I return another time, then?' Richard suggested. He was all too aware that she was embarrassed by his arousal when she last changed his wound.

Emma shook her head emphatically. 'Why no, Sir Richard. I can re-dress your wound.' Then she looked directly at him and smiled. 'I would like to if you would permit me.'

He followed her through to the room and lay down on the couch while she went and brought all that she needed for the re-dressing.

'I heard that there will be another court

tomorrow,' she said, as she unwound the bandage. 'Have you found something out, Sir Richard?'

Strangely, he wanted to tell her, to confide in her, but he would not permit himself to. 'I need to go over some things. We shall see how it goes.'

She nodded. 'Of course, Sir Richard. I did not mean to presume. It is just that I wondered if you would need to see my husband again.' She pulled back the mouldy leather padding and let out a little exclamation of delight. 'It is healing very well indeed.' She looked up and found him gazing at her. 'W . . . will you need him, sir?'

Richard coloured, conscious of the attraction that was developing. He coughed. 'It is likely, yes.'

'I worry about him sometimes. He works so hard and he is not getting any younger.'

Richard looked around the room. 'But he obviously looks after you very well.'

Emma had applied another piece of mouldy leather and was beginning to wind the bandage back on. She looked up and nodded enigmatically. 'He does his best, Sir Richard. But one day I would like to have a child.'

Richard nodded sadly. 'Everyone desires to see their line continue. I lost my wife in childbirth and my son a few days after.'

'So you are all alone, Sir Richard?'

'All alone, yes.'

She looked at the floor for a moment then looked up at his face with a nervous smile. 'Shall I rub your leg again, Sir Richard? To help clear the toxic humour?'

Richard had previously debated with himself how he should answer such a question, should she ask it again.

'Please,' he replied.

* * *

Hubert had jumped at the opportunity to return to the Bucket Inn to try to smooth Beatrice Quigley's ruffled feathers. The particular message that Sir Richard had entrusted him with, however, hardly seemed likely in his mind to further his amorous cause.

'And just why exactly does your master want us all to attend the court?' Beatrice demanded, as she stood facing him with her hands on her hips in the middle of the crowded inn.

Hubert thought that she looked magnificent when she was riled. Yet that moment was not, he decided, a suitable time to tell her.

'He is reviewing the case of the murder

— and — er — other matters.'

Beatrice eyed him askance. 'What matters?'

'I — er — am not at liberty to tell you,' he replied. 'But he was emphatic that he wants you, Matilda Oxley, and the young Lillian to be there.'

'But Lillian is still weak!'

Hubert nodded his head sympathetically. 'He was clear about it. She must attend even if she has to be carried.' He put on his most beseeching look and added, 'I will happily come and carry her for you if needs be.'

At this, Beatrice could not help herself and her defences crumbled. 'You are a merry rogue, I will give you that.' She held out her hand and took his. 'Come, I will let you buy me a cup of mead.'

A few minutes later they were happily drinking each other's health in the inglenook. Beatrice put her cup down. 'But on a different note, you had better take care of yourself. You have upset George-a-Green the pinder. He stopped in a while ago in a rare temper.'

Hubert merely grinned. 'Do I detect a note of concern for me?'

Beatrice pursed her lips. 'Maybe a little. But seriously, he is a strong lad and not one to cross.'

Hubert took a deep draught of ale. 'Nor

am I, my dear. And I just hate being crossed by bully-boys like him.'

'George-a-Green isn't a bully, Hubert. He is big and bluff and speaks his mind. Maybe it has to do with the fact that he spends more of his time with cattle than with people. I do know that he hates to see injustice.'

'Still, he needs to learn some manners. Maybe it will be up to me to teach him.'

Beatrice smiled. She liked Hubert's rugged good looks and his self-assurance. 'Can you teach many things, Hubert?' she whispered coquettishly.

'A whole lot, Beatrice,' he returned, his breathing noticeably speeding up. 'Just give me a willing pupil.'

Beatrice ran her eyes appreciatively over his face. 'I expect that your master Sir Richard will not need you all night,' she said after a moment. 'Why don't you call back here at curfew time?'

Hubert tweaked her knee and stole a kiss before draining his ale.

'At curfew time it will be, Beatrice. I will see you then.' He stood up and winked. 'But first I must attend to any other business my master may have in store for me.'

★　★　★

Richard seemed to be in a merry humour when Hubert met him as previously arranged in the office of the Moot Hall. Richard was going over some administrative matters with John of Flanshaw, the bailiff.

'I have another commission for you, Hubert,' Richard said, as he sat back in his chair and tossed a document on the table. 'I want you to go back to Sandal Castle and tell Sir Thomas all that has happened today. Tell him that I am reopening the Manor Court tomorrow at ten o'clock and will be viewing the body.'

John of Flanshaw coughed politely. 'Did you say you would be viewing the body, Sir Richard? What body? William Scathelocke?' He wrung his hands at the thought. 'I was going to ask you about this, Sir Richard. He is already starting to smell.'

'He will be buried soon enough,' Richard replied. 'But actually, we shall be viewing the body of the Pardoner. Although his crime was going to be tried by a consistory ecclesiastical court, his murder makes this a case for me to investigate.' He looked sternly at the bailiff. 'But you are to say nothing of this to anyone.'

John of Flanshaw hurriedly nodded his head and studied the documents before him.

'Are you not returning to Sandal Castle tonight, Sir Richard?' Hubert asked.

Sir Richard shook his head. 'Not tonight. Father Daniel has offered me his hospitality so I shall stay in Wakefield.'

Hubert wondered whether his master's decision had anything to do with whatever the minstrel Alan-a-Dale had been hinting at in his song that morning. 'Then I should be back in Wakefield before curfew,' he said, lightly.

'No Hubert, I want you to stay at the castle tonight.'

'But, Sir Richard, I — '

'No buts, Hubert. I also want you to have a chat with that friend of yours, Adam Crigg. Find out how many men are truly reliable and loyal to the King in the castle. That is what I want to know.'

Hubert eyed his master and was about to ask why he wanted to know this, for he had already told him of Adam Crigg's feelings about Sir Thomas Deyville's men. Yet he detected something in Sir Richard's countenance that would not brook questioning. 'When shall I go, Sir Richard?'

'Now, good Hubert. This instant. Offer to escort Lady Wilhelmina tomorrow morning if she has a mind to attend the court.'

It was with a sense of frustration and disappointment that Hubert called at the Bucket Inn on his way to Sandal Castle. It was not often that he felt like cursing his master, but this was one of them. He planned what he was going to tell Beatrice as he tied his mount up in front of the Bucket Inn.

But Beatrice was not in.

Then he did curse Sir Richard under his breath. He had been looking forward to being a teacher to Beatrice Quigley. As well as being a willing pupil himself.

*   *   *

Father Daniel's house was a neat three-storeyed building with its own garden enclosed with wicker fencing on top of the hill overlooking the Ings, where the township archery butts were located.

A servant met him and took his horse while a serving girl curtseyed and led him through an anteroom into a cluttered study. For some minutes he stood looking out of the window which was not yet shuttered, breathing in the scent of hollyhocks, columbine and calendula. Beyond the garden the hill ran down to the village of Thornes, which was in turn overlooked by the deserted motte of an early castle erected in the days of King Stephen. In the distance was the New Park and the dense woodland that eventually linked up with the Barnsdale Forest. All in all, it seemed a fine view for Father Daniel to contemplate as he sat and wrote.

Richard turned as the serving girl returned with a tray with a flask of wine and two pewter goblets.

'The master will be with you soon, my lord. He sent word for us to begin supper preparation at six o'clock.' She curtsied again. 'My name is Susan, Sir Richard. Anything you need, I am to see to.'

Richard smiled and poured himself some wine once she had gone, then he ambled about the room with the goblet in his hand. It was a comfortable room, and clearly that of a scholar. A large table and chair occupied the area in front of the window. Its surface was covered with piles of manuscripts, an astrolabe, a huge illuminated Bible, ink-pots, quills and all the paraphernalia of the writer. Shelves strained with the weight of tightly wound scrolls, caskets, and yet more piles of fresh vellum and parchment. Maps of the locality and of the manor, of the country of England and even one of the lands beyond the channel were nailed to three walls, while beside the window a large plain cross was pinned to the wall above a small praying stool. The floor was stone-paved and bedecked with lavender, fleabane and yarrow.

Richard picked up a parchment from the

desk, admiring the bold handwriting. Yet as he scanned the words he found himself admiring even more the bold sentiments that they contained.

A fine poet indeed, he mused to himself.

He lay the parchment back where it had been and looked at another that lay beside it, clearly written in a different hand. He began to read it and realized immediately that it was a poem, written by a woman, he presumed. And clearly written to express love for the reader. Realizing that it was a personal piece he dropped it back on the desk. A moment later he heard the door open behind him and the tread of a boot on the rushes.

'Sir Richard, thrice welcome to my humble abode. You do me a great honour by supping with me and staying the night.'

Richard shook his head abruptly. 'Indeed, Father Daniel, I assure you that it is you who does me a service in giving me shelter tonight. It is frankly a relief to be away from the castle.'

Father Daniel inclined his head diplomatically. 'Yet I fear that my conversation will not be up to that which you are used to, Sir Richard. I know little about politics and lofty affairs, such as you might discuss with Sir Thomas Deyville.' He bowed humbly. 'I am after all a simple scholar and priest.'

Richard gave a short laugh. 'I have heard a lot about your modesty. You are a man of many parts, it seems. Parish priest, castle chaplain, nun's priest, scholar, guildmaster and — '

'And playwright,' Father Daniel volunteered. He smiled. 'And in the last you discover the real me, Sir Richard. The writer is the true Daniel, the one that believes he can make a humble contribution to the world.'

Richard turned to the desk and pointed to the piles of manuscripts. 'Ah yes, and I am told by Lady Wilhelmina, Sir Thomas Deyville's daughter, that you are already famed as the Wakefield Master.' He accepted the seat that Father Daniel offered and took a sip from his goblet.

Father Daniel poured himself a goblet of wine. 'I fear that is a kindly title that I do not deserve, Sir Richard. I see myself as a scholarly scribe, little more than that. The words I write come to me from . . . a higher source.'

'From divine inspiration?' Richard suggested.

There was a tap at the door and Susan entered to let them know that the meal was prepared in the solar upstairs. Richard let Father Daniel lead the way upstairs to the solar, which had an even better view of the countryside beyond Wakefield. Yet it was the sumptuous meal that lay before them that most demanded his attention, and he realized that it had been many hours since he had last eaten.

They ate in relatively polite silence, enjoying a capon brewet, and a civet of hare, finished off by a frumenty of figs and nuts.

'You seem to live well, Father Daniel,' Richard sighed at last, sipping his goblet.

'I am conscious of my blessings, Sir Richard. But whatever we do not eat shall be received by whatever poor vagabonds and street urchins are already congregating at my gate.'

'Have you always lived in Wakefield?' Richard asked.

'No, Sir Richard. I took my orders in York, but I also travelled in my youth. To Padua where I studied languages and theology, and to Oxford, where I studied our own great language. But I was born in Wakefield and was happy to get a living and patronage here.'

'And are there many educated folk of your station here?'

'Lady Katherine, the Prioress of Kirklees is learned in many things, Sir Richard. She has a firm grasp of literature and an unparalleled knowledge of the scriptures.'

'And the Mystery Plays, how far on are you with them?'

Father Daniel bent his head. 'We will be ready, Sir Richard. It is a struggle getting folk to remember their lines, I will not deny, for they have to have them read to them until they remember.'

'It is a problem that so few people can read and write, I agree,' said Richard. 'But it is a feather in Wakefield's cap that his majesty is planning to come to watch the performance on Corpus Christi Day. How did that come about?'

Father Daniel sipped his wine then lay the goblet down. 'A strange matter, that, Sir Richard. To be honest, I have no idea. He has been invited every year, but so far he has never expressed an interest, and I never thought that he would. But this year he sent word himself to Sir Thomas Deyville.'

'Another Wakefield Mystery, then?' Richard asked with a smile.

As they both laughed at his little joke Richard was mentally chiding himself. There seemed too many mysteries in this town. And he fully intended to find out about them soon.

9

Pardons and Relics

Sir Richard was woken by the noise of the town slowly coming to life. First of all he heard the servants rising from their pallets, the sound of water being sluiced about, then the rattle of shutters and doors. From somewhere close, he presumed from the Parish Church of All Saints, the dawn bell rang out, and then from about the town came the noise of pigs, cows and assorted fowls being taken from undercrofts and stables to the pastures outside town. Shops and businesses began to open noisily and the trundle of carts and the clopping of horses filled the air.

There was a tap on his door and Susan, the comely maid-servant, came in upon his command, smiling sweetly.

'Father Daniel sent me to invite you to accompany him to mass at the church before breaking your fast, Sir Richard.'

Ten minutes later Richard had his first sight of the interior of the church of All Saints. On the way there Father Daniel told

Richard of its history from Saxon times. It was a fairly simple building as churches went, the tall tower of which was surrounded by scaffolding for repair work after its partial collapse in 1315, the year of the Great Famine. Understandably, the local townsfolk had taken the collapse, coinciding as it did with the suffering caused by the famine, to be a sign of God's displeasure. Accordingly, work to reconstruct the tower at the public expense had been going on ever since and slowly the walls of the aisles and the tower itself were beginning to take shape.

As Richard took his place on a front pew while Father Daniel disappeared to robe up and prepare for the service, he nodded his head approvingly at the size of the congregation, for he believed that a God-fearing community was likely to be a law-abiding community. That could make his task easier, he felt.

There were two aisles on the north and south of the nave, with the chancel beyond the ornate rood screen, and the altar and sanctuary visible beyond them.

And as he looked through he was aware of a couple of men, clearly felons, skulking in the sanctuary. He had no idea, of course, what crimes they had committed that had driven them to seek the forty days of sanctuary allowed by the church, but he expected that in due course of time he would find out. Inevitably, however, his thoughts went from the two sanctuary claimants to the Pardoner, Albin of Rouncivale. In a sense he had claimed sanctuary from the law when he claimed benefit of clergy. It seemed ironic that he might have been safer if he had sought sanctuary.

As Father Daniel's voice reached him, as he sang out to begin the service Richard felt a surge of guilt. Perhaps if he had been more rigorous in his initial handling of the court he might not have delivered him into the hands of his killer. And with the first surge of guilt it seemed to mount up inexorably. Like most men, he was not free of guilt himself. It made him feel determined. If he could not bring the Pardoner back to life, at least he could discover his murderer.

★　★　★

After breaking his fast with gruel and a mug of ale Richard bid Father Daniel farewell until the court session at nine bells. He then went directly to the Roll's Office in the Moot Hall where John of Flanshaw was already preparing the documents from the last session for Richard to peruse. Richard leafed through them, then leaned back in his chair, closed his eyes and pondered.

John of Flanshaw, supposing that Richard was falling asleep stopped writing and lay down his quill, for he feared that the scratching noise would disturb the Sergeant-at-Law. Yet he need not have worried. Although Richard looked to be on the verge of slumber, yet his mind was anything but inactive. He was going over all of the events that had taken place since he and Hubert had travelled through the Outwood to Wakefield. And the more he thought about it, the more he began to worry. He needed to talk to Hubert, to find out what, if anything, he had found out.

At about eight o'clock Hubert arrived. Richard snapped open his eyes, dispelling any suspicion that he had been asleep, and immediately dismissed the bailiff to make the court ready.

'How now, Hubert?' Richard asked. 'You have a peevish look about you this morning.'

Hubert scowled, and then grinned sheepishly. 'I was peeved as it happens, Sir Richard. You see, I had an *opportunity*, last night.'

Richard's mouth formed a silent Oh. Then he smiled and asked, 'Mistress Quigley?' When Hubert nodded assent, he went on, 'I thought that I had noticed an exchange of regard between the two of you.'

Hubert slumped onto a stool. 'We had a sort of assignation, but I am willing to wager that I am no longer in her favour.' Then his eyes twinkled and he added, 'And you may not be in another lady's favour either, my lord!'

Sir Richard stared at him, then nodded his head to encourage him to tell all. 'Well, go on! What mean you?'

'The Lady Wilhelmina seemed both anxious and a little vexed that you did not return to the castle last night.'

He did not add that the minstrel Alan-a-Dale had greeted him at breakfast with another of his suggestive little compositions on the lute. Like the previous morning he had followed it up by doing a disappearing act when Hubert turned away.

'And what of Sir Thomas's men? What had occurred yesterday morning?'

Hubert was immediately non-plussed, since he had expected Sir Richard to have been more concerned about Lady Wilhelmina's reaction. He forced his mind back on the subject.

'Ay, yes, it was the Hood and his men. Sir Thomas's men had been sent out to prepare an ambush on either side of the Wakefield trail through Barnsdale Forest, only they were lured into a trap. A group of mendicant friars came up the road, led by a big fat one, that they called Friar Tuck. They challenged them, then immediately found themselves caught by two groups of bowmen who had outflanked them.'

Richard chuckled. 'A pincer move! He has brains, this Robert Hood.'

'They stripped them of their mail and weapons — which the Hood claimed as their toll for using the forest trail — and sent them back to the castle on foot.'

Richard ran a finger over his beard. 'And what was Sir Thomas's reaction to all of this?'

'Rage! He flailed about with that whip of his. Gave a couple of the men, including the sergeant-at-arms, a few bruises. The brute! Then he vowed that he would take the outlaw.'

Sir Richard looked worried. 'And so tell me about the castle and how many men are loyal to the King. What did Adam Crigg say?'

'Well, my lord, you may recall that Adam did not hold a high opinion of Sir Thomas's men. He is still of that opinion, yet he cannot say whether they would be loyal or not. But there are thirty original men of the guard and he feels that they would know exactly what to do if the castle was attacked. The castle can certainly be secured and it would take an army with proper siege weapons to take it.'

Richard looked relieved. 'So it is unlikely that a simple company of bowmen could cause a problem. Yet this Robert Hood shows that he has a tactical brain, so he cannot be taken for granted. Yet the thing that worries me is that there may be many dissatisfied former Lancaster supporters who have been declared wolfshead. If they joined together and were organized . . . '

Hubert's eyes widened. 'I see what you mean, my lord.' Then he shook his head doubtfully. 'But surely no such thing could happen?'

Richard shrugged. 'Who knows? If there actually is an organized outlaw band, it could just take something to set it off. Wakefield is some three miles from the castle and is relatively poorly defended. And remember what the Hood said to us in the Outwood: if justice was not done, perhaps he and his men would take it into their own hands.'

They looked at one another for a moment.

'Perhaps he already has,' Sir Richard suggested.

* * *

John of Flanshaw tapped on the door and entered as the nine bells were ringing out.

'All is ready, Sir Richard,' he said. 'And Sir Thomas and Lady Wilhelmina have just taken their seats at the bench.'

Richard and Hubert followed the bailiff through into the crowded hall. Hubert took a stance at the end of the bench and Richard sat down beside Sir Thomas, having first bowed to Lady Wilhelmina, who gave him an enigmatic half-smile.

Hubert caught sight of Beatrice, Matilda and Lillian in the middle of the crowd and was rewarded by a look of disdain from Beatrice. Then she studiously ignored him and he groaned inwardly.

Immediately, Richard rapped his gavel on the bench.

'This special session of the Manor Court has been convened to investigate three dire criminal cases. First, the murder of William Scathelocke. Second, the alleged rape of Lillian Fenton by one Albin of Rouncivale, who, as the court heard yesterday, was granted benefit of clergy.'

There were murmurings of disapproval, although no one made any outright show, presumably recalling Richard's warning of the day before. Richard ran his eyes over the crowd, noting the presence of Simon the Fletcher, and of Wilfred Oldthorpe the Apothecary, his wife Emma and their servant

210

Gilbert, the dribbling hunchback.

He rapped his gavel again. 'And also the murder of Albin of Rouncivale, a Pardoner, which happened yester evening by the hand of a person as yet unknown!'

This announcement was greeted by an eruption of surprise and what almost sounded like several exclamations of pleasure. A couple of men gave short laughs.

Richard rapped his gavel firmly. 'There will be no disrespect shown in this court! A man's murder is no cause for hilarity and any inappropriate displays will be dealt with severely.'

The crowd was silenced immediately and Hubert was aware that the faces of many of the audience registered anger, alarm and obvious resentment directed at Sir Richard.

'Bailiff, we shall begin by swearing in the jury members again. The same men as yesterday step forward.'

The twelve men were duly sworn in and took their stools.

'Yesterday,' Richard continued, 'this court saw the body of William Scathelocke. We also heard testimony from Simon the Fletcher, regarding the murder weapon. An arrow.' He turned to John of Flanshaw. 'You have this arrow?'

'It is on the bench, my lord.'

Sir Richard glanced at the cloth that covered the gory arrow on the bench in front of Lady Wilhelmina, and noticed the look of revulsion as she stared at it. She in turn saw his glance and raised her chin defiantly.

'The case against the Pardoner, Albin of Rouncivale was, as I just informed you, not investigated because he had been granted benefit of clergy. His murder changes this. Please record that in the rolls, Bailiff.'

He watched John of Flanshaw scratch away on the parchment.

'So now we shall hear the facts about the murder. Call Constable Ned Burkin.'

At his name the Warrengate constable came forward and took the witness pen. Then to Richard's interrogation he described the journey towards Kirklees Priory.

Following this, the men of the watch were also questioned, and then Father Daniel gave his version.

'I thank you, Father Daniel,' Richard said, as the priest took his place at the front of the audience again. 'Men of the jury, note that all of the witnesses say that the murderer cried out, directly addressing the Pardoner, and that as he turned, he was shot in the throat with an arrow.'

He waited a few moments, watching the reactions of the crowd before continuing. 'We shall now view the body of the victim. Bailiff, arrange for the body to be brought before us.'

The reaction of the crowd to the entrance of the body of the Pardoner was clearly different to the way they had greeted the entry of William Scathelocke's body the day before. The crowd parted willingly, showing no remorse, faces showing derision, as if the sight of the wrapped bundle carried between two men of the watch indicated that justice had already been served.

The corpse was laid before the court bench.

'Raping bastard!' someone called from somewhere.

Richard immediately rapped his gavel. 'I said before that no display of disrespect will be tolerated!'

At this, Sir Thomas Deyville slapped his hand on the bench. 'By the blood of the Martyr! This man committed a heinous crime. He raped a girl!'

'A crime that he had not been tried for, far less found guilty!' Sir Richard retorted with frosty coolness. 'This is an English law court and I swear that Albin of Rouncivale, though he is dead, shall have a fair hearing. We shall look at his alleged crime in due course. But first we shall look at his own, all too clear murder. Now please, Sir Thomas — no more interruptions! I am conducting this court.'

The two knights glared at each other. Sir Thomas finally flounced back in his chair and folded his arms. 'So be it,' he said sullenly.

Richard inclined his head politely.

'Call Wilfred Oldthorpe, the apothecary.'

Moments later, when the apothecary had detached himself from the crowd Richard addressed him. 'Master Oldthorpe, examine the body please, and then give us your opinion on the cause of death.'

As the apothecary knelt and pulled back the horsehair blanket from the corpse Richard's eyes met those of Emma Old- thorpe. No words or even expressions were exchanged, yet in their eye contact Richard took slight comfort in having at least one pair of friendly eyes upon him, apart from those of his man, Hubert.

There were many utterances of horror at the sight of the murdered Pardoner's naked body, for his clothing had been cut by Richard and peeled back with the blanket. The arrow through the throat had not been touched, just as Sir Richard had directed.

Wilfred Oldthorpe grimaced and looked up. 'The cause of death most certainly was caused by this arrow wound, my lord.'

Sir Richard nodded. 'Please examine the rest of the body.'

The crowd watched with morbid fascination as the apothecary bent to his task and ran fingers and hands over the naked body, prodding the skin and peering close to check on the stagnation of blood in the white and purple mottled skin. At last he looked up again.

'This man has no manhood, my lord,' he announced. 'His testicles have either never fallen, or he was gelded as a child.'

'Explain what that means to the jury,' Richard directed.

'It means that he could grow no body hair, no beard, and he would never have been able to have children.'

'Could he have raped a woman?'

'I doubt it, my lord. He would have no desire for it.'

Richard directed his attention to the jury. 'Mark this well, jurymen. It may be important.'

He noted with some satisfaction when he saw that the bailiff was busy writing everything down.

'Now look at the arrow, Master Oldthorpe. I would like you to remove it.'

The apothecary's Adam's apple bobbed up and down, as he clearly did not relish this task. Yet he did not flinch. Grasping the shaft of the arrow he pulled, exerting a steady traction so that it came away with a horrific sound, as if its barbed point scraped on bone and cartilage as it was removed.

'I thank you, Master Oldthorpe,' Richard said. 'Please leave it upon the bench here, and then you may step down.'

Once the apothecary had returned to stand by his wife, and Gilbert, their servant, Richard instructed the bailiff to call Simon the Fletcher.

'Now, Master Fletcher,' he said, when the large, surly craftsman had taken the witness pen. 'I would like you to compare these two arrows.' He gestured to Hubert, who moved forward and carried them over to the witness pen for the fletcher to examine.

Simon the Fletcher hefted them, ran his fingers over the head, checked the flights and looked down the length of each of them. At last, he said, 'They were made by the same hand, my lord.'

'And do you know whose hand that could have been?'

The fletcher shook his head. 'All I can say is that they are arrows made for accuracy, by one skilled in fletchery — but not by me.'

'Do you know of anyone who is so skilled?'

The fletcher shrugged. 'In these days there may be many, my lord. All men are obliged to train with the yew bow.'

Richard nodded and dismissed him. Then he rapped his gavel and directed John of Flanshaw to record the fact that the two murders had been committed with arrows made by the same hand, according to the testimony of Simon the Fletcher.

'Now let us consider the murdered man's possessions,' Richard went on. 'Constable Burkin, show the court all that you found upon Albin of Rouncivale when you arrested him.'

Ned Burkin lifted the sack and staff that had been brought in with the body of the Pardoner and laid the sack on the bench.

'First of all, my lord, he had this staff with a metal cross atop it.' He held it aloft for all to see. 'And you can see it has been studded with pieces of coloured glass, to look as if it is embedded with jewels.'

At a sign from Richard he laid it on the bench then reached into the sack and drew out a purse.

'He had this purse with fifteen shillings in it.'

Richard's eyes narrowed momentarily. 'Record that please, Bailiff.'

Constable Burkin delved into the sack again and drew out a bundle of clothing, a wallet and three small earthenware jars. He opened the wallet and drew out a sheaf of papers.

'There is writing on them, my lord. I think they are — '

But Richard had snapped his fingers and held out his hand for them. After rifling through them he declared, 'As I thought, these are Indulgences written in Latin.' He held one up. 'People call these pardons,' he explained. 'The Pardoner is permitted by the law of the land and by church law to sell these indulgences which, while not pardoning the buyer from a transgression of some sort, are believed to reduce their load of guilt upon their day of Judgement. Or so they say.'

There was a titter of amusement from the crowd, which was immediately silenced when Richard rapped his gavel on the bench. He eyed the crowd censorially and went on sternly, 'This court is investigating a murder, which is no cause for amusement. Now this Pardoner, Albin of Rouncivale sold many of these pardons, I want anyone who bought one to put his hand up now.'

Slowly and reluctantly, several people held up their hands.

'After this session all of these people will be interviewed. Under oath, they will tell me why they had need of purchasing a pardon.'

There was a good deal of shuffling of feet, as indeed Richard had supposed there would be. He imagined that people would at that very moment be preparing alternative reasons. He had little doubt that he would be able to sort out the real from the imaginary.

He nodded to Constable Burkin who picked up the first of the three earthenware jars. Pulling out the bung he poured out a number of small bones into his hand. Once more Richard gestured for them to be handed to him.

'I imagine that the Pardoner claimed that these bones were holy relics of some saint,' he announced. 'And that for a price he permitted sinners to touch them to receive the pardon of the saint.'

There was a gasp of amazement from the crowd and a tall man dressed in the garb of a tanner cried out, 'That is just so, my lord. They are the small bones of the hand of St Christopher himself.'

Sir Richard let the bones stream back into the jar. 'These are pig bones,' he said to the tanner. 'And you shall tell me later the nature of the sins that you needed divine help with.'

At a nod from Richard, Constable Burkin pulled the bung out of the second jar and poured out a number of wood chippings.

'These I expect were said to be slivers from the true cross, or chippings of the coffin of some saint.'

Again there were gasps of surprise from

several members of the audience and Richard nodded to Hubert to pinpoint them so that they too would be called to give testimony to him later.

'The third jar, Constable,' Richard prompted.

The constable opened the jar and poured out two small white objects. 'Teeth, my lord.' He handed hem to Richard who looked at them one at a time.

'Ugh! How disgusting!' exclaimed Lady Wilhelmina. Richard permitted himself a smile at her look of repugnance.

'Master Oldthorpe,' he called. 'Your opinion on these, if you please.'

The apothecary came forward and bent over the teeth in Richard's palm.

'They are human and fairly fresh, my lord. One is a dog tooth,' he said, indicating one of his own, next to his two front incisors. 'And the other is a molar, one of the grinding back teeth.'

Lady Wilelmina had leaned forward and commented, 'They look fairly healthy.'

The apothecary looked at her with an expression of respect. 'Her ladyship is quite correct, I believe. They seem to have been good teeth.'

Richard nodded. 'Yet not the teeth of a saint.' He eyed the crowd. 'Who here paid Albin of Rouncivale to gain a pardon by touching one of these teeth?'

But there was no reply from the crowd.

Richard handed the teeth back to Constable Burkin and brushed his hands together. 'So no one knows ought of the teeth? So be it. Now we come to the investigation of the murder scene itself. Yesterday morning Father Daniel, my assistant Hubert of Loxley and I came back along the road that Albin of Rouncivale had been taken. It is through the forest towards Kirklees Priory. We have already heard the testimonies of Father Daniel, Constable Burkin and his men of the watch who accompanied the prisoner. We heard that the murderer had called to them and that everyone had looked round. At that moment the murderer shot his arrow and hit Albin of Rouncivale through the throat. He fell off his donkey into the dusty trail. We saw the exact spot, and from that I was able to work out the position of the assassin. I investigated a spot in the undergrowth just off the trail and from my findings I am able to give some information about the assassin.'

He waited a few moments, watching the faces in the crowd as he spoke.

'This was a ruthless murderer. He was on his own and not accompanied by others. He was a militarily trained man of above average height, who had been waiting there for some time. Moreover, he had waited there with the single purpose of killing the Pardoner, yet undoubtedly would have dispatched the rest of the party had they shown any sign of attempting pursuit.'

There was stunned silence in the hall for several moments. Then Sir Thomas broke it by thumping the bench with his fist.

'Nonsense! How can you say any of those things without having been there and witnessed it all yourself?'

Richard turned and gave his challenger a thin smile. 'Simply because I looked for the signs and found them. Then I used my brain and built up a picture.' He turned and faced the court.

'Firstly, the point he had chosen for his ambush was well thought out. He did not aim to disturb the undergrowth too much, yet he made sure that he had enough room to retreat swiftly should the need arise. He had prepared well by being there some time before the party arrived along the road. He had a horse tethered in the forest some fifty yards away, far enough away to be fairly sure of silence, yet close enough to reach swiftly to get away. Indeed, he was there so long before that he felt the need to relieve himself, which he did by passing urine against the side of the oak tree that he was sheltered beneath.'

'And how do you know that he was tall?' Sir Thomas demanded.

'By the top of the trail of urine on the side of the tree,' Sir Richard explained.

'And what about being there just to kill the Pardoner? How did you know that?'

'For the same reason that I know that he had some military training. I found six small holes in the ground.'

'Now I know you are mad!' Sir Thomas exclaimed.

Richard shook his head. 'I repeat, there were six small holes in the ground where the assassin had stuck his arrows in the ground. That is what a trained bowman would do, so that he could reload swiftly without having to reach for a quiver. So he was trained. Also, he shot only one arrow, and spared the rest of the party when he could without doubt have dispatched them all.'

Running his eyes over the crowd he saw Constable Burkin and his two men of the watch shuffle about. The Warrengate constable paled visibly and swallowed hard. Further along, Father Daniel made the sign of a cross over his heart.

Sir Thomas scowled angrily. 'You could have said so straight away, Sir Richard. But what all this amounts to is that the killer, whoever he is, felt that he was doing what this court should have done in the first place — punish the rogue!'

Richard shook his head. 'We still have not got enough evidence to say one way or the other.' He rapped his gavel and addressed the jury. 'This case is not yet closed, but will be returned to at a later time. The same jurymen will be called again.'

He then addressed the bailiff. 'Since we cannot come to a conclusion over the Pardoner's murder, we shall now reconsider the Pardoner's alleged crime. The rape of the Wakefield maid, Lillian Fenton. Call her and her cousin, Matilda Oxley.'

John of Flanshaw duly did so and Matilda, Beatrice and Lillian threaded their way through the crowd. Sir Richard pointed to Matilda, then to the witness pen. She took her place, her head held high. Dressed in a green gown and with her head covered in a wimple she made an impressive sight.

'You are Matilda Oxley?' Sir Richard queried. 'What is your relationship to the accuser?'

'I am, my lord. I am kinswoman to Lillian Fenton.'

'And you live at the Bucket Inn together?'

'We do, my lord. And we do not understand why you are bothering to investigate the Pardoner's crime. Is it not best to allow Lillian to get over her ordeal? As you know, she has suffered and — '

'I will ask the questions, Mistress Oxley,' Richard interrupted. 'You are betrothed, I understand. Give your betrothed's name to the court.'

'Robert Hood, my lord.'

Sir Thomas leaned forward, his face suddenly suffused. 'The contrariant! Then why is this woman not already in the Tolbooth herself?'

'Because this court will not permit it, Sir Thomas,' Richard said patiently, yet firmly. He went on, 'You were ill the night of the alleged rape?'

Matilda looked down, her face registering both anxiety and embarrassment. 'I had a flux of the bowels, my lord.'

'And your cousin went out to meet someone after the curfew time. Who was that?'

Matilda looked at him beseechingly.

'You need have no fear in answering,' Richard urged. 'You are safe here. We merely wish to get to the truth.'

'It was to meet my Robin.'

'Outrageous!' Sir Thomas thundered.

'You may stand down,' Sir Richard said. 'Bailiff now call the maid, Lillian Fenton.'

It was clear to all that Lillian was reluctant to appear before the court. Most people were aware of her bandaged wrists, and the reason for the bandages. Richard tried to put her at her ease. Apart from her blue gown and grey wimple, she looked very much a younger version of Matilda Oxley.

'Your cousin tells us that you went to meet her betrothed. Where were you to meet him?'

'In the town cemetery, my lord. But I could not see anyone. And then . . . and then — '

'Tell us,' Richard urged.

'I was grabbed from behind, sir,' Lillian replied, her voice quavering as she replied tremulously, tears only a moment away. 'Someone grabbed my neck and forced me to be still. I . . . I believe that he would have snapped my neck. And then — he lifted my clothes and entered me — from behind, like a dog!'

'He used you, and then left you?'

'I . . . I didn't dare move for many minutes, my lord. But when I did dare to look up he had gone.'

'Do you know who this man could have been?'

Lillian's voice quaked. 'I . . . I do not know — '

'Who do you think it was?' Richard asked sternly. 'You are here under oath and must answer truthfully before God.'

'I . . . I think it could have been . . . Robin.'

Matilda Oxley gasped, and then cried out in rage. 'Liar! Traitor!' And it looked as if she would throw herself upon her kinswoman, except that Hubert took a step forward in case.

'Why do you think this?' Richard asked.

'I had seen Robert hold a deer just like that, my lord. By the neck so that it couldn't move.'

Matilda began pushing her way through the crowd, but was intercepted by Beatrice, who threw her arms about her.

Richard rapped his gavel. 'This court accepts that Matilda Oxley may be justifiably distraught. She may leave and may go back to the Bucket Inn.'

Sir Thomas let out a gasp of surprise. 'Ah! I see what this is all about now. Clever, Sir Richard, clever! It was the contrariant, Robert Hood. And you think he was trying to silence the Pardoner. To make it look as if he was meting out punishment when it was really to conceal his own crime.'

Lillian Fenton had dissolved into tears. Richard rapped his gavel. 'I am adjourning this court for today. Bailiff, record that it is the court's urgent desire to speak with the outlaw Robert Hood.'

For the first time Sir Thomas laughed. 'Oh don't worry about that, Sir Richard. I will be true to my word. I will bring this dog before you.'

The court gradually filtered out of the great oak-beamed hall and Richard noted that Emma Oldthorpe had gone quickly to comfort the distraught Lillian. He watched her guide the younger woman out of the court, with her arm about her shoulders.

Lady Wilhelmina caught Richard's sleeve as her father left. 'Don't you think that you were a little cruel this morning, Sir Richard?' she asked, with one eyebrow raised sardonically.

'I am afraid that sometimes you have to be cruel to be kind, my lady. And sometimes to learn the truth you have to be even crueller still.'

10

Ambush

Between them, Sir Richard, Hubert and John of Flanshaw spent a good three and a half hours rounding up, interrogating and recording the accounts of all the people who had bought pardons from Albin of Rouncivale. There were some fifty-eight in total and by the end of the session the bailiff's writing hand felt cramped and his wrist was beginning to pain him.

The reasons for purchasing the pardons varied immensely, although for the majority they seemed banal to Richard. The folk of Wakefield seemed to have felt guilty about all sorts of misdemeanours, including being suspicious of a new husband, wishing a plague of warts on a neighbour, and wishing impotence on a rival in love. For the most part Richard felt that he could dismiss most of these, yet others, such as the baker who was worried about having given short measure to his customers, and the draper who was concerned about giving less than the legal length of cloth to his customers, he made a mental note to instruct the bailiff to arrange for them to have random checks. And for those who had clearly made up reasons that were fabrications, he decided to let them depart in the belief that they had successfully fooled the circuit judge. When they were recalled over the next day or two he would ensure that they told him the truth.

Richard dismissed the bailiff and sent Hubert out to bring back a couple of meat pies and a flask of ale, which they ate in the Roll's Office.

'I am going to return to the castle tonight, Hubert,' Richard said, as he brushed crumbs of pastry from his tunic.'

Hubert looked crestfallen.

'But I want you to stay at the Bucket Inn,' he went on. Hubert immediately cheered up.

'You need to keep an eye on Matilda Oxley and the maid, Lillian Fenton. I fear that they may not be over-friendly from now on.'

'It would be a mystery if they were, my lord.' Hubert took a gulp of ale. 'I was surprised that you brought it all out in the open court.'

'It had to be done, Hubert.' Then, without explaining further, he opened his purse and handed over a number of coins. 'This should pay for your bed tonight.'

'It will certainly pay for a mug or two of

ale, my lord.' Hubert grinned, for he hoped that his bed would not cost him over-much, if anything, that night.

★ ★ ★

Richard went from the Moot Hall down the Westgate towards the apothecary's premises. Gilbert, the Oldthorpe servant was laying fresh reeds on the earthen floor of their undercroft when Richard entered. Seeing Richard, his eyes opened wide with alarm and he strove hard to get words out of his dribbling mouth.

Richard felt sorry for his discomfiture and tried to calm him with gently upraised palms. 'Have no fear. Your name is Gilbert, is it not?'

The hunchback nodded his head vigorously, a trail of saliva dropping from his lips.

'Is your mistress in?'

There was the crunch of a foot on a reed and Richard turned quickly, expecting to see Emma Oldthorpe, but instead found himself facing the apothecary himself.

'You wished to see my wife, Sir Richard? I am afraid that she has been called to a childbirth.' He gestured at Gilbert, who hobbled gratefully from the room.

'No,' Sir Richard lied. 'I came to thank you both for your care. I think that my wound is well healed now, and I came to pay you for your services.'

'We are always pleased to be of service, my lord.'

Richard opened his purse and drew out more coins. Already his mind was thinking of ways that he could legitimately call upon the apothecary's wife.

* * *

Hubert had gone to the Bucket Inn as quickly as he could. He had a powerful thirst on him and somehow felt at home as soon as he pushed open the door of the inn and entered its smoky, crowded interior.

The surly-looking potman, whose name Hubert had since learned was Hap, presumably on account of his welcoming demeanour, was knocking the spike out of a fresh barrel of ale. 'Mistress Quigley is upstairs, Master Hubert,' he announced. 'She is with the upset women-folk. And small wonder they are upset, what with all the misery that has befallen this inn of late.'

Hubert ordered a jug of ale and offered to buy Hap one as well, which was greeted with a curt nod and a grunt of thanks when he tossed a coin on the barrel top. His drink appeared a few moments later and Hubert took it and sat at a vacant table.

'There is a bad smell in the Bucket today,' came a deliberately loud voice from a group of men at the neighbouring table. Hubert recognized two of the group of five as having been with George-a-Green the pinder the other day when they threatened to eject him. The speaker was the one with a cloth round his head, covering one eye. 'Beatrice Quigley is letting all sorts of scum in here these days.'

Hubert slammed his mug down noisily. 'Was that remark meant for me, *One-eye?*'

'It might have been — if you are the cause of the smell!' retorted the other.

An older man with a bald pate prodded him in the side. 'Have a care, Hector. That is the judge's man,' he whispered to him.

The man called Hector shrugged him away. 'I know who he is,' he said, his voice now noticeably slurred. 'I don't like the way that judge handles things and I don't like the way he didn't come out with it and say what everybody knows.'

'You should listen to your wise friend,' said Hubert. 'And you ought to hold your counsel.'

'Why? What you going to do? Have me put in the stocks, like poor old Will Scathelocke?'

The other three members of the group made placating noises to Hector, but he waved them aside as well. 'Even that wicked fool Sir Thomas Deyville saw what was going on, but what did your judge do? Nothing!' he sneered. 'And the Hood is free.'

At this there were murmurs of agreement from the others at the table, as well as from several other tables. It was clear to Hubert that there was a tide of feeling against the man called Robert Hood.

'He raped Lillian,' someone cried.

'He murdered Scathelocke!'

'And that Pardoner, the poor sod!'

And almost like a flame that suddenly erupted from a smouldering ember the anger in the room became palpable. And it was stoked up by the inebriated Hector.

'Enough!' cried Hubert, jumping to his feet, his hand going to the hilt of his sword. 'The man called Robert Hood is wanted for questioning, as you all heard this morning. But my master, Sir Richard Lee, is a Sergeant-at-Law; he knows every scrap of the law, and the fact that he hasn't accused this Robert Hood is because there is not enough evidence against him.'

Hector rose unsteadily to his feet and faced Hubert. 'And I say he's not as clever as you think. I say — '

Hubert shot a hand out and grabbed Hector's tunic. 'You have had too much to drink, fellow.' With his other hand he slapped him hard across the cheek. 'No one insults my master, in my presence. Now I give you one chance. Go home and get sobered up. And next time we meet, be polite!'

He gave Hector a gentle push as he released him, but he stumbled and somersaulted over a stool to lie on his back. Then he was on his feet and rushing at Hubert with his arms flailing like windmills. But Hubert merely sidestepped, ducked a wild punch then delivered a couple of short blows to his midriff before following up with an almighty wallop that lifted him off his feet and catapulted him onto the table among his cronies.

'Does anyone else want to insult my master or the King's law?' Hubert demanded.

In answer there was a mighty belly laugh from the door. Hubert looked round to see the burly figure of George-a-Green, the pinder, standing half bent with amusement. 'A fair beating you have given Hector there,' he said, advancing towards him.

'Go . . . get . . . him, George,' rasped Hector.

'Why?' returned the pinder. 'I heard what he said, and I heard what you said. And if I had been here earlier I would have cuffed you myself. You bloody fool. Robert Hood is no murderer. This judge seems to have some idea of justice. Now get you home, Hector, before Beatrice Quigley sees you and really boxes your ears.'

Hector sneered and made suggestive thrusting movements with his pelvis. 'I'll box her, and no mistake.'

At this Hubert took a step towards him, but he was restrained by George-a-Green.

'Just get out now, Hector Lunt, before I put out your good eye myself!' the pinder replied threateningly. 'Beatrice Quigley is a good woman, you remember that.'

As Hector's cronies helped him towards the door, the pinder extended a ham of a fist to Hubert. 'I like the way you disport yourself, stranger. That Hector is not as bad as he sounds, except when he drinks too much. But come now, let us have a drink together.'

Half an hour later, and three mugs of ale each found Hubert and George-a-Green the best of friends, all previous animosity forgotten. It surprised Beatrice Quigley when she came downstairs and found them laughing and joking together.

'This is a good fellow, Beatrice,' George-a-Green said. 'He knows how to fight and set Hector Lunt right when he went on about Robert Hood being a murderer.' He drained the last of his mug and stood up. 'And now I must be away.' He slapped Hubert on the shoulder and blew a kiss at Beatrice, then departed.

Beatrice sat in the pinder's vacated seat. 'Now there is a turnaround. I was sure that you two would end up tearing each other's arms off.' She took a sip of his ale. 'I must say that I am pleased. And I am pleased that the judge only wants to talk to Robin Hood. That Sir Thomas Deyville would like to see him brought in dead.'

'And how go things here, Beatrice?' Hubert asked.

'Do you mean with us?'

'Aye, with us, my sweet. I tried to call in and tell you that my master had ordered me away last night, but — '

She silenced him with a kiss that took him by surprise. 'I know. Hap told me later. And so maybe we can make up for it tonight?'

Hubert stroked her knee through her gown and returned her kiss. 'Not even my master could stop me tonight. But to return to the other matter: how are things between Matilda and her cousin Lillian?'

Beatrice sighed. 'I wonder if things can ever be right between them. Matilda is furious and will not talk to Lillian. And yet Lillian feels that her kinswoman should at least listen to her. I feel like the pig in the middle.'

Hubert put his hand round her waist and squeezed. 'No one could ever call you anything so base, fair Beatrice. Tonight, I shall show you how much you are admired.'

Beatrice kissed him again and gently ran a hand up the inner surface of his thigh. 'I will hold you to that promise, my fine lad,' she replied, with a sweet smile. Then she clamped a hand on his thigh and whispered in his ear, 'But if you disappear again like last night I promise you, you'll end up as well equipped as was that Pardoner!' And with that she was up and off collecting mugs.

★ ★ ★

Lady Alecia seemed to be in pain at dinner that evening. Even grasping her knife seemed to cause her discomfort, Richard noted.

'My joints have pained me these last two years,' she explained, as she produced a small vial and poured a powder into her wine goblet. 'If it was not for Master Oldthorpe and his potions I doubt if I would be able to get out of bed some mornings.'

'My mother is a fine musician and that is what really pains her,' Lady Wilhelmina added. 'She used to play the lute, but can no longer.'

Richard pointed to the empty minstrel's gallery. 'Where are our musicians, by the way?'

'They are practising in Wakefield,' Lady Alecia said. 'For the mystery plays. They are only a few days away, after all.'

'Ah yes, I supped with Father Daniel last night and he told me much about the mysteries.'

'Yes, we missed you last night,' Lady Alecia remarked, with a faint smile in her daughter's direction. 'Is that not so, Wilhelmina?'

In answer, Lady Wilhelmina gave a curt nod. 'I am sure that Father Daniel provided stimulating conversation.'

'He did indeed,' replied Richard. 'Yet I had need to talk to him. I had to ask him some pertinent questions about my investigations.'

Sir Thomas gulped some ale, and then gave a short laugh. 'I am sure you did, Sir Richard. I have to admit that I had doubts about you when you first sat in the court. I thought you were too lenient, but this morning I saw another side. Methinks that you have a shrewdness about you.'

Richard bobbed his head in acknowledgement of the compliment.

'And while I may not be the shrewdest of fellows,' Sir Thomas went on, 'yet I have a certain cunning. I used that cunning today

239

when I set about the job of catching the outlaw Robert Hood.'

'Another trap?' Richard asked.

'No trap. Rather a disengagement.'

Richard raised his eyebrows quizzically. 'You will have to explain, I fear.'

'I had words with Midge the Miller. His son is a contrariant and a member of the Hood's band, as you know. Well, I told him that if he wanted his son to be pardoned, he had the means in his hand. All he had to do was to get word to him that Robert Hood was wanted for murder and for the rape of Lillian the maid.'

'That is cunning, Sir Thomas, but not entirely legal.'

'Damn this legal nonsense. We need a result. These dogs are traitors, but no man likes a rapist. I wouldn't be at all surprised if they didn't cut off his balls and send him to us in a sack.'

Richard took a deep breath and willed himself not to lose his temper at his host's table. 'But I need him alive. I need to talk to him.'

Sir Thomas took another hefty swig of ale, and then wiped his beard with the back of his hand. 'I shouldn't worry, Sir Richard. After all, as we heard this morning, a man can live without his balls.'

At that he fell into a laughing fit, despite the blushes of his wife and daughter.

★ ★ ★

Richard lay on his bed later that evening, staring at the circle of light on the plastered ceiling above him. The castle had long since gone to sleep and he himself had unsuccessfully tried to get to sleep. Yet there were so many thoughts that kept intruding upon his consciousness. So many unanswered questions.

He heard the tap on the door and was immediately upon his feet, his hand instantly to his dagger as he threw open the door.

Lady Wilhelmina was standing there in a long cloak.

He opened his mouth to speak but she advanced swiftly, pushing him back as she did so. She closed the door behind her, and then turned, reaching up to unfasten her cloak, which fell to the floor to reveal her naked body.

'Wilhelmina!' he whispered. 'Wh — '

She stepped close to him, one hand pushing his hand with the dagger aside. 'I want you to ravish me!' she said, as she snaked an arm about his neck and drew him towards her waiting mouth.

Hubert and Beatrice had made love throughout most of the night, and finally rolled apart,
their bodies bathed in perspiration, to lie in
dreamy post-coital bliss until cockcrow.

'You think a lot of that master of yours,
don't you?' Beatrice asked, as she stirred back
to wakefulness.

Hubert yawned then turned on his side to
stroke her hair. 'I do. He has been good to me
and we have fought several battles side by
side. If it were not for our ranks we might be
counted friends.'

Beatrice sighed. 'Friends! Matilda and I
have been friends for most of our lives. I hate
to see her in this state.' She bit her lip. 'And
now with all this business between Matilda
and Lillian I don't rightly know what to say to
her.' She shook her head. 'But I just cannot
believe that Robin could — '

There was a sudden commotion from
along the hall, then a door slammed and they
heard footsteps running along the corridor.

'Beatrice! Beatrice!' called out a voice, as
someone started rapping on the door. Both
Hubert and Beatrice sat bolt upright as the
door was thrown open and Lillian, dressed in
a long loose cotte rushed in. She gasped at
the sight of their naked bodies, then put a

hand over her eyes and turned her back on them.

'A thousand pardons! I . . . I am scared. I thought I heard . . . I heard Matilda leave her room in the night. I . . . I was too afraid to check until daybreak. Then I went to see. But . . . but she has gone!'

'Gone?' Beatrice repeated. 'Gone where?'

In answer, Lillian dissolved into hysterical tears and Beatrice pulled a blanket about her and went to comfort her. Hubert pulled on his tunic and charged through the door. 'Which is her room?' he asked over his shoulder.

'The end of the corridor then first left,' replied Beatrice, patting Lillian's back as if she were comforting a distraught child.

Hubert ran down the corridor and looked in the open door. The room was empty, the blankets on the bed neatly folded and a spare pair of shoes protruding from underneath the bed. A cupboard contained some gowns, but the simple table was bare of all the usual womanly trinkets and paraphernalia that Hubert expected to have been there.

'It looks as she has truly gone,' Hubert said, as Beatrice and Lillian appeared in the doorway. 'Do you have any idea where she could have gone to?'

Beatrice pouted. 'I wager she has gone to Robin.'

Lillian began to sob anew at this. 'But she must not! It . . . it is not — '

'It is not what, Lillian?' Hubert demanded. 'Not safe?'

Lillian simpered. 'I am . . . afraid for her. He . . . he . . . ' She did not finish, but ended up screaming hysterically.

Beatrice frowned and slapped her hard across the face. 'That is enough, Lillian! Robin would never have raped you. You are mistaken and now look what you have done.'

Lillian had stopped screaming, but at this reaction from Beatrice she stared at her in total confusion. Then she lapsed into rhythmic sobbing.

Hubert shook his head in consternation. 'This is my fault! Sir Richard will have my hide for this. It was my charge to ensure that she stayed safe.'

Beatrice put a hand on his arm as he ran his hands through his hair in agitation. 'And my fault as well, fair Hubert. I had a part in this, in case you had forgotten, and I have failed my friend.'

Hubert patted her hand on his arm, when he really wanted to take her in his arms, but could not because of Lillian. He sighed, then said, 'I had best get back to Sandal Castle and alert Sir Richard. He will need to know about this at once. Have you any idea where

244

she could have gone? Did they have any special meeting place?'

Beatrice shook her head. 'I don't know. I am sure that she will have left the town and gone to Barnsdale Forest. The town watch would not have stopped her if she was determined to leave. But as to where . . . ?'

'I . . . think I may know,' Lillian stammered.

'Then tell us quickly, Lillian,' Beatrice demanded urgently. 'Matilda's safety could depend on it. There are others in the forest apart from Robin and his men. Dangerous men!'

Lillian stared back at her like a frightened rabbit. 'They used to meet at a charcoal-burner's hut. It . . . it is not easy to get to, but I think I can draw a map for you.'

'Then let us have pen, ink and parchment,' said Hubert, 'for I must be off.'

★ ★ ★

Hubert rode fast, bent low over his horse's neck as he let it have its head on the road towards Sandal. Yet before he was halfway there he saw a rider trotting the other way towards Wakefield. It was Sir Richard.

He drew to an abrupt halt in front of his master and garbled a good morning.

'I slept poorly and was coming to meet you,' Richard began to explain. 'I had an idea that — '

'My lord, Matilda Oxley has gone!' Hubert blurted out.

'That is what I feared might happen,' Richard said, smiting his fist into the palm of his other hand. 'When did she leave? In the night when you were all asleep, I presume?'

Hubert flushed. He was all too aware that he had probably been far from sleep, yet far from alive to anything that was happening outside Beatrice's bedchamber. 'The maid Lillian thought she heard something, but was too afraid to investigate in the night,' he volunteered, guiltily. And he recounted his findings and all that had happened that morning, apart from the fact that Lillian had discovered Beatrice and himself in bed.

He was surprised that Sir Richard seemed so phlegmatic in his response.

'She will have gone to meet the Hood,' he said. 'Have you any idea where they could be meeting?'

Hubert drew out the parchment from his tunic. 'The maid Lillian thinks that they might meet at an old charcoal-burner's hut.' And he showed Richard Lillian's rough map.

'Then let us go quickly,' said Richard. 'We cannot afford for any ill to befall Matilda.'

* * *

The map was good enough to give them a general idea of their direction, yet insufficiently detailed to give them an exact path, for the way was off the marked forest paths into parts that were probably completely uncharted. They rode beneath a green canopy of oak, beech and giant sycamores and a ground-screen of brambles, bracken and coarse grass.

'How was the Lady Wilhelmina?' Hubert asked at last.

'Why do you ask?' Richard snapped back, unexpectedly.

'Why, just because she seemed pale at the court yesterday morning, my lord,' Hubert replied, surprised at the heat in his master's query.

'She was well,' he returned, without embellishment. 'How far do you think we have to go to this charcoal-burner's hut? Is it still used?'

Hubert shook his head. 'It has not been used for years, my lord. That is apparently why they used it for their assignations. I think it is only a hundred yards or so distant. It looks as if there is a clearing up ahead.'

And indeed the forest did open up into a clearing at the far side of which was a simple hut with an overgrown mound beside it that looked as if it had been a charcoal burning mound in days gone by.

'Shall I call out, my lord?'

'No, we shall ride up to it quietly.'

'Is that wise, my lord?' Hubert asked as they entered the clearing and advanced towards the hut.

Suddenly, a flock of birds took to the air and started flapping towards the tree tops.

'Curious,' Hubert stated.

'Worrying,' replied Richard, turning in his saddle.

The arrow shot just past his ear and he reacted instantly. 'Ride as fast as you can, Hubert. Make for the hut.'

Another arrow narrowly missed Hubert as they spurred their mounts towards the hut and then hurled themselves from the saddle to dive simultaneously for the entrance. They rolled inside in a tumble of limbs, crashing into the far wall.

'We are safe enough for a while, at least,' said Hubert.

'That we cannot be sure of,' said Richard, coming instantly to his feet and flattening himself against the wall to peer through the doorway, the only way in or out. 'We may have fallen into a trap.'

He ducked back inside as an arrow

embedded itself in the doorpost, inches from his head.

A moment later the first of several flaming arrows shot through the air to land on the dry wood and moss-covered roof. The crackling of burning wood and the sudden filling of the hut with smoke made the desperateness of their situation all too clear.

From somewhere on the other side of the clearing they heard an unpleasant, almost maniacal laugh.

11

After the Funeral

The hut filled up with smoke at an alarmingly fast rate, so that within a couple of minutes both Sir Richard and Hubert were coughing and forced to cover their mouths and noses by pulling up their neck-cloths. Their eyes were smarting, and the heat from the burning roof was well nigh unbearable, besides threatening to collapse within moments.

From outside they could hear the taunting laughter.

'We will have to make a run for it, Hubert,' Richard rasped. He drew his sword and Hubert followed suit. 'This madman has us pinned down.'

'Then I will go first, Sir Richard,' Hubert returned, his voice equally rasping. 'Remember, I have the advantage with my talisman from Antioch! Come straight after me, and then dive left towards the undergrowth.'

'Hubert, no!' Richard cried, as his assistant charged outside, sprinting straight ahead towards the other side of the clearing, all the while yelling a blood-curling battle-cry. He knew all too well that Hubert meant to sacrifice himself and in that split second of reasoning knew that he must follow Hubert's instruction, for it was sound logic that he make for cover. He bent low and dashed after Hubert out of the doorway, ran a few feet before dashing leftwards towards the undergrowth of nettles and bracken.

An arrow swished overhead and embedded itself in the side of the charcoal-burner's hut. Without looking round he felt relief, for the arrow had clearly missed, or had not been aimed at Hubert. At any rate Hubert's intimidating battle-cry was echoing through the air. Within a few seconds he had crossed the ground to the undergrowth and launched himself into it. Almost simultaneously he heard Hubert cry out.

Richard landed in the greenery and rolled over, parting the bracken fronds enough to spy Hubert lying face down, motionless on the ground. Instantly, he saw red and instinct urged him to charge their assailant to hack him to pieces with his sword. Yet military training stayed his hand. Hubert's sacrifice would amount to nothing if he acted so rashly. He needed to locate exactly where his adversary was in the first place.

And then there was the sound of a hunting horn from somewhere behind him and before he knew it; it seemed as if the air suddenly became thick with arrows. And they came from several points, all aiming at the area where he thought the assassin lurked.

There was an exclamation of anger, then a noise of breaking branches and rustling, as of a man running away through the greenery. Moments later he heard a horse retreating fast.

Richard stayed crouched where he was until he was sure that the shooting had stopped and then he called out. He was answered immediately and ordered to stand and walk into the clearing. He complied, still holding his sword, yet not wielding it threateningly.

From several points nearby men broke out of the forest, several with yew bows bent and with arrows ready notched. Three of them ran across the clearing, one stopping to check on Hubert while his fellows made for the point where the assassin had been.

'You must be Sir Richard Lee?' came a voice from the forest. A moment later a portly friar came out of the forest, a broadsword in his hand and a helmet upon his head. 'I am Tuck, a friar, once of Fountains Abbey, yet now the leader of this goodly band of — *contrariants*.'

'I thought that the man they called Robert

Hood was their leader.'

'He was until he turned raping dog and murderer!' said another voice. And a small stocky man with a warty growth on his nose came out of the greenery. 'I am Much, son of Midge the Miller. My old father got word to us of all his crimes.'

'This man is alive,' a voice cried, from the middle of the clearing. Richard spun round, overjoyed to see the outlaw help Hubert to his feet.

'There is some blood here!' called one of the men from the undergrowth on the far side of the clearing. 'Looks like we hit him. Not badly though, for it is just a trickle.'

'Do you know who it was?' Richard asked Friar Tuck.

The corpulent friar nodded. 'It was almost certainly the Hood.'

'He's gone mad,' said Much, with an emphatic nod of his head.

'Hubert, thank God you are alive,' said Richard, as the outlaw, a burly fellow with a mane of red hair helped Hubert over to them.

Hubert grinned as he rubbed a rapidly rising bump on his forehead. 'Fool that I am, I stumbled in a coney-hole and knocked myself out as I fell.' Suddenly recovering himself, he grasped his master's shoulders and shook him hard. 'But you are safe, my lord, and that is all that matters.'

Friar Tuck chuckled. 'How he missed you, my friend, I will never know. Robin Hood is probably one of the finest shots in the country and you made a good target dashing straight for him.'

Hubert gave a lop-sided grin and pulled out his talisman. 'It was because of this.' He winked at Richard and then replaced it under his tunic. 'It deflects arrows,' he explained to the friar and the rapidly assembling group that had gathered around them. Others began beating out the fire as the roof collapsed and fell inwards.

Richard prised one of the arrows out of the doorframe and handed it to Hubert for safe keeping.

'We came after Matilda Oxley,' Richard explained. 'Have you — ?'

'She is in our camp,' Friar Tuck explained. 'We managed to get to her before Robin did and we took her back to our latest camp. She doesn't believe that Robin could have done the things it is claimed that he did, but perhaps this will convince her.' He looked at the other outlaws, then back at Richard again before going on, 'I think you will be safe now.'

But Richard shook his head. 'I think that we had better take Matilda back for her own safety. If you let me talk with her I am sure that I can persuade her that coming back to Wakefield would be sensible. According to Hubert here, her cousin is distraught.'

Friar Tuck pondered for a moment, and then nodded his head. 'But first we shall blindfold you. We are all outlaws and you are the King's man. We wouldn't want to tempt you, my lord.'

'I am not a man to be tempted,' Richard replied.

Hubert said nothing, although he was far from convinced about that.

★　★　★

Hubert ate some bread and cheese and drank a mug of ale with Much the Miller's son and a few of the outlaws while Richard and the friar went to talk to Matilda in one of several bivouacs that had been constructed deep in the forest. When they came out and prepared to leave, Matilda said nothing. Hubert thought that it looked as if she had been crying, and that she was in a state of disbelief. Indeed, the three of them hardly said a word as they rode through the forest and back to Wakefield.

Upon Richard's instructions, Hubert escorted Matilda back to the Bucket Inn and briefly told a surprised Beatrice of their adventure.

'We will be back later, my love,' he told her. 'My master will probably want to have more words with you all.'

Beatrice shivered slightly. 'Do you think it would be best if I keep them apart?'

Hubert scratched his chin. 'Frankly, I don't think so. Matilda is obviously going to take the whole thing as a bitter blow, but I believe that she understands that her man has gone mad — or bad — or both. If Sir Richard didn't convince her then I think that the friar and the other outlaws would have.'

She kissed him and squeezed his neck. 'Come back soon, my love.'

Richard was waiting for him in the Roll's Office of the Moot Hall.

Hubert pinched his nose as he came in. 'The air is none too pleasant around here, my lord.'

Richard nodded in agreement. 'Aye, the stench comes from the Tolbooth. Both bodies are, I imagine, starting to putrefy. They need to be buried before too long.' He held out his hand. 'Have you the arrow?'

Hubert produced it and Richard laid it beside the two other arrows that he had taken out of the chest that had been put aside to hold the evidence of the recent crimes that he was investigating.

'It is exactly the same,' Richard mused.

'Which means that Robert Hood is guilty of all of these crimes,' said Hubert. 'Yet I can't help thinking that it does not make sense! Why would he want to kill us?'

Richard stroked his beard pensively. 'That was concerning me all the way back. It can only have been to remove me from the scene. I suspect that he thought that if he could do that then it would be an end to the matter. Instead, it would just result in someone else coming to fill my place.'

'What about Matilda? Surely he would never have meant to harm her?'

Richard shrugged. 'Who can say what a madman may do? To rape his betrothed's cousin, then kill in cold blood someone who may have seen him — William Scathelocke, I mean!' He clicked his tongue. 'That is hardly what an honest and sane man would do.'

'But it is what an evil man would do,' suggested Hubert. 'But where would the Pardoner come in?'

'Hmm, that was another thing that worried me. But I think I may have the answer. The Pardoner may have talked with Scathelocke before he was shot. He may have pardoned him, when Scathelocke confessed his sins to him.'

'But wouldn't there be a pardon, one of those papers on his body?' Hubert queried.

'Not necessarily. Not if the Pardoner just took pity on a wretch in the stocks. Such things are possible. And it would fit the case.'

Hubert bit his lip. It was clever, and fitted, he had to admit, but usually his master was able to convince him more so than he had. He felt unsure as to whether Sir Richard believed his version himself.

'But until we can actually question Robert Hood we still don't know anything for certain,' Richard went on. 'But at least we know that Matilda is safe.'

'But why should he wish her harm, my lord?'

Richard shook his head. 'If he is mad, and as good a shot as they say, then no one is safe until he is brought before the court.' He sighed. 'It pains me to say it, Hubert, but we might need Sir Thomas to finish off the job he promised to do and bring him in.'

* * *

They both covered their noses as they left the Moot Hall and quickly made their way from it. As they passed the parish church they saw Emma Oldthorpe and her servant Gilbert crossing the street in front of them. She strode in front and he hobbled slowly behind her with a basket laden with various bottles and jars, presumably delivering medicines to some of her husband's housebound patients.

'I think I am in love, my lord,' Hubert said, abruptly. Richard had been about to hail Mistress Oldthorpe, but at his words he stopped in his tracks and stood staring at his assistant.

'Beatrice Quigley?' he ventured.

Hubert shuffled his feet and flushed with colour. 'Aye, my lord. She is the sweetest, the most comely of buxom wenches.' Then he frowned at his choice of words and corrected himself, 'I mean, she is a beautiful lady.'

'And does she feel the same way?'

'Aye, my lord. We slept together.'

'You have slept with many women since I have known you, good Hubert, but this is the first time you ever used the 'love' word.'

Hubert beamed at him. 'I know, sir. Yet it is the first time that I have ever felt like this.' His expression grew sheepish. 'It is all right, isn't it, sir? Me falling in love, I mean.'

Richard gave him a look of mock seriousness until his expression grew sad. Then he cuffed him playfully on the side of his head. 'Of course, it is all right. And if she feels the same I am glad for you both. She is, as you say, a beautiful woman.'

As they walked on Richard was disappointed to see that there was no longer any sign of Emma Oldthorpe and Gilbert. 'Let us go to the back of Bread Street,' he said, walking faster. 'The yard behind the manor bakehouse is being used by the guilds to rehearse their Corpus Christi plays. The pageants are all there ready. I need to talk to Father Daniel and he told me that he would be there this afternoon.'

As they approached the great manor bakehouse, which was almost perpetually in use, for most of the township were obliged to have their bread baked there, they heard the sound of a lute and a familiar voice singing. He sang of a beauteous lady, a ravishing beauty and of a man with lust in his heart.

They turned the corner and saw Alan-a-Dale sitting on the top of a flight of wooden steps, strumming his lute. He looked up at them, smiled and touched his prodigious forelock.

'Hm, that fellow always seems to crop up,' said Hubert, once they had passed him. 'Methinks he seems to know when I am coming and his songs always seem to have a suggestive edge to them. Mayhap I shall have words with him sometime.'

Richard shook his head. 'Leave it, good Hubert. He is a minstrel and they always either sing of love, lust or the pursuit of either. Think nothing of it.' He himself would have preferred to let the matter drop, but Hubert clearly had love in mind.

'Your pardon, my lord,' he began, 'but it has been a year since your wife, my mistress died. Have you not seen any . . . ladies, who tempt you?'

Richard was taken aback by the question. Indeed, since coming to Wakefield he had thought a great deal about the fairer sex. And that thinking had been associated with much guilt.

'Hubert, I — ' he began. But he was cut off as they turned the corner again into the great yard and were immediately spotted by Father Daniel, who hailed Richard. He came running across.

'Sir Richard, I heard about your misadventure!' he said, turning his head and pointing to the figure of Lady Katherine, the Prioress of Kirklees Priory, who was standing in front of two pageants on which men in costumes were rehearsing their parts in their respective plays. 'The prioress and I were most upset to hear of it. Are you quite unhurt?'

'We are all well, I thank you. Matilda Oxley has been recovered and taken back to the Bucket Inn. I am, however, most surprised to know that you had intelligence of it.'

Father Daniel bowed. 'Wakefield is a small town, my lord. Especially after all the violence of the past few days it is not surprising that virtually everyone is taking note of anything untoward.'

They had walked across to join Lady Katherine. Richard and Hubert bowed to her, and she bowed back as became her position as a prioress.

After reiterating her concerns for their welfare Lady Katherine held up the neatly written parchment in her hand. 'We are running through two of the plays,' she explained. 'Here on the left is *The First Shepherd's Play*, by our Guild of St Oswald, and on the right is the Guild of Grocers with their play *Herod the Great*. After that we are going to go through our *The Talents* and the Grocers *The Deliverance of Souls*.'

Richard made appropriately approving noises about the pageants themselves with their elaborate stages. Each pageant was about twice the size of a normal wagon, built as were all of the pageants dotted around the great yard, by the guilds of carpenters and wheelwrights. The Guild of Grocers in particular was the most impressive, since it had two tiers, and a façade that looked like a face.

'The lower part drops, you see,' Lady Katherine explained, 'so that it looks as if the mouth of Hell has opened. This is for *The*

Deliverance of Souls play, when the fiends emerge from Hell's mouth to consume the world.'

'You will be glad when it is all over, I am sure,' said Richard. He pointed to the parchment in her hand. 'Are these the stage directions?'

'My notes,' returned Lady Katherine with a smile.

Richard nodded approvingly. Yet he seemed distracted.

'You look somewhat puzzled, Sir Richard,' Father Daniel commented.

'Did I? My apologies. I was just admiring Lady Katherine's handwriting. It looks familiar — and yet unfamiliar.' Then he gave a short laugh. 'But I must not keep you from your work. I actually came to ask you something, Father Daniel. About the two murdered men.'

Both Father Daniel and Lady Katherine looked ineffably sad, almost professionally sad. 'How can I help you?' he asked.

'By allowing me to have their bodies buried — temporarily, I mean — in consecrated ground. They are beginning to putrefy and I think they should be laid to rest.'

'Of course, Sir Richard. But why only temporarily?'

Richard shrugged. 'It is just that they might

need to be reexamined.'

They all looked round as Lady Katherine gave a short gasp. Then they saw her slowly slide to the ground in a dead faint.

★ ★ ★

It was early evening before Richard and Hubert arrived at the Bucket Inn. Lady Katherine had recovered to find herself surrounded by three concerned male faces, and was given a cup of wine by one of the Grocers guildsmen. She had been embarrassed and admitted to having felt overcome by the thought of the bodies starting to putrefy. After that they stayed to watch the first rehearsal of two of the plays, while one of the carpenters prepared two large rough coffins. Then Richard accompanied Father Daniel to the town cemetery while Hubert trundled off on the carpenter's cart with the two coffins to collect the two bodies. Ned Burkin happened to be the constable on duty and he marshalled a couple of watchmen to locate two of the town gravediggers.

'There have been many deaths in the last few years, I see,' Richard remarked, as he and the priest watched the gravediggers prepare two shallow graves.

'The great famine of 1315 caused a lot of

it, and then we had an epidemic that took many children.'

Hubert approached with his neck-cloth drawn well up to cover his mouth and nose. 'Are you sure you don't want them a bit deeper, my lord?' he asked. 'They are pretty ripe, the pair of them. We had a devil of a job getting the coffin lids shut.'

Richard pulled up his own neck-cloth. 'That is why I had the carpenter build large coffins. The gases inside their bellies will have swollen them up to almost twice their normal size. But no, they must be shallow enough for us to exhume them if the need arises.'

Father Daniel said a short blessing once it was all over, and then excused himself to get back to the rehearsals. Richard dismissed the others then he and Hubert stood looking down at the two fresh mounds.

'This burial ground is well protected from animals,' Richard commented, pointing at the surrounding trees and mulberry hedging. 'And it is not visible from the streets with all these bushes.'

'You mean that you could see how the rape of the maid Lillian could have taken place?'

'Exactly. And the Pardoner, Albin of Rouncivale who confessed to the crime, but who was murdered, lies here. As beside him lies William Scathelocke, who was cruelly murdered while a captive in the stocks. It is a bitter irony that it is likely that neither of them had anything to do with the crime.'

'And meanwhile Robert Hood goes free.'

'Hardly free, Hubert. He is an outcast now. An outlaw thrown out by his fellow outlaws.'

'Yet he came close to adding us to his tally, Sir Richard,' said Hubert, shivering despite himself. 'We could be lying there this evening.'

Richard punched his arm playfully. 'Yet we are here to tell the day. And so now let us retire to the Bucket Inn, for I need to have words with the women there.'

Beatrice met them as they came into the busy inn. Her expression registered all too clearly the fact that she was happy to see Hubert, Sir Richard noted with some pleasure.

'I would like to have words with the three of you, Beatrice,' Richard told her. 'May we come up?'

The atmosphere in the upstairs room was fraught, as expected, but Richard was heartened to see that Matilda no longer glowered at her cousin. Indeed, they sat together on a settle, both of them red-eyed from recent tears. As Richard told them of his suspicions about Robert Hood Matilda reached out and squeezed Lillian's hand.

'I know what you are saying, Sir Richard,' she said. 'It is just hard to believe that my Robin could have turned so wicked. I can only think that it is this business of being declared a contrariant. He is' — she gulped hard as fresh tears threatened to flow — 'he was a good and kind man. But I must now look to protecting my cousin.'

Seeing them somewhat reconciled Beatrice led the two men downstairs again.

'I think we should sup here,' Richard said, 'then I think that I shall stay the night in Wakefield.'

'Are you not expected at the castle, my lord?' Hubert asked.

He was suddenly knocked forward and, turning rapidly, found himself looking into the bleary eye of Hector Lunt. The man swayed on his feet.

'Your pardon — *my lords!*' he slurred, sarcastically. 'I have drunk my fill and now I must go, for I do not like the smell around here.'

'Why Hector Lunt, you drunken fool!' said Beatrice between clenched teeth. 'How dare you talk to my guests like that?'

Hubert was about to grab him, but Richard stayed his hand.

'You would do well to get home before it gets too dark, my man,' Richard said. 'Or you

267

may find yourself in front of me in court. And possibly might find yourself facing a spell in the stocks.'

Hector's one eye opened wide in alarm and he gave a drunken bow and staggered towards the door. As he did so, George-a-Green detached himself from the group he had been sitting with and came over.

'He isn't a bad fellow, my lords,' he explained. 'He just can't say when he has had enough ale.' He looked at Beatrice with mock accusation in his eyes. 'Your ale is too tempting.'

Then he bowed to Richard. 'I am sorry if I have seemed rude, my lord. My friend Hubert here set me straight about a lot of things. We need the law around here. It is that that keeps us all safe.'

From somewhere outside, a blood-curdling scream rang out. It was followed moments later by a second, shorter and more muffled cry, and then silence.

Hubert and George-a-Green were out of the tavern door in seconds, followed by Richard and half of the clientele of the Bucket Inn. The light was fading fast, but up a side street some fifty yards from the inn they found the bodies of two men.

One was Hector, lying on his back with an arrow through his chest. Half-sprawled on top of him was the body of a well-built man in a cloak and hood.

Hubert and George-a-Green lifted him off Hector and laid him on his back. He was dead, that was clear, for the gaping wound in his neck where his throat had been cut from ear to ear no longer pumped blood. Beside him was a bow.

'He shot Hector!' gasped George-a-Green.

'And then Hector slit his throat in defence when he was leaning over him,' said Hubert, pointing to Hector Lunt's hand, in which was still grasped a bloodstained knife.'

Suddenly, Hector's eyes fluttered open and he coughed up blood.

'He took my life!' he gasped. 'He . . . he said . . . '

Richard bent down and gently lifted his head. 'What did he say? Tell me and we shall get help.'

'He . . . said . . . it was for the eye . . . and for . . . the tooth. He . . . took my . . . '

He clutched at Richard's tunic, his open eye staring into eternity as his death rattle proclaimed the passage of his soul.

'A revenge killing?' Hubert suggested.

'I don't know about that,' volunteered George-a-Green, pointing at the face of the other dead man. 'But that man has been about the town for a day or two. Why, I think he was drinking in the Bucket Inn earlier on this evening, and the other night as well. He's not from round here, though. I reckon he's a foreigner, from Pontefract or thereabouts.'

Richard did not say anything immediately, for he seemed to be trying to work something out in his mind. Then he stirred himself from his momentary reverie.

'Hubert, I know it is late, but I want you to summon the bailiff, John of Flanshaw. I want the town alerted. There will be a court session at nine bells tomorrow. We have two more deaths to investigate.'

Hubert sighed and pointed to the two corpses. 'It is just as well that we emptied the Tollbooth, my lord.'

12

The King's Eye

John of Flanshaw had done a good job, having risen at four o'clock to marshal the constables, their men and the town reeves to ensure that the townsfolk all turned out for the extra session of the court. The Moot Hall was packed by the time that Sir Thomas Deyville and his daughter, Lady Wilhelmina arrived and took their places behind the bench on the dais.

As the nine bells of All Saints rang out Sir Richard entered from the Roll's Office. He bowed to them both then took his seat.

'If I did not think better, I would declare you a jinx, Sir Richard,' said Sir Thomas with a cold smile. 'Death seems to follow you.'

'Father!' Lady Wilhelmina whispered protestingly. 'Two men died last night: it is no time for your jokes.'

Suitably rebuffed, the Deputy Steward slumped back in his chair and Richard gave the Lady Wilhelmina a grateful smile, which she accepted with a slight nod of her head and the hint of a returned smile.

The bailiff had already assembled the jurymen who waited by their stools.

'This special court is now in session,' Richard announced with a rap of his gavel. 'It is my sad duty to announce that last night, as many of you will no doubt already know, there was a double killing. It took place up Greenwood Street, but fifty yards from the Bucket Inn.'

And he described how he himself had seen Hector Lunt in the Bucket Inn, in an inebriated state, and of how he had left after having been given a warning. Then he described the two screams; the first loud and blood-curdling, the second more muffled and shorter.

'When we investigated we found the two bodies in Greenwood Street. Hector Lunt was lying on his back with an arrow in his chest and the other man was sprawled half over him. His throat had been cut. It looked as if he had shot Hector Lunt with an arrow and it seemed as if his throat had been cut, by Hector, before he collapsed. It is possible that the second man, the bowman had been leaning over what he thought was a successful kill. At any rate, Hector Lunt had a knife in his hand.'

The crowd made suitable noises of alarm and horror, yet without any of the rowdiness that had occurred in the first court session.

Richard went on, 'The bowman was dead when we arrived, but Hector Lunt lived and managed to blurt out something about an eye and a tooth.'

He noted Father Daniel's presence in the crowd. He was standing with Lady Katherine. 'Can you tell the court where that expression comes from, Father Daniel?'

The priest nodded. 'I believe he would have been referring to the Gospel according to Matthew, Sir Richard: '*Ye have heard that it hath been said, An eye for an eye, and a tooth for a tooth.*' Its meaning is, I think, quite apparent.'

Richard nodded. 'It sounds as if he was saying that it was an act of vengeance. Well, those are the facts of the case, or so they seem. Bailiff, have the two bodies brought in.'

The crowd moved about restlessly as people craned necks to see the entry of the men of the watch with the two bodies, both wrapped in old blankets. They were laid down before the bench.

'We will start with the body of Hector Lunt. Uncover him,' Richard ordered. He scanned the crowd and saw Wilfred Old-thorpe standing as usual with his wife, Emma and their servant Gilbert. Emma's expression seemed somehow strained, as if she, like him, would like to have had words in private. She put a hand on Gilbert's shoulder and patted it gently, like a mother comforting a child.

'Master Oldthorpe, the court would again like to call upon your services. Step forward please and examine the body.'

The apothecary made his way through the crowd, bowed to the bench and then bent to inspect the body. As before, the arrow had been left in place and the blood-soaked clothes had been left as they were.

'This man died of his arrow wound, my lord. It is a high wound on his chest on the left side. I think that it must have missed his heart, but would almost certainly have punctured a lung and probably severed his main blood vessel from the heart.'

'Would this be consistent with him living for several minutes after he was struck?'

'Absolutely. Men can live for hours after the lung is punctured, but if the blood vessel was leaking he would have died once the blood filled his chest.'

Richard nodded grimly. 'Remove the arrow if you will.'

'I shall need to use some instruments,' the apothecary replied, taking off his shoulder bag and delving inside for a thin knife and a pair of forceps. 'First I will need to remove his clothes, my lord.'

Richard gestured to begin and the crowd

strained to watch Master Oldthorpe begin his grisly work. He laid his instruments down on the floor and gingerly opened the tunic as far as he could. Then he cut the clothes around the arrow so that he could peel them back to reveal the chest and the gory wound with the arrow protruding from it. Before he made a move to remove the arrow he ran his hands expertly over the exposed torso and neck.

'There is a curious cut at the side of his neck, Sir Richard,' he pointed out. 'I would say that it could have been from a chain or a string. It could have been made if something like a medallion had been torn from around his neck.'

Richard nodded to John of Flanshaw. 'Record that, please, Bailiff.' Then he turned to Master Oldthorpe. 'Now the arrow, if you please.'

Lady Wilhelmina and most of the women in the crowd looked away as the apothecary worked on the tissue around the arrow shaft to loosen it. Then grasping the shaft, he pulled and it came out with a sickening sucking sound. As it came away, old dark blood spurted from the chest and oozed for a moment over the alabaster white chest of the corpse. He rose with the arrow and, at Richard's indication, laid it on the bench beside three other arrows, two of which were as blood-stained as the new one.

'And now, please examine the other body and give us your opinion.'

The apothecary stepped over Hector Lunt's corpse then bent again and drew back the blanket from the second body. At the sight of the corpse with its gaping throat wound and still staring eyes there were many gasps and oaths, and two members of the crowd fainted and had to be carried out.

Wilfred Oldthorpe remained detached and leaned close to inspect the wound. 'Clearly this man would have died almost immediately, Sir Richard. He was killed by a mortal wound to his throat.'

'A knife cut?'

'A terrible wound, Sir Richard. His main blood vessels and his windpipe were severed.'

'Could it have been done while he was leaning over the first body?'

'It could.'

'And could it have been done by Hector Lunt, as he lay there with an arrow in his chest?'

The apothecary pursed his lips pensively as he considered the question. 'It could,' he replied hesitantly, 'if he flailed out, but even so, I fear it would have sapped his remaining strength.'

'Quite so,' Richard commented. 'Yet on battlefields you see such feats of strength even at the point of death. Thank you, Master Oldthorpe, you may stand down.'

Richard rapped his gavel to silence the crowd, for several sections had begun whispering and speculating. 'Does anyone recognize this man? Can he be identified?'

People leaned forward or craned above their neighbours to try to get a better view of the bodies. A few men, including George-a-Green volunteered that they had seen him in one tavern or another over the last few days, but in general there was much head-shaking. No one seemed able to put a name to him.

'Very well,' said Richard. 'Before we proceed, I am going to report on another thing that occurred yesterday.'

And he gave an abbreviated version of his and Hubert's trip into Barnsdale Forest and of the way that they were ambushed and of how they took refuge in the charcoal burner's hut, which their assailant set on fire with blazing arrows. He made no mention of Matilda Oxley or of their rescue by the outlaws.

'I tell you this because we brought back one of the arrows that narrowly missed us.' He picked up the single arrow that was not bloodstained from the bench. 'Here it is. Now call Simon the Fletcher.'

John of Flanshaw duly called the fletcher, who took his place in the witness pen.

'You have already examined two of these arrows, one of which was removed from the body of William Scathelocke and one from the body of Albin of Rouncivale. Please now compare them with the one that has just been removed from Hector Lunt and this one that was fired at us yesterday.'

It took a matter of moments before Simon the Fletcher replied, 'They are all made by the same hand, sir.'

'Thank you. You may stand down, Simon the Fletcher.' Then to John of Flanshaw, 'Record that if you please.'

Richard sat forward and tapped his fingertips together. 'So this is what apparently happened. Hector Lunt left the Bucket Inn, was followed by this unknown man and shot with an arrow. As he lay dying the bowman came and leaned over him and possibly pulled something from his neck, if the apothecary is correct. Then with his failing strength Hector Lunt lashed out with his knife, which was found in his hand, and cut his murderer's throat. Does this sound likely?'

He waited for a reaction, scanning the

crowd before going on, 'I do not believe that this happened!'

'And why not?' Sir Thomas demanded.

'For several reasons,' Richard replied suavely. 'First, I find it hard to believe that an assassin armed with a bow would only come with a single arrow. He had a bow, yet no quiver, no other arrow in case he missed.'

'If he killed all three men, then clearly he was a marksman!' exclaimed Sir Thomas.

'Yes, if he was,' said Richard. 'But I am not convinced that he was a bowman at all, far less a marksman. Constable Burkin, lift the man's right hand.'

Ned Burkin did as he was instructed and people in the crowd murmured their under-standing.

'He has lost his second finger!' exclaimed a youth at the front.

'Exactly!' said Richard. 'Hardly likely then to have been an archer, no matter whether he was right or left-handed. This man had an accident of some sort in the far past, for the wound is healed. And secondly, if he had taken something from about Hector Lunt's neck, what was it? And where is it?'

Sir Thomas had been sitting nodding his head as he followed Richard's argument. 'Clever, Sir Richard. Clever!'

'And lastly,' Richard said. 'I am not

convinced that Hector Lunt would have been able to cut his throat. Not from his position on his back.'

Wilfred Oldthorpe nodded his head. 'You are right, Sir Richard. I see that now. This wound would be more consistent with someone grabbing his head from behind, so that his throat was exposed, then a blade was applied from one side to the other.' He made movements with his hands, as if dealing such a mortal wound to an invisible adversary.

'Exactly my belief,' said Richard. 'I think that our mysterious bowman slew Hector Lunt, then the unknown man went in to check the kill, and while he was leaning over the dying man, he had his throat slit by the bowman who had crept up behind. Whatever was taken from Hector Lunt was taken away, the bow was dropped by the body and the knife was planted in Hector Lunt's hand to make it look as if no one else was involved.'

'But why was he killed in the first place?' Lady Wilhelmina asked.

Richard glanced towards Beatrice, Matilda and Lillian, who were standing at the back of the crowd. 'I think that there is enough here which suggests that one man may have had a motive for some if not all of these killings. That man is Robert Hood.'

There were angry murmurings from the

crowd and much nodding of heads. Yet a few steadfastly shook theirs.

'If Robert Hood was guilty of the crime of rape, he could have a motive for silencing a man who was once a rival in love, and who had seen him leave the cemetery. The Pardoner may have given him a pardon upon hearing his confession, yet when the Hood thought about it he may have come after him. Hector Lunt had publicly abused Hood's name. And this unknown man — well, it looks as if he had been in league with the bowman, until the opportunity presented itself for him to remove him as well. By doing so he effectively removed all potential blame from him.'

The crowd considered it all and this time Richard did not stop them from talking among themselves. He noticed that the twelve jurymen also were murmuring to each other.

'I go back to our adventure of yesterday,' Richard continued, when the hubbub settled. 'You do not need to know the details, but my assistant and I were attacked, we believe, by Robert Hood while we took refuge in the hut. It almost cost us our lives and we were only saved by his former fellows who chased him away. I should add that the reason they had chased him away is because he is an outcast among the outlaws that he led until yesterday.

281

The reason for this was a spectacularly clever plan by the Deputy Steward, Sir Thomas Deyville.'

Sir Thomas stared at Richard in wonder, then, when he found himself being applauded, he beamed and slapped the table with his hand. 'It was my pleasure, Sir Richard,' he roared.

Richard gave him a thin smile, and then went on, 'All of this leads me to believe that it is ever more important to bring Robert Hood to justice. His crimes are great and we need to hear him in person. I therefore make this proclamation, which John of Flanshaw shall copy and have read out and nailed up in writing for any who can read, in every village and hamlet around the town of Wakefield. It shall also be posted at every road leading into the Barnsdale Forest and the Outwood.' He paused, then dictated slowly:

A proclamation, in the name of King Edward the Second, of Caernarvon, a reward of five guineas for the arrest of the outlaw Robert Hood, to be taken alive. If this arrest is made by an outlaw or group of outlaws, they shall earn full pardon. If it is made by any who are not freemen, they shall by this deed gain their freedom.

Sit Thomas thumped the bench with his fist. 'By God's blood, we shall have the dog by nightfall, I wager! I will send some men out to the forest roads straight away.'

The crowd in the Moot Hall were carried away by the Deputy Steward's exclamation and began to jeer the name of their former townsman, and to cheer at the reward for his capture.

Hubert had been watching the crowd all this time and he noted the gleam in the eye of Midge the Miller. He assumed that the news of the proclamation would reach Barnsdale Forest before the proclamations were dry on John of Flanshaw's parchments.

Richard was about to close the court session when there was the sound of a horse outside and a commotion from the outer members of the crowd. Moments later a young messenger dressed in the unmistakable royal livery appeared at the door and made his way through to the bench.

He doffed his hat and bowed. 'Greetings, sirs. I seek Sir Thomas Deyville and bring him a message from His Majesty the King. I rode to Sandal Castle but was informed to ride here.' He drew from within his tunic a sealed message.

Sir Thomas hesitated for a moment, and then gestured to Richard. 'My eyes are strained this morning, Sir Richard. Would you be so kind as to read it for me?'

Richard held Sir Thomas's eyes for a moment, then nodded with a genial smile. He took the message, opened the seal and read the message. Then he leaned closer to the Deputy Steward and whispered in his ear. Sir Thomas coloured, asked a couple of quiet questions then stood up.

'His Majesty the King and his special adviser Hugh le Dispenser are staying at nearby Rothwell Castle, but have decided to dine and stay at Sandal Castle until Corpus Christi in two days when he will watch the Wakefield Mystery Plays.' He beamed proudly. 'This is a great honour for Wakefield and to mark it I invite all of the Wakefield burghers and the heads of the guilds to sup with us, his majesty and his adviser this evening at five o'clock.'

He was still beaming proudly some minutes later, once the court had cleared, when Lady Wilhelmina brought him down to earth.

'Father, we should make haste. My mother will be all of a fluster. Honoured though she will be at entertaining his majesty, yet I fear she will be less pleased at having to entertain half of Wakefield.'

★ ★ ★

Richard was dressing and Hubert was looking out of his tower room when the royal party rode up the hill towards Sandal Castle. At the head of the party of some twenty men rode two trumpeters, then two banner carriers, and behind them, a tall dark-haired man of about thirty years, somewhat foppishly dressed, with a pill hat that barely covered his cascading locks. Beside him was the unmistakable figure of the King, Edward II of Caernarvon. Resplendent in blue tunic and hose, with a breast-plate, a flowing fur collar on his purple cloak, and a light crown upon his head. Even at a distance the strange three-forked beard that he cultivated was evident, and he cut a dashing figure. The two men laughed as they rode, clearly enjoying the afternoon sunshine and each other's company. Behind them rode a column of heavily armed men.

'His majesty comes, my lord,' Hubert announced. Then he gave a soft whistle. 'So that is his special adviser, Hugh le Dispenser.'

Richard joined him at the window and looked down. 'Indeed. He seems rather a fine peacock of a fellow, does he not?'

Hubert scratched his chin. 'And you say that he is the new Gaveston, my lord?'

'That is what they say. The King calls him his *King's Eye*.'

Hubert hummed. 'They seem close enough that is for sure.'

'Too close for many of the King's opponents,' returned Richard. 'And indeed, too close for her majesty Queen Isabella, for she had him and his father banished, until only this year. Now that he is back she has been sent on a diplomatic mission to France. But still, that is up to his majesty. Our purpose is to uphold the King's justice. And it would not do for us to be absent when the King arrives, so come, we had best take our places.'

Richard completed his change of clothes then swiftly made his way down to the courtyard where Sir Thomas, Lady Alecia and Lady Wilhelmina were already waiting to receive the king. The castle staff was assembled at a discreet distance.

'A great honour for you, Lady Alecia,' Richard said with a smile.

Lady Alecia smiled back nervously. 'Yet a daunting challenge, Sir Richard. I wish that his majesty had given us more time.'

'It will be fine, my lady,' said Sir Thomas. 'A great opportunity for — all of us.' His eyes fell on his daughter and Richard imagined that there was sadness in his regard. 'Alas, he will probably not be over interested in my daughter's beauty.'

'Father!' Lady Wilhelmina hissed beneath her breath.

Trumpets called from without the walls of the castle, then there came the sound of horses crossing the outer drawbridge as the royal party entered the castle. The trumpeters and the two officers rode up to the waiting Deputy Steward and his group, then they broke apart to reveal the King and his adviser, Hugh le Dispenser.

The King looked down as Richard and Sir Thomas bowed and the ladies curtsied. And behind them, the castle staff echoed their moves.

'Excellent! Most excellent!' King Edward laughed, elegantly swinging a leg over his saddle and nimbly dropping to the ground. 'Isn't this the most delightful little castle, Hugh?'

Hugh le Dispenser followed suit and came to stand beside his monarch and friend, for their relationship was immediately apparent to be more that of two close friends than sovereign and humble subject. He looked round at the barbican, the inner moat and then at the keep beyond. 'An interesting design, Edward, I give you that.' He nodded his head as if agreeing with his own statement. 'Quaint, but functional, I would say.'

'And this must be Sir Thomas Deyville, the Deputy Steward that I have such high hopes of.'

Sir Thomas bowed and kissed the outstretched fingertips. 'Your loyal servant, Your Majesty,' he returned, obsequiously.

'And these beauties must be your wife and daughter,' went on the King. He pouted, and then added, 'But which is which? They are both so enchanting that they could be young sisters.'

Lady Alecia giggled and blushed. 'Your Majesty is too kind. I am Alecia and this is my daughter, the Lady Wilhelmina.'

Both the King and Hugh le Dispenser bowed in unison.

'And how are you, Richard, my good and trusty Sergeant-at-Law?' asked the King.

'I am well, Your Majesty.'

'Your wound is healed?'

Richard looked puzzled for a moment, then said, 'Quite healed, sir. There is an apothecary here in Wakefield so skilled that he cured it days ago. I had forgotten.'

'Maybe you will be fit enough to hunt with us tomorrow then, Richard. Hugh here is keen to stick a boar or two in this Great Park that we have heard so much about.'

'Or a deer,' said Hugh le Dispenser with a yawn. 'I quite fancy exercising my bow arm.'

Richard inclined his head. 'I would beg to be excused from a hunt, Majesty. I still have pressing law work to take care of. Yet I am sure that Sir Thomas would be a more than able guide to the park here.'

'Indeed, Your Majesty,' began Sir Thomas. 'I would — '

'Pah! The law!' interrupted Hugh le Dispenser. 'It is so boring. So dusty, don't you think?'

King Edward smiled indulgently on his adviser. 'I think you are too artistic to understand the law, Hugh. But my realm needs good law and just law. That is why Richard here is the perfect man for me. He breathes the law. Isn't that so, Sir Thomas? Has he taught you much?'

'Indeed, your Majesty. In fact — ' Sir Thomas began again.

'But we must not stand here gossiping,' cut in the King. 'These ladies must be tired. Let us to our rooms, to refresh and then to supper.'

Lady Alecia curtsied. 'We have prepared a meal for you, Your Majesty and we have invited the local dignitaries to eat with us. I hope that is to your satisfaction.'

Hugh le Dispenser yawned again, but the king smiled. 'It will give me great pleasure, Lady Alecia. A king must ever be pleased to meet his subjects. Especially when they are as beautiful as you and your daughter.'

Richard permitted himself a smile as he looked at the two ladies. Of the two, the mother was clearly more susceptible to flattery.

★ ★ ★

The King clearly enjoyed the feast in the Great Hall, for socializing was one of his great pleasures, and something that he excelled in. He gave the impression to all, as they filed past and were introduced to his royal personage, that he was intensely interested in each person that he spoke to, even though it was unlikely that he would ever remember their names afterwards. He talked knowledgably about art and playmaking with Father Daniel and Lady Katherine; about physic with Wilfred Oldthorpe and about forestry and falconry with John Little, of the Guild of Foresters. Hugh le Dispenser, on the other hand, showed little interest in anyone except the King or himself. He was an easy man to despise, Richard concluded.

The talk at the head table was mainly trivial. Although the King had shown some interest in the affairs of the Manor of Wakefield, yet he did not care to hear about details of any cases that were under investigation.

'I appoint men such as you Sir Thomas, and Richard here to look after my interests,' he said with a grin at Hugh Le Dispenser. 'And while you are looking after those interests, I can take a healthy interest in this splendid feast and the affairs of my people.'

'Quite right, Edward,' agreed le Dispenser, dipping his fingers in a fingerbowl. 'Why keep a chicken and cluck yourself!'

'So speaks the King's Eye! Am I not lucky to have such a friend? Mayhap I should call him my *mouth*?' And both of them guffawed, as did those about them as if le Dispenser was the greatest wit in the realm, matched only by his sovereign.

For his own part Richard spied out Emma Oldthorpe with her husband on one of the lower tables and would have dearly liked some opportunity to have words with her. He was also pretty sure by a look on Lady Wilhelmina's face that she had caught him more than once sneaking a glance in Emma's direction. She did not seem happy about it.

Indeed, that evening after the King and Hugh le Dispenser had retired to their rooms in the Great Chamber beside the Great Hall, and Sir Thomas and Lady Alecia had repaired to their lodge, Richard sat in his room musing over the events of the day. He still had much to do and he was glad that he had been permitted to be excused from the hunt in the morning.

The knock on the door made him jump up.

Lady Wilhelmina was standing there in a hooded cloak when he opened the door.

'Wilhelmina, what are you doing here?' he whispered. 'This is madness, I told you before.'

She pushed past him and turned once he had closed the door. 'Why, Sir Richard?' she asked.

'I don't understand?' he replied.

'Why do you keep putting me off? The other night when I came, naked, to this chamber, you thrust me away. And the time before that you turned me around and sent me away. Why will you not lie with me?'

He looked aside. 'Wilhelmina, it is not easy.'

Her eyes opened wide in shock. 'Are you — like his majesty? Do you prefer other men? Is that why he calls you Richard?' As she fired questions her eyes became wider still, almost round. Beautifully round, he thought. 'So is your manservant — Hubert — is he more to you than a servant?'

He gave her a thin smile and shook his head. 'No, Wilhelmina, it is nothing like that.'

'Then what? Is there someone else?'

He said nothing.

Suddenly she looked crestfallen. 'I saw you looking tonight. Why not at me? I come every day to your court. I sit beside you at dinner. Am I not desirable?'

He hung his head. 'Wilhelmina, I think you ought to go,' he said.

She forced back a sob as she pulled up her hood. 'Damn you, Sir Richard. Damn you! You will regret this some day.'

When she had gone he leaned with his back against the door. 'I think I do already, Wilhelmina,' he whispered to the empty room. 'There is just so much at stake.'

★ ★ ★

Richard slept little that night and was grateful when the first light of dawn permitted him to rise, do his ablutions and then get ready to take his leave. As he expected, Hubert was up, breakfasted and pacing across the bailey courtyard awaiting his orders. The place was buzzing with activity as men prepared horses and weapons for the hunt that had been arranged for the King and his adviser.

'We will go to Wakefield straight away,' Richard said. 'But first I need to speak with the Deputy Steward.'

Hubert pointed behind Richard and he turned to see Sir Thomas coming down the steps from his lodge.

'Ah, Sir Thomas, a word,' said Richard. And they retired again to the Deputy Steward's office.

'I am concerned for the King's safety, Sir Thomas,' said Richard.

Sir Thomas looked puzzled. 'As am I, Sir Richard. As should every good Englishman. We go hunting this morning and I will have men all around him, to say nothing of his own. He could not be safer.'

'And what of tomorrow, at the Mystery Plays?'

'The same. We shall have him well protected.' His cunning eyes narrowed. 'Why this all of a sudden, Sir Richard? Do you suspect some attempt on his life?'

Richard shook his head. 'It is just as well to be prepared for any eventuality. What of the men you were going to send into the forest?'

'They have gone, and they are better prepared than before. That blockhead who led them last time has had a lesson in tactics.'

Hubert had been standing silently at the door. He grinned inwardly, for his friend Adam Crigg was in the contingent sent into the forest. He had told him the extent of the tactics given to them by Sir Thomas. It was simply, keep an eye behind you and don't get hoodwinked.

Once they reached Wakefield, Richard sent Hubert off to check on Matilda and Lillian, which he did with great willingness. He himself rode to the parish church of All Saints and tethered his mount outside. Then he went inside the church and walked up the aisle to the altar, where he knelt and said a silent prayer.

It was eerily quiet and slightly cold. He gripped the hilt of his sword, testing it for swift unsheathing if necessary, then he walked into the shadowy sanctuary beyond the altar.

He stood in the centre and turned to look back at the altar.

From behind him he heard a rustle of cloth from somewhere in the shadows, then a voice whispered his name.

'I was hoping to find you here,' Richard whispered back.

13

Mysteries

His Majesty, King Edward II had enjoyed his day's hunting in the Great Park. He had shot two deer and stuck one boar, all clean kills. By contrast and much to his chagrin, Hugh le Dispenser had taken one deer, but messily, so that it had to be dispatched by one of the foresters. The evening meal with the Deputy Steward, his family, and Sir Richard had inevitably been a splendid dinner of boar and venison prepared to perfection by Gideon Kitchen, whose beaming presence was called for by the King himself.

'How is it, Master Kitchen, that I have not heard of your skills before? Methinks that your talent may be wasted up here in the wilds of Yorkshire. How think you of coming to London to cook for us?'

Gideon Kitchen beamed anew, his cherubic cheeks seeming to bulge with pleasure. He bowed, stumbling slightly as he did so, because of his lame leg. 'Your Majesty does me great honour, yet I am not the person to ask. Your Majesty, the Deputy Steward may have — '

'The Deputy Steward may have other ideas?' Edward interjected. He laughed lightly, and waited in the expectation that the others would also find his words amusing, which they dutifully did.

'And I expect that is so, am I not correct, Sir Thomas? You would not like to lose so accomplished a cook.'

Lady Alecia volunteered a reply. 'I would hope that our good Gideon Kitchen would stay with us, Your Majesty, so that we could entice you to favour us with further visits in the future.'

Hugh le Dispenser laughed. 'Well said, madam. And to be frank, I would suggest that you keep him here, Edward, for I would like to hunt these woods again, despite my bad luck today.'

'Then the cook shall stay!' the King announced, taking a large mouthful of wine. 'And who knows, perhaps someday the Deputy Steward will not just be a deputy,' he said suggestively. 'I am liking this Sandal Castle. I quite see why the Earls Surrey and Lancaster both had a liking for it.'

Sir Thomas beamed. 'I hope that I will merit the trust you have placed in me, Your Majesty.'

The king laughed again. 'Oh, I am sure that you will.' He was smiling, yet there was no mistaking the fact that the smile was only a movement of the mouth, for there was no laughter evident in his eyes. 'After all, everyone knows what happens to those who cross me.'

Hugh le Dispenser was dangling his knife in his right hand. He smiled and suggestively waved it in front of his neck. 'Look what happened to Lancaster, the last 'owner' of Sandal Castle.'

The minstrels up in their gallery came to the end of their music and it seemed that an eerie silence fell upon the diners. It was broken after a moment by the King.

'And tomorrow we shall see these Mystery Plays that Wakefield seems famous for.' Suddenly, he turned to Richard. 'What say you, Richard? You have been quiet all evening?'

Richard was taken unawares. 'My apologies, Your Majesty. My mind has been with more mundane matters than this. I am sure that you will be mightily entertained by it all.'

*　*　*

The whole of Wakefield was up before daylight for the Corpus Christi celebrations. The day before, the pageant wagons had been hauled into place to form a semi-circle around the one side of the Bull Ring and all of the market-stalls had been taken down. The plan was to start the celebration at nine bells with a mass at All Saints before the procession of the players through the town, to end up at the Bull Ring, where the crowd would be eagerly waiting.

Hubert met Richard as agreed at the Roll's Office in the Moot Hall a good hour before the mass was due to start.

'My Lord, I . . . I have a favour to ask,' he said.

Richard was sitting at the desk tapping the lid of a chest containing some of the artefacts from the recent court cases. He was preoccupied and replied distractedly. 'Ask then, good Hubert.'

'May I . . . may I have your leave to marry?'

Richard looked up in surprise. 'You wish to marry Beatrice? But you have only known her a few days?'

'A few days, a couple of nights. What does it matter? I love her with my soul. I love her when I see her across the Bucket Inn, I love her when she scolds me, and I love her when we make love. When I close my eyes I see her, as she is in bed, naked, looking down at me, smiling with those beautiful lips. I love those lips, that gap in her teeth, the way she — '

'Hubert, stop! That's it!'

'That's what, my lord? Have I said too much?'

'Teeth, Hubert! Teeth! Go and find George-a-Green the pinder. Bring him to me.'

'But my lord, what about — ?'

'Now, Hubert!'

It took Hubert a good twenty minutes before he returned with the bewildered looking pinder. He was dressed as a shepherd, ready to perform in one of the plays.

'You wanted to talk to me, sir?' he asked. 'Will it take long?'

'I want to talk to you about Hector Lunt. You must have been one of his closest friends. I want to know if he bought a pardon from Albin of Rouncivale.'

A muscle twitched in the pinder's strong jaw and Richard thought that he detected a glint of anxiety register in his face. 'No, sir, he didn't buy a pardon, but he did buy something else.'

Hubert interjected. 'Why didn't you say so before?'

'I didn't see that it was important.'

'It was a tooth, wasn't it?' Richard pressed. 'I imagine he paid a goodly sum for it.'

The pinder looked amazed. 'It was, and he did. He said it was the tooth of a sainted nun and that he was fully protected because of it. He became really cocky and all. But how did you — ?'

'That will be all,' Richard returned coldly. 'I have no time to explain, but you will probably have to explain in court some time.'

When the pinder departed sheepishly Richard tapped the casket in front of him and opened it. 'Teeth, Hubert! Fool that I am, I did not recognize the significance of the teeth.' He drew out one of the Pardoner's small jars and poured from it the two teeth. 'Look at them, Hubert. What do you notice about them?'

Hubert bit his lip and concentrated. 'They look fresh and they look good.'

'Exactly! No rot. Just as Lady Wilhelmina said. These are not the teeth of a peasant.'

'So could they be the teeth of a saint, as the Pardoner claimed?'

'No, they were the teeth of a noble. Someone who ate and lived well.'

'But who lost their teeth?' Hubert asked, still bemused.

'These teeth had been pulled out, Hubert. After death, I am sure.'

Hubert snapped his fingers. 'A noble killed in battle?'

'No! One who died by decapitation.'

It took Hubert a moment, then he stared at

his master in disbelief. 'The Earl of Lancaster?'

'Precisely. And now I think it fits. Or much of it. The Pardoner came to Wakefield from Pontefract, that we know. I believe that he bought some teeth from the headsman and probably sold them off to people who believed that they needed special pardoning. Probably because they were racked with guilt, or because they were afraid that some crime might be discovered.'

'Like Hector Lunt?'

'Like a man who had raped a girl in the town,' Richard mused. 'And who confessed to the Pardoner. Then later Hector must have panicked and tried to get the tooth back. And that was why the Pardoner gave himself up to the watch and confessed that he had committed a crime. He blurted out that he had committed the crime that had been confessed to him, and which was obviously in his mind at the time. He felt threatened and needed to gain the protection of custody. Albin of Rouncivale's crime was not rape, but greed.'

'So where does Robert Hood come in?'

So deep had they been in discussion that they had barely noticed the sound of people milling about outside, of horses clopping up the streets. Then the bells of All Saints started to ring.

'Never mind the Hood,' Richard said. 'The thing that Hector Lunt gasped when he lay dying is of the greatest importance now.' He thumped the side of his head and cursed. 'I have been such a blind fool! Hubert, we assumed he was just saying an eye for an eye, a tooth for a tooth. What he was actually saying was that his killer had taken his tooth, his protection. And also something deeper than that. Remember, Scathelocke had been shot in the eye! An eye for an eye.'

'I don't understand, my lord.'

'No, I do not fully understand it myself. Yet there is something here that worries me deeply. And it concerns the King. He used to call Piers Gaveston his Eye. And now he calls Hugh le Dispenser the same thing.'

'You think that someone means to kill le Dispenser?'

'I think it is possible. The King still has many enemies and le Dispenser is as unpopular as ever Gaveston was. We must be vigilant.'

'What do you want me to do, my lord?'

'I want you to stay close to his majesty and le Dispenser. I will have a word with Sir Thomas and make it all right. Also, keep an eye on me. If you hear me call out, guard the King and Le Dispenser.'

'Should we not say something to his

majesty?' Hubert asked.

'There is no time,' Richard replied. 'We must to church straight away.'

★ ★ ★

Richard shuffled up the aisle and sat down beside Sir Thomas Deyville who was sitting behind the King and Hugh le Dispenser. Richard whispered his concerns to the Deputy Steward, but as he expected he found that he was less concerned than he thought he should be.

'The King could not be better protected,' he whispered back. 'There is a small army in the town. You stick to the law, Sir Richard, and leave this to me. I will allow your man to shadow the King, but otherwise I shall take care of his protection.'

Richard looked past him and bowed his head to Lady Alecia.

'Where is the Lady Wilhelmina?' he asked.

'She is unwell this morning,' Lady Alecia whispered back. 'A sickness. I have sent word for the apothecary to call later today.'

Richard nodded guiltily, feeling sure in his own mind that he was partly responsible for her absence.

Father Daniel conducted the Corpus Christi mass after which Lady Katherine and her nuns sang while the King, Hugh le Dispenser and the congregation filed out of the church. The King and his party, now including Hubert walked the short distance to the Bull Ring and took their seats in the special high carved chairs that had been set up on a canopied dais for them to observe the plays as they were performed in the temporary amphitheatre.

The procession of players, musicians and singers meanwhile marched through the streets, snaking their way into the Bull Ring, to take up their places behind the pageants of their guilds.

A drum rolled and Father Daniel walked into the main area before the dais and welcomed the royal party and the crowd of spectators that had formed round about. As he did so Richard noted Sir Thomas and Lady Alecia sitting on either side of the King and le Dispenser, and Hubert standing at attention behind the King's chair. He also stood surveying the rows of armed men within easy reach of the king. He knew too, that more armed men were located around the town boundaries, so there would be no chance of an armed assault by anything less than an organized army while they were there, for, of course, the town was built on a ridge, with good views in most directions. He ran an eye across the tops of the buildings, checking that no one could be secreted on a rooftop or in a garret. Beyond the Bull Ring stood the scaffold-surrounded tower of All Saints, from whence the bell pealed every few minutes, as Father Daniel had instructed.

Perhaps he was wrong, Richard wondered. Perhaps there was no connection and he was worrying needlessly. He began to relax as the plays began.

★ ★ ★

The opening play of *The Creation* was performed by the Guild of Haberdashers and was as expected a colourful piece. There were great flashes of coloured cloth and much banging of drums, as God, resplendent in flowing robes and prodigious beard appeared and began to create the heavens and the earth and the water upon it. Dancers appeared on the pageant and around it to portray the fish, the birds and the animals of the wonderful Garden of Eden. And then, tastefully dressed in garments depicting no garments at all, Adam and Eve appeared.

The great apple tree of knowledge was wheeled on and Satan dressed as a snake tempted them to eat apples, with the result that they realized their nakedness and garnished their private parts with fig leaves.

The audience enjoyed it, as did the King and his party, their appetites whetted for more with the play *The Killing of Abel*, performed with gusto by the Guild of Butchers.

And so it went on for three hours, each subsequent play moving on to the next pageant, and then round again. *Noah*, *The Procession of the Prophets*, *The Flight into Egypt*, and *The Arrival of John the Baptist*; all of the well known Biblical stories were enacted, cheered, and enjoyed by the royal party and the people of the town without a break, until the King raised a hand and a trumpeter blew a royal fanfare which silenced the cheering crowd and drew everyone's attention to the royal dais.

Father Daniel appeared from the side where he had been busily directing.

'My good Wakefield Master,' said the King, 'I am enjoying this fine day and these fine plays, but nature is calling and I — '

There was a creaking noise from the pageant wagon on the right of the royal dais, the one used to portray the Face of Hell. Slowly the huge face that formed its backdrop began to open.

Everyone knew that from the jaws of Hell the demons and lost souls were eventually supposed to pour out. It was assumed that some fool had allowed the mechanism to open prematurely.

'As I said,' his majesty went on, irritably, 'I need to — '

Suddenly the jaws of Hell dropped fully open and a masked figure dressed as a demon in scarlet jumped forth. But instead of the usual fork that he was supposed to brandish, he held a bow, already notched and bent back.

''An Eye for an Eye, sayeth the lord'!' he cried. 'Thus die tyrants, traitors and their spawn!'

Richard cried out, 'Hubert!'

Hubert of Loxley reacted instantly. Thrusting himself between the King and le Dispenser's chairs, he spun round, grabbed le Dispenser by the neck and dragged him towards the king. Then in one movement he encircled them both in his arms and threw all of his weight forwards to topple the King's chair backwards. So great was their momentum that they all tumbled over the back of the chair.

There was a swooshing noise and an arrow shot over them and skewered a man at arms through the thigh. It knocked him off his feet and he fell to the ground, a severed artery pumping blood.

'Hood!' Richard cried, unsheathing his sword and dashing, as were several soldiers of the king's guard, in the direction of the scarlet demon-clad bowman.

Immediately a figure appeared atop the scaffolding of the tower of All Saints, a bow and arrow at the ready.

Richard sprinted, aware that the demon had calmly reached to a quiver on his back and had already drawn and notched another arrow. He drew back the cord and the yew bow began to bend.

'Die!' he bellowed.

But before he released it, it looked as if he had been struck with a battering ram. With a sickening thud an arrow thumped into his shoulder amid a splurt of blood. The bow fell from his hand and the arrow went wild as he was hurled backwards to fall into the jaws of Hell.

A soldier of the guard ahead of Richard vaulted onto the pageant and grasping his sword in both hands raised it above his head to cleave the assassin in two. Richard leapt up, crying 'No!' — and thrust his sword forward in time to parry the soldier's downward blow.

'He . . . must . . . be taken alive!' he yelled.

And, as the soldier swung his sword up again, his training to protect the King at all costs, Richard turned his sword broadways and struck the unfortunate soldier across the chest with the flat of the blade, knocking him sideways to fall over one of the great wagon wheels of the pageant.

Other soldiers had by now mounted the pageant and were homing in on the assassin who lay, writhing in agony, twitching feebly at the arrow embedded in his shoulder. Richard wheeled on them, his sword at the ready.

'Hold your swords!' he cried. 'I am Sir Richard Lee, Sergeant-at-Law. I need this man alive!' He swung the sword menacingly. 'Now hold, or I will maim any man who moves.'

Such was the savagery and determination of his order that the men held their arms. They surrounded the prisoner and hauled him roughly to his feet.

Only then did Richard allow himself to turn to see what had happened. The crowd had panicked and people were trying to escape the confines of the Bull Ring. With relief he saw Hubert, the King and le Dispenser rising from behind the tumbled chair. Casting an eye at the church tower he noted with relief that there was no one there.

He turned at the gasps of pain from the prisoner, who was receiving no sympathy from the hardened soldiers.

Richard reached for the assassin's mask and pulled it away.

His eyes widened in surprise.

'You! Surely it cannot be?'

14

Revelations

It took some time for the soldiers, mainly under Sir Thomas Deyville's directions to settle the panicking townspeople and allow them to leave the Bull Ring in an orderly manner. Difficult though that was, Richard had a harder task. It took all of his powers of persuasion to prevent the summary execution of the assassin on the King's orders, for his temper was furious, believing as he did that the assassin had been sent by his wife, Queen Isabella. So it was that the prisoner was manhandled by soldiers to the Tolbooth and thrown into the cell next to the one containing the two dead bodies.

Father Daniel offered the use of his home for the King and le Dispenser to take refreshments, an offer which was less than graciously taken up.

'I need to get Wilfred Oldthorpe to remove that arrow from the assassin,' Richard said to Sir Thomas.

'I think we should let the cur rot. Why make death less appealing?' Sir Thomas replied.

Lady Alecia was looking pale and badly shaken. She put a hand on Richard's wrist. 'The apothecary may not be in the town. We sent for him to look at Lady Wilhelmina, if you remember.'

Richard thanked her and excused himself. He soon found Hubert with Beatrice Quigley's arms about him.

'Good Hubert, you were magnificent and truly saved the King today. That arrow must have missed you by inches.'

Hubert grinned and produced his talisman. He kissed it. 'It was my crusader's arrowhead, sir. That arrow could never have reached me.' He shook his head. 'Which is more than can be said for that poor fellow who was standing there guarding the King's back. He was bleeding like a stuck pig.'

Richard put an arm about Hubert's shoulders and guided him aside. 'I shall return him soon, Beatrice,' he said to her. 'I still have need of Hubert's services.' Once they were a few paces away he whispered, 'I want you to go to All Saint's Church and look in the sanctuary. There is someone there who deserves the sanctuary of the church, and who must not be taken.'

'You mean Robin Hood, my lord?' Hubert asked with a smile. 'I fancied that you had some game up your sleeve. Trust me, I shall

313

go and no one shall know why I go.'

Richard slipped away, noticing with a smile that Beatrice was quick to take Hubert in her arms again and shower him with the kisses reserved for heroes and lovers.

He went quickly to the Westgate and headed for Master Oldthorpe the apothecary's premises. The door was closed but opened easily at his shove. He called out then went through to the apothecary's treatment room.

Master Oldthorpe, the apothecary, was there. He was lying on the reed floor in a pool of his own blood. By his side was a large flask that had been used to stave in the back of his skull.

★　★　★

Richard rode like the wind towards Sandal Castle. Fearing that he had no time to waste, he had set off immediately and let his mount have its head on the long undulating road south towards Sandal. By the time he began the snaking climb up the hill towards the castle the horse was lathered and snorting heavily.

'Just a little further, then you shall rest,' he whispered, as he bent low over its ear. Halfway towards the top he dismounted behind some trees and tethered the horse so that it could crop some of the grass by the verge of the trail. He proceeded on foot, his nerves on edge and his heart racing.

There was no challenge from the battlements as he jogged along the side of the outer moat towards the gate. The drawbridge was down and the portcullis was up. Again, there was no challenge from within.

Richard edged across the drawbridge and peered round the door of the gatehouse. Slumped in a corner lay two men; the gatehouse-keeper and one of the guards. Richard checked them and found that they were both deeply unconscious. Two mugs lay on the floor with half their contents spilled over the stone flagstones. He had no doubt that the ale they had been given had been drugged, hence the lack of challenge and the raised portcullis.

'I pray that I am not too late,' he whispered to himself, and moved off to enter the seemingly deserted castle, looking about him all the time. Upon the battlement wall he spied the collapsed forms of two more guards.

The door of the steward's lodge was standing ajar and he went through the passage and mounted the steps.

He heard the noise of someone retching

and vomiting upstairs.

Step by step he went up, wary lest the creaking of timber should give his presence away. Along the corridor he went to an open doorway. He looked inside and saw Lady Wilhelmina lying on her side in bed, a vomit-bowl by her side. Standing over her, dressed in a man's surcoat, hose and riding boots was Emma Oldthorpe. On the bed was the unmistakable shape of a pewter bleeding bowl and in the apothecary's wife's hand was a long, thin, phlebotomy knife.

'Have you come to bleed Lady Wilhelmina?' Richard asked, stepping in the door.

Lady Wilhelmina's face was alabaster pale. She looked up weakly and gave him a thin smile.

'Sir Richard, what a pleasant surprise,' purred Emma Oldthorpe. 'Are you not at the Mysteries?'

'No, I came to visit Lady Wilhelmina. I heard from Lady Alecia that she had sent for your husband.'

'He was unable to come so he sent me. I have skills with a knife.'

'I saw him, Emma,' he said. 'Did you kill him?'

There was a creak on the stairs and then running feet. 'You were right,' called out

Gideon Kitchen. 'I have it. It was just where you said it — '

He came in the doorway and stopped short when he saw Richard. In one hand was a small sack and in the other a wicked-looking short sword.

'You have what, Gideon Kitchen?' Richard asked. 'More drugs? It was you who drugged the guards, I take it?'

The normally beaming face took on an ugly, aggressive expression.

Emma laughed at his look of discomfiture. 'Yes, it was Gideon, my faithful assistant here. One of our little group. And he gave the Lady Wilhelmina the mix which nicely incommoded her today and kept her away from the Mysteries. I knew they would send for Wilfred.' She nodded her head casually. 'And in answer to your question, did I kill Wilfred — no! That was Gilbert, my dear younger brother.'

'A good disguise,' Richard commented. 'He really looked like a hunchback.'

Emma shrugged. 'It was an uncomfortable contraption, but it served its purpose.'

'And he killed all those men, didn't he?'

She nodded her head appreciatively. 'You are a clever man, Sir Richard.' She pouted. 'And more attractive than most. I almost wish that I had slept with you.'

Lady Wilhelmina raised her head, almost with an expression of horror on her face. Then she sighed and bent her head over the bowl again. Emma patted her back with the hand still holding the knife. 'There, there, my dear. Soon I will put you out of your misery.'

Richard looked anxiously at the knife. 'It had much to do with teeth, did it not? Teeth belonging to the Earl of Lancaster, unless I am mistaken. Pulled from his decapitated head by the executioner.'

Gideon Kitchen shuffled uneasily. 'Why are you telling him all this, Emma? We should be getting away.'

'Silence!' she hissed. 'Sir Richard has a perfect right to know. He has reasoned out so much that I am intrigued, and I appreciate intelligence, since I so rarely meet anyone with any.' She reached up to her neck with her free hand and pulled from under her surcoat a necklace. 'And here they are. When he had my half-brother Piers murdered and decapitated I vowed that I would wear a necklace of his teeth.' She gave a short laugh. 'But the greedy fool of a headsman sold three to that Pardoner.'

Richard nodded. 'So the Gaveston family was larger than anyone knew.'

'Our father served the old King in Wales. Gilbert and I were brought up as the children of a merchant in Caernarvon. When he died and Piers had become Edward's lover, Piers found us and 'favoured' us. Gilbert was devoted to him. When Piers was foully murdered we promised that we would make them all pay. First we made it to Warwick, where I married that fool Wilfred, who taught me so much of medicines and poisons. And that is where we managed to get to Earl Warwick and poisoned him for his crime, for he was supposed to have protected Piers. Instead of that he let the dog Lancaster drag him from his castle.'

'And so the Pardoner had to die in case his story led to the headsman and then to you?'

'That is right. We had our mission. First to take back the jewels that Earl Lancaster stole from Newcastle when he and his band of cutthroat nobles chased Piers and the King. I knew that the bastard would hide them here in Sandal Castle. It would have given him pleasure to hide them here in his old enemy's former home.' She nodded at Gideon Kitchen. 'Tell him where they were, Gideon.'

'In the bell in the Earl's Chapel,' the cook said truculently.

'Of course, the blacksmith who died suddenly!' said Richard.

'After he gave me the information he had. I had to encourage him, a little.'

'You seduced him?'

She turned up her nose. 'Oh no! That would have been as bad as sleeping with my odious old husband. Let us just say that I stroked his manhood a little. Then Gideon dispatched him with a little hemlock in his stew.'

'Emma, I really think we — ' Gideon Kitchen began.

'And Hector Lunt, did he also have to die because he bought one of the Pardoner's fake relics, a tooth of a saint?'

'Very good,' she purred. 'Guisley, that fool of a headsman! He had to go too, just in case.'

'And when your brother killed them both, he said that it was 'an eye for an eye and a tooth for a tooth.' He really meant that, didn't he?'

It was Emma Oldthorpe's turn to look surprised. 'Gilbert can be so foolish sometimes. But he is passionate. Just as he was passionate about his archery and his skill with the bow. He has really cared about nothing else except getting even with them all for what they did to Piers. Yes, we took Lancaster's teeth and we planned to take Edward's new *Eye*, for that is what he calls his creature le Dispenser. But first we needed to kill that bastard King for being so weak after Piers was murdered.'

Richard frowned. 'But why Scathelocke? Why did he kill him so cruelly?'

She shrugged. 'Practice, that was all. He was a pitiful specimen of a man and he just put him out of his misery. Target practice.'

Wilhelmina retched into her bowl. 'You w . . . witch!' she gasped.

Emma laughed. 'And by now Gilbert will probably have dispatched both of them. He should be with us soon.'

Richard shook his head. 'He will not be coming, Emma. He was shot and taken. The King and le Dispenser are safe and your brother lies in the Tolbooth with an arrow in his shoulder.'

Her face contorted with rage. 'You lie!'

'I pulled the demon mask from his face myself.'

'Kill him now!' she cried.

Gideon Kitchen dropped the sack and thrust his sword at Richard, who dodged, kicked out at the cook's wrist and tried to draw his own sword. Yet the cook, lame though he was, knew a trick or two. He swung his sword round and slashed sideways in a scything action, going for Richard's legs. Richard immediately jumped, then, as soon as he landed, closed in on the cook, breaking his nose with a straight-armed punch to his face and following with a vicious upward blow to his jaw that lifted him off his feet and deposited him in an unconscious heap in the corner of the room.

'Stand where you are!' Emma cried, as he spun round to face her.

Richard stared in horror at the sight of her with one hand enmeshed in Wilhelmina's hair and the knife pressed against her throat.

'You know that I will use this. Now take out your sword and drop it out of that window, then kick the sack over by the door.

Richard did as he was bidden. 'So you are going? A common robber, betraying your fellows.'

She sneered. 'Gideon can escape if he comes round in time. Me, I shall ride far and without hindrance.'

'Leave Wilhelmina,' Richard pleaded.

'Move over by the bed. She is coming some of the way with me. You, I am afraid will be locked in here.' She wrinkled her nose. 'Just think, Richard, if things had been different you could have enjoyed me in a bed like that.'

He eyed her distastefully. 'I had a lucky escape then.'

She laughed and hauled on Wilhelmina's hair. 'Get up, my lady. And take a care, for this knife is sharp.' And to prove her point she pressed the blade slightly so that a trickle of blood flowed down Wilhelmina's throat. Wilhelmina gasped in pain, but dared not move. 'Now bend slowly and pick up this sack.'

They moved as one and then Emma backed out of the doorway, dragging Wilhelmina with her.

'D . . . don't hurt me,' Wilhelmina whimpered.

Emma sneered. 'Like so many ladies, gutless!'

'Yet she has many womanly qualities,' said Richard. 'She likes music, for one thing.'

'What?' Emma demanded.

As if by magic there was the sudden strumming of a lute from the corridor and Emma slackened her grip and turned her head to see the smiling minstrel, Alan-a-Dale standing there with his lute in his hands.

Wilhelmina grasped the sack with both hands and swung it upwards with all her strength. It arced over her shoulder and caught Emma on the temple.

The knife fell from her hand and she crumpled unconscious to the floor.

'Find something to bind her with,' Richard instructed Alan-a-Dale, while he strode over in time to catch Wilhelmina who had started to fall in a dead faint.

When she came round some moments later

and found Richard's concerned face staring down at her tenderly she smiled. Then her expression changed to one of consternation. 'What did she mean you *almost* slept with her? Why not with me?'

He laughed. 'Wilhelmina, this is not the time for such talk.'

'But I want you, Richard. I have wanted you from the first moment I saw you. I want you to — '

'Hush, Wilhelmina, you must rest. I have things to do first. Important things, but in a few days I will be able to — woo you.'

Her eyes fluttered and as she drifted off to sleep a smile spread across her lips.

★ ★ ★

There came the sound of horse's hoofs from without and Richard quickly straightened and crossed to the window in time to see Alan-a-Dale heading towards the drawbridge. The minstrel grinned up at him and raised his hand. Dangling from it was the sack containing the jewels.

Richard gave a silent curse and was in two minds to go after him, yet he dared not leave Wilhelmina alone with Emma Oldthorpe, even although she was still unconscious and had been bound hand and foot by the minstrel. So thinking, he went over to the crumpled heap that was Gideon Kitchen and, unbuckling the cook's belt, turned him over and bound his hands behind his back.

He was just straightening up again when he again heard the sound of a horse outside the lodge. This time when he looked out he was surprised to see two people upon the one horse: Robin Hood with Matilda Oxley behind him.

'Hail, Sir Richard!' cried Robin Hood, upon spying Richard's face at Wilhelmina's chamber window. 'Is all well?'

'It is now,' returned Richard. 'I have the other traitors! The cook, Gideon Kitchen and Emma Oldthorpe, the apothecary's wife.'

Matilda gasped. 'Emma Oldthorpe! It cannot be! Sir Richard, you are mistaken.'

Richard shook his head sadly. 'There is no mistake, I am afraid.'

'The King is unharmed?' Robin Hood asked, concernedly.

'Aye, thanks to you. So what now, Robin Hood? Where are you going now?'

The handsome, bearded outlaw glanced over his shoulder at Matilda and grinned. 'We head for Barnsdale Forest again, and mayhap as far as Sherwood.' He nodded his head. 'Our plan worked well enough, did it not?'

'Thanks be to God,' Richard returned.

'Will we ever be able to return, Sir Richard?' Matilda asked, her hands tight around the waist of her lover.

'I shall be petitioning his majesty about it,' Richard replied. 'When the time is right.'

Robin Hood nodded. 'Then we must be away. My men will have released Sir Thomas's men — after charging them a suitable toll — and they will be with you as soon as their feet will carry them.' He raised his hand in a salute. 'Farewell, Sir Richard Lee.'

'Wait!' Richard cried. 'Did you pass the minstrel Alan-a-Dale? I fancy that he has some property belonging to the King.'

Robin laughed. 'We did — and he has.' He winked. 'Let us just say that it is the King's property, which we will look after for him, until he chooses to pardon the brothers of the Greenwood.'

Richard grinned as the outlaw wheeled his horse round and they waved before galloping for the drawbridge.

★ ★ ★

Emma Oldthorpe groaned and Richard turned to look down at her with sadness and distaste. He was aware that his feelings of attraction to her had been transformed into utter revulsion.

'Will you let me go, Sir Richard?' she asked, her voice neither pleading nor showing any sign of fear. 'And if not, will you spare me the worst?'

He felt the bitter nausea of bile rise in his throat. He shook his head sadly.

'I am afraid that I can do neither, Mistress Oldthorpe. You must face the law.'

To his amazement she smiled. 'The King's law?' she asked. She tossed her head back and spat.

'God damn the King!'

Epilogue

Richard had not been surprised to learn that Hubert had not found Robin Hood in the sanctuary. He had told him of their subsequent meeting at Sandal Castle and of all that had happened. Hubert had, of course, felt slightly put out that Richard had not informed him of the subterfuge, yet when Richard explained that he needed him to convince Beatrice, he cheered up. And, of course, having the prospect of wedding the beautiful Beatrice filled him with total joy.

His Majesty King Edward II decided that he had experienced enough of Wakefield and of Sandal Castle and left for Rothwell Castle before heading on to York with Hugh le Dispenser. The conduct of the court he left to Richard.

The cases did not take long. The evidence was so strong, there was no need for any pressure, despite Sir Thomas's view that a little torture would speed things up and satisfy the King's subjects' blood lust. Yet this Richard would not allow, for although he was gladly accepted as a suitable suitor for Sir Thomas's daughter, he was determined not to be swayed by his potential father-in-law in his pursuit of fair justice, as befitted a Sergeant-at-Law.

Yet the sentences gave Richard no pleasure at all. Gideon Kitchen and Gilbert Gaveston, if that was his name, were to be hanged, drawn and quartered, as the law proscribed for commoners found guilty of treason against the King. Emma Oldthorpe was sentenced to be burned at the stake.

When the execution day arrived, crowds gathered from Wakefield and all the surrounding villages and hamlets of the Manor of Wakefield. The site chosen was Sandal Common.

A great pyre was erected in the centre of the common, atop which Emma Oldthorpe was bound. The intention was that she should watch the barbaric deaths of her brother and henchman before she was sent to the fires of Hell herself. Symbolically, the pageant that they had used for their assassination bid had been smashed up and used to fuel the pyre.

All three of them looked in a piteous state, having had neither appetite for food or water for several days. The quick deaths that they had asked for had been denied.

The two men died hideously with much gore and accompanied by much jeering from the crowds. Throughout it all Emma Old-thorpe screwed up her eyes as she tried to blot it all out of her mind.

Richard as the presiding judge was obliged to watch, feeling helpless when the lighted brands were finally tossed on the pyre and the dried branches began to smoke and burn, until flames were licking at her.

Then seemingly from out of nowhere, an arrow flew and pierced her heart. She gasped once, then her head fell and mercifully she knew no more.

Richard made the sign of the cross over his heart. So many deaths, so much hate. Yet for this last death he was grateful. He was pretty certain that he knew who had fired that arrow.

God save the King! He mouthed, then rose to leave.

He had a lady to woo.

Historical Note

The Pardoner's Crime is a work of fiction, yet the location, some of the main characters and certain events are real.

In 1313 the jewels referred to in this tale were indeed taken at Newcastle by the Earl of Lancaster, amid great controversy.

In 1316 Robert Hood (Hode) appeared before the Manor of Wakefield Court and was fined for failing to take up arms on behalf of John de Warenne the Earl of Surrey. He is believed to have been one of the 700 bowmen who fought at Boroughbridge under Thomas Earl of Lancaster, and was subsequently declared a contrariant and outlaw. It is thought that he was subsequently pardoned by King Edward II, for he and his wife Matilda returned to live out their days in the house that he built on the Birch Hill.

In November 1326 Hugh le Dispenser, the King's favourite, was taken prisoner and tried for treason, then executed at Hereford by being hanged, drawn and quartered.

On 21 September 1327, King Edward II, who had been forced to abdicate in favour of his son (King Edward III) was murdered in

Berkeley Castle upon the orders of his wife, Queen Isabella, and her lover Roger de Mortimer, first Earl of March. It is said that the assassins were instructed to leave no mark upon the King's body. A horn was inserted up his rectum and a red hot spit was thrust into it to penetrate and burn his entrails.

England in the fourteenth century was a dangerous place to be. Great acts of barbarism occurred and not even kings were safe.

Glossary

Apothecary
The medieval equivalent of a pharmacist and doctor. They were originally members of the Grocers' and Spicers' Guild.

Ashlar
Dressed stone blocks, often rectangular or square, used to make castles and cathedrals in medieval times.

Bailiff
An official of a town, court or large estate.

Ballista
One of the great siege weapons. The earlier Roman versions were essentially giant crossbows, but in medieval times they were capable of propelling arrows or missiles.

Beaver Hat
A classic medieval male hat. It was round with an oval brim of fur.

Benefit of Clergy
In the early days of the English legal system

clergymen could claim the right to be tried in a consistory or ecclesiastical court according to canon law. Originally this right was restricted to churchmen, but it was extended to any who could read and write a passage from the Bible. Thus such people as Pardoners, Summoners and Vergers could evade the harsher sentencing of secular courts.

Bollock Dagger

A knife in common use between the thirteenth to the eighteenth centuries. It had a distinctly shaped haft, with two oval prominences resembling genitalia. It was used for dispatching unhorsed knights by stabbing through the visor.

Burgher

A freeman or landowner within a township.

Chantry Chapel

Chantry Chapels were common in medieval England. They were special chapels within church buildings or on private land where priests could chant masses. There were four Chantry Chapels standing on the four main entrances to medieval Wakefield — St Mary Magdalene's on Westgate, St John the Baptist on the Northgate, St Swithens on the road to York, and St Mary the Virgin on Wakefield

Bridge. Only the latter has survived to this day.

Coif
A close fitting lawn or silk cap that covered the top, back and sides of the head. It was the badge of office of the Sergeant-at-Law in the fourteenth century.

Consistory Court
A church or ecclesiastical court. One claiming benefit of clergy could be tried by this court.

Constable
The senior member of the town watch. In medieval times there were four watches in Wakefield.

Contrariant
After the Battle of Boroughbridge in 1322 King Edward II declared that the remnants of Thomas Earl of Lancaster's army should be declared 'contrariants' and thereby outside the law.

Cote-hardie
A tight-fitting garment for both men and women. For women it was a long garment that reached to the ground, with slimming seams from the shoulders to the hips and

often with loose sleeves. The man's cote-hardie was close-fitting in the waist.

Doctrine of Humours

The Ancient Greeks had developed the Doctrine of Humours or the Humoral Theory, which was the dominant medical theory of medieval times. It was believed that there were four fundamental humours or body fluids (from the Latin *umor* or *humor*, meaning 'moisture' or 'fluid') which determined the state of health of an individual. These humours were blood, yellow and black bile and phlegm. Treatments aimed at removing excess of illness-producing humours by bleeding, purgation and the use of emetics.

Fletcher

An arrowsmith.

Garderobe

A medieval toilet. In castles these often took the form of seat-covered holes with long drops into cess-pits, or shafts dropping into the moat. Buckets for handfuls of moss were used as cleaning agents.

Greave

Lower leg armour covering the shins or sometimes encasing the whole of the calf.

Groat
A silver coin worth four pennies during the thirteenth century.

Hauberk
A chain mail tunic, originally worn down to the knee, but later as a defensive tunic. Sometimes worn under a surcoat.

Honour of Pontefract
One of the great medieval estates with its centre around Pontefract Castle. Originally owned by the de Lacy family, it was gained in marriage by Thomas Earl of Lancaster.

Hue and Cry
In medieval times the law said that upon discovering a felony the individual was obliged to raise the hue and cry. Everyone hearing the call was equally obliged to join in the chase to catch the miscreant.

Liripipe
A long peak hanging from a hat or hood. A classic head garment of the medieval era.

Manor of Wakefield
One of the great medieval estates with its centre at Sandal Castle. Originally owned by the de Warenne family, it was forcibly taken

from John de Warenne, the Earl of Surrey by Thomas Earl of Lancaster after his wife had been abducted by one of the Earl of Surrey's squires.

Manor Court Rolls

The Wakefield Manor Court Rolls are still existent and cover the entire period from 1274-1925. They contain an immense amount of detail about people, places and events in and around Wakefield, and give a valuable insight into the working of the legal process in medieval Wakefield until the early twentieth century. The manor court house was held in the Moot Hall, situated opposite the south side of the parish church of All Saints.

Marcher Lords

The Marcher Lords were powerful barons appointed by the king to guard the borders with Wales and Scotland. The greatest Marcher Lords along the Welsh border included the earls of Chester, Gloucester, Hereford, Pembroke, and Shrewsbury. Their counterparts along the Scottish border were the earls of Northumberland and Durham.

Onager

A war machine used in the medieval era. It

consisted of a large catapult with a fixed bowl for firing either single or multiple missiles.

Ordainers
In 1311 a baronial committee of twenty-one Lords Ordainers drew up a series of ordinances, whose effect was to substitute The Ordainers for the King as the effective government of the country.

Pantler
The servant in charge of the bread and the pantry.

Pardoner
A pardoner sold pardons or indulgences. These were certificates of remission of penance. They were introduced in return for gifts to an ecclesiastical charity, but the system became chaotic and unregulated. Unlicensed Pardoners made a handsome living by going from town to town selling pardons and indulgences and false relics of the saints. Geoffrey Chaucer introduces such a character in *The Canterbury Tales*.

Pillory
A wooden framework on a post with holes for the head and hands, in which offenders were

locked, so that they could be exposed to public ridicule and humiliation.

Pinder
The keeper of the township's cattle. George-a-Green the Pinder of Wakefield was mentioned in one of the earliest poems about Robin Hood.

Rouncivale
The hospital of the Blessed Virgin Mary at Charing Cross. Some Pardoners, such as Albin of this tale, would claim allegiance from there, thereby dignifying their position.

Sanctuary
A fugitive or suspect could claim forty days sanctuary within the 'sanctuary' of a church.

Sergeant-at-Law
A now extinct legal title. A Sergeant-at-Law (*servientes ad legem*) was a senior barrister in medieval times. They were often appointed as circuit judges or as judges, but were still permitted to plead in the courts. Geoffrey Chaucer has a Sergeant-at-Law as one of his pilgrims in The Canterbury Tales.

Soke
One of the feudal rights of the lord of a

manor. In the Manor of Wakefield the Lord had the right to have all corn ground in his (soke) mills, or to have bread baked in his bakehouse.

Solar
A private room, usually upstairs, in a medieval home.

Surcoat
A surcoat was an outer garment commonly worn in the Middle Ages. It can either refer to a coat or tunic worn over other garments or the outer garment of a person.

Steward
One who managed a castle, property or estate on behalf of a Lord or King.

Stocks
Punitive hinged, wooden framework, in which a person's feet were locked in place, and sometimes as well their hands or head. The victim was thus kept in a sitting position, a ready target for passers-by to pelt with dung or rotting vegetables.

Undercroft
The ground floor of a medieval building, often used for storage or to keep livestock.

Wimple
The classic medieval head garment for women, consisting of a cloth which went over the head and round the neck and chin.

Wolfshead
An archaic term for outlaw. As an outlaw someone was considered outside the law and could be hunted and killed.

We do hope that you have enjoyed reading this large print book.

Did you know that all of our titles are available for purchase?

We publish a wide range of high quality large print books including:
Romances, Mysteries, Classics
General Fiction
Non Fiction and Westerns

Special interest titles available in large print are:
The Little Oxford Dictionary
Music Book
Song Book
Hymn Book
Service Book

Also available from us courtesy of Oxford University Press:
Young Readers' Dictionary
(large print edition)
Young Readers' Thesaurus
(large print edition)

For further information or a free brochure, please contact us at:
Ulverscroft Large Print Books Ltd.,
The Green, Bradgate Road, Anstey,
Leicester, LE7 7FU, England.
Tel: (00 44) **0116 236 4325**
Fax: (00 44) **0116 234 0205**

Other titles published by
The House of Ulverscroft:

THE MAJOLICA MURDERS

Deborah Morgan

Ex-FBI agent and antiques picker Jeff Talbot asks his friend Lanny to scout out some antique majolica as a present for his wife, with no idea just how costly it will be. Jeff is shocked when Lanny is arrested for murdering an antiques dealer, and discovers that Lanny quarrelled with the dealer after she sold two pieces of majolica she was supposed to hold for him — uncharacteristic of the caring and trustworthy man Jeff knows. As he investigates Lanny's claims of innocence, Jeff learns the majolica has a long history — one that someone is determined to keep quiet.

THE DEATH OF AN AMIABLE CHILD

Irene Marcuse

Social worker Anita Servi's world is turned upside down one morning when Clea, her five-year-old daughter, discovers the body of a homeless woman who had occasionally slept on a landing in their apartment building. It seems clear to Anita that a crime has been committed. Lillian Raines, also known as 'the lady of the landing', had been an enigma to those, including Anita, who had tried to help her. Determined to find and notify the family, Anita begins to piece together Lillian's story. Was she as rich as rumoured? Why did she spend so much time by the memorial to the Amiable Child in Riverside Park? Anita must use her contacts and intelligence if she is to get justice and peace of mind.

DEAD CENTRE

Joan Lock

It is 1887, the year of Queen Victoria's Golden Jubilee, and London is in turmoil, particularly at the dead centre, Trafalgar Square. Here, the angry unemployed gather daily to protest and nightly to sleep. The police are tired and bitter about accusations of brutality from the protestors. Then a prominent member of one of the socialist organizations leading the protests is found dead at the foot of Nelson's Column and Detective Inspector Ernest Best catches a fleeting glimpse of Stark, a man he knows was guilty of a dreadful crime in Whitechapel. Tension builds. Something terrible is about to happen . . .

FEET OF CLAY

Ruth Birmingham

PI Sunny Childs is the hard-nosed, fast-talking lead detective at Atlanta's Peachtree Investigations. When her cousin Lee-Lee, a documentary film maker who's set to interview convicted murderer Dale Weedlow, invites Sunny along for the ride, Sunny knows her very presence will probably convince her cousin that he's been framed. But Sunny goes and finds that things are not as they seem. Behind the local politics, business and law enforcement looms evidence of a cover-up, and Sunny finds herself deep into the original murder case. But with no cooperation from the locals, and the convict's execution rapidly approaching, Sunny has to hurry if she's going to get to the bottom of the six-year-old murders of two girls whose feet had sunk deep into the Southern clay.

DEADLY OBSESSION

Peter Conway

Professor Helen Vaughan was a top scientist in the field of DNA research, and still only in her middle thirties. But she's found slumped over her desk in her office at the City Hospital, bludgeoned to death by a severe blow to the side of her head. Acerbic and both feared and disliked by her colleagues, she had a colourful private life featuring sado-masochistic games — as the police were soon to discover. Investigation into that, her traumatic upbringing and hospital tensions begin to reveal the deadly obsession that led to her death and the person responsible for it . . .